The Devil's Paintbrush

THE
DEVIL'S
PAINTBRUSH

Jake Arnott

SCEPTRE

First published in Great Britain in 2009 by Sceptre
An imprint of Hodder & Stoughton
An Hachette Livre UK company

I

A CIP catalogue record for this title is available from the British Library

Hardback ISBN 978 0 340 92270 5
Trade Paperback ISBN 978 0 340 92316 0

Typeset in Monotype Sabon by Ellipsis Books Limited, Glasgow

Printed and bound by Clays Ltd, St Ives plc

Hodder & Stoughton policy is to use papers that are natural, renewable
and recyclable products and made from wood grown in sustainable forests.
The logging and manufacturing processes are expected to conform to
the environmental regulations of the country of origin.

Hodder & Stoughton Ltd
338 Euston Road
London NW1 3BH

www.hodder.co.uk

For Stephanie Theobald

Part One
FIGHTING MAC

I

Paris, 24th March 1903

A GREAT, SIMPLE, LION-HEARTED man with the spirit of a child, thought the Beast as he caught sight of Hector Macdonald taking lunch alone in the dining room of the Hotel Regina. The General sat to attention, ramrod-straight, at first glance looking so strong and resolute. Only one of his hands betrayed him. It clawed at the white linen tablecloth, as if grasping at a ledge.

The Beast sniffed instinctively, alert to the scent of something rotten. Scandal, yes, that was it. Wasn't everyone talking about this? The rumours of a general's return to London from Ceylon in disgrace. There had been some talk of it in Le Chat Blanc the night before. Wild gossip of some terrible sin yet to be made public. That's what must have brought him here. To Paris. Like so many others.

He felt a delicious thrill at having spotted the great hero. Fame was a lure to the Beast, especially where it seemed tainted with dishonour and notoriety. The General had the air of a fugitive in his pitiful attempt at travelling incognito. The funereal suit he wore, as if in mourning, was not even that well cut. But perhaps here was a man that did not fit the clothes, the type of soldier that should never be out of uniform. So good on parade yet so awkward in mufti. One cruelly lacking the subtle distinction of a civilian gentleman. He looked like a Tommy in his Sunday best.

He was low-born, the Beast knew that. Risen up through the ranks, into the highest echelons of the British Army. And yet despite the drab flannel, he was unmistakable. The great Empire Man. Major-General Sir Hector Archibald Macdonald. 'Fighting Mac' it was, or, rather, the hollow image of him. The same stern jaw, steel-grey hair and moustache, the beetle brows that furrowed deep-set brown eyes. Those features that had been reproduced countless times in the illustrated newspapers, on cigarette cards and imperial memorabilia, framed by the scarlet tunic and a dazzling phalanx of medals, so proud and expectant. Now he looked simply to be waiting. Waiting for a fate that he could not quite bear.

What a sad sight, thought the Beast, such a poignant tableau. And what monstrous fun could be had as a witness to such degradation. He mused fleetingly on some marvellously wicked anecdote that he might relate to the exiles at Le Chat Blanc, an outrageous story that he could concoct over the dinner table. Fighting Mac's glory was so great, he had become a modern archetype, like a trump card of the *major arcana*. But suddenly it all meant more than that to the Beast. This melancholy image of Macdonald brooding hopelessly like a wounded animal at luncheon appeared to him as a sign. One who had ascended to the command of heaven now awaiting terrible depths in his fall. He felt a peculiar urge to go to his aid.

The Beast had only come into the Hotel Regina by chance, for a quick drink before a saunter through the Tuileries. But there was no such thing as chance, he concluded. Destiny had brought Sir Hector and himself together; this circumstance must be connected with his greater purpose. The imminent battle with Mathers, his former master. This fortuitous event was no mere distraction. The General was somehow part of his struggle, he decided.

To meet Macdonald now seemed urgent and portentous. He would introduce himself, make himself known to the renowned warrior. He would use his full title: Laird of Boleskine and Abertarff. It was a form of address he had rather neglected of late but he was certainly entitled to it. After all, the estate in Scotland had cost him over two thousand pounds.

As he reached the table Fighting Mac was staring straight ahead, listlessly picking at his food with his unclawed hand.

'Sir Hector?'

Macdonald looked around, startled. As if frightened by his own name. He saw the bright green suit with brocade lapels and a jewelled waistcoat sparkling gaudily beneath. Then, as he looked up he saw a bull neck bulging out of a loosely tied silk cravat. The head was bald but for a froth of oily hair garlanding the crown, the glabrous pate hinting at a tonsure, making him appear like a degenerate monk. The Beast was young, still in his twenties, but burdened with a corpulence that aged him. Heavy jowls made a once handsome face bestially sensual. His whole countenance was disturbingly naked. The lips protruded, heavy and moist. Expectant. Macdonald felt a pang of recognition that he could not quite place.

'I don't think I have had the pleasure,' he began.

'Laird of Boleskine and Abertarff,' replied the apparition and held out a fan of heavily ringed fingers.

The General took the proffered hand, which was limp and slightly damp. Soft, like everything else about this man. Except the eyes. Pale blue and unfaltering, they seemed the hardest part of him. It was hard to meet their gaze in that it was difficult to gauge where exactly they focused. They seemed to look beyond, to meet at a point behind one. They had an enveloping emptiness. Glaring somewhere between infinity and the middle distance. Seeing nothing, but giving the impression of great depth.

'May I?'

'Please,' said the General, scraping back his chair with involuntary recoil. Giving easy ground as he had rarely done in the field. 'Be my guest.'

The Beast swiftly sat down opposite Fighting Mac, and haughtily scanned the dining room.

'It's on the banks of Loch Ness,' he declared nonchalantly.

'I beg your pardon?'

5

'My manor.'

Macdonald frowned. The man's voice was like crushed velvet.

'Close to your part of the world I believe,' the Beast went on.

'My part of the world?'

A waiter appeared and the Beast ordered champagne. Macdonald glowered at the ridiculous dandy sitting opposite him. An English fop playing at Highland nobility. God knows what garish tartan he would wear at his country estate. My part of the world, indeed, he thought.

'I was born in Rootfield in Ross-shire,' Macdonald suddenly boomed. 'My folk were nae lairds.'

The Beast tossed his head and let out a short peal of laughter, amused at how swiftly Sir Hector's speech could go from the clipped tones of the officer class to the rich brogue of his forefathers.

'Of course,' he rejoined. 'A crofter's son. No shame in that. My grandfather was a brewer.'

'I'm not sure that I like your tone, sir.'

'Oh, I meant no offence. You must forgive me. I'm only rather clumsily pointing out those things we might have in common.'

'I hardly think we have much in common.'

'Oh, you'd be surprised. I was in Ceylon too, you know.'

'What?'

'Studying Buddhism, yoga and,' the Beast's blue eyes glowered, 'other things.'

'Look—'

'I know all about you,' the Beast said softly.

His eyes became hypnotic again in that slightly unfocused way. Macdonald felt a sense of revulsion at being drawn into this man's gaze. He knew now that he did recognise something about him. Not from his waking past but from some flicker of prophecy hidden amid the horrors he had witnessed. He was a vision of what was to come. What he had always dreaded.

'Listen,' Macdonald began, his eyes darting about the dining room, as if seeking a way out.

The Beast leaned across the table, conspiratorially.

'It's all right,' he whispered. 'I want to help you.'

'Who are you, sir?' Macdonald demanded.

The Beast sat back in his chair and placed a bejewelled hand on the table.

'I'm a poet,' he declared. 'Of some repute. A mountaineer, too, of course. But my principal vocation is thaumaturgy.'

'What?'

'I am sir' – the Beast lifted his hand and opened it with a little flourish – 'a magician.'

'A theatrical performer?' Macdonald asked.

'Oh no. A real magician.'

Macdonald gave a deep-throated laugh. The Beast smiled.

'Of course you are,' the General went on. 'But what is your name, sir?'

My name? thought the Beast. He had so many. Apart from Boleskine and Abertarff, there was his ceremonial name Perdurabo; the pseudonym George Archibald Bishop he had used as an author of obscene poetry; he had taken to calling himself Count Vladimir Svareff for a while. So many names, and there would be many more. He was the Beast, of course, but that was just the name he had for himself. The secret name his mother had called him.

'Crowley,' he announced suddenly, as if remembering it. 'Aleister Crowley. At your service, sir.'

II

MACDONALD FOUND HIMSELF IN Le Jardin des Tuileries with Crowley, who had suggested a post-prandial stroll. Macdonald had agreed, he needed air. His head was fuzzed with champagne and the florid talk of his unexpected guest. But even in the open Crowley's presence could have a stifling effect, like some hothouse creeper, oozing a sickly scent, choking all the life around him. Macdonald watched him gazing at the statue of a centaur, his wet mouth jutting salaciously.

'Catherine de Médicis built a palace here,' the Beast commented languidly as they strolled along the gravel path. 'She was reputed to have been a sorceress, certainly a poisoner. It is said that she held black masses here.'

'Is that so?' Macdonald muttered low, not wanting to encourage him.

'The occult has always been a feature of Parisian society. Satanism is terribly fashionable here at the moment, you know.'

'No, I didn't.'

'But Scotland has always been the place for witchcraft, hasn't it?'

'I wouldn't know. I was raised in the United Free Presbyterian Church.'

Crowley laughed.

'My dear fellow, my father was a lay preacher in the Plymouth Brethren. I too was brought up with the hell-fire of the Low Church. But we can all break free of religion. We are going to have to.'

'And what are we to believe in then?'

'Why in magic of course.'

'Och, man, you're having a joke with me.'

'I'm perfectly serious. Haven't you noticed? This strange time we are living in. Just when positivism reaches its peak, everyone is suddenly fascinated by the occult. In the past century rationalism and atheism have overthrown all religions, all forms of mysticism. Except magic. Magic is about to reassert itself. It's the beginning of a new aeon. Can't you just feel it?'

'I'm not sure if I can, no.'

'It's about power.'

'Aye.'

'And the will.'

'You mean willpower?'

'Yes, but when people say that they usually mean restraint. I don't mean that. I mean the opposite of that.'

'I'm not with you.'

'Well . . .'

The Beast began to stumble in his argument. He had been working something through in his mind for a while. He was looking for an idea. It did not have to be a particularly good idea, just a strong one. It would be to do with the will. What he wanted was a verbal formula, a spell that could enchant. Something that could shock the whole world.

'Power,' he tried to explain to the General, to himself. 'It can come out of restraint, yes?'

'Aye.'

'Like steam power. That will soon be out of date. In the modern age there will be more expressive forms of power. The internal combustion engine, electricity.'

'Well, you're talking about science now.'

'Science and magic, they're the same thing.'

'You're not making sense, man.'

'I'm talking of the supernatural. Look, under Victoria all the power of the Empire came out of repression. For machines, for men also.'

'What do you mean?'

'I mean the application of pressure. Building up a head of steam, if you like. Do that to an iron engine and you have the means for a railway system. Do it on the emotions of men and you can power a whole empire.'

'Well, I don't know about that,' Macdonald retorted.

'Repression, it's been the fuel of expansionism. Now we are entering a new age. We are free now that our Great Mother Victoria is dead. The fog is lifted. Now is a time for expression.'

They had left the park and were crossing the Seine. Macdonald looked down at the swirling water. There was a choking sensation at his throat. He felt the vertiginous nausea of his predicament.

'I am talking of energy,' the Beast went on. 'Energy that can no longer be sublimated.'

Macdonald staggered on, his head reeling, his stomach full of bile, his gorge burning with the acid of the champagne. The Beast followed him, the moist mouth horribly close.

'Sexual energy,' he whispered in the General's ear.

'Please,' he begged.

'Don't be afraid,' the Beast said. 'I understand. I want to help.'

They had reached the other side of the river now and were walking past a line of shoddy bookstalls. That this absurd man might share the knowledge of his terrible crime filled Macdonald with horror.

'My dear fellow,' Crowley went on. 'You must realise, you are not alone in Paris.'

'What?'

'The night Oscar Wilde was arrested the boat train here was packed with gentlemen of a certain type. Many of them are still here.'

'But—'

'I know you think that what you have done is unspeakable. But everyone is talking about it.'

'Oh God,' Macdonald gasped.

'And not just the exiles.'

'But nothing has been—'

'Of course, of course,' the Beast interjected impatiently. 'It's all a great puzzle. They love that. Despite the endless gossip, the indulgence in every sordid detail, they want a different kind of revelation. Their greatest thrill is to imagine something hidden.'

'I don't understand.'

'The sex act has the magic of a secret. Like a sacred mystery would have been to medieval peasants. This is the power that should be harnessed in the future.'

'The power?'

'The power of the secret. Imagine if we could unlock that. Unleash it.'

Crowley's face tightened into a beaming grin. His eyes bulged with energy. Macdonald struggled to understand, to work out what this curious man was saying. Was it just idle talk? He found himself desperate for any kind of succour, no matter how obscure or peculiar.

'You said you could help me,' he reminded Crowley.

'Yes, of course,' the Beast replied.

'But how?'

'Well, we can help each other. You've come to the right place, after all.'

Macdonald was about to say something else but the Beast had swiftly moved in on a grubby-looking cart displaying racks of postcards.

'Here,' the Beast beckoned him over.

Crowley was plucking at an assortment of photographs and daguerreotypes as a surly stallholder remonstrated with him. He handed one to Macdonald. Then another. And another.

'Look,' he insisted. 'It's all here.'

One showed two youths entwined in a gymnastic posture, their smiling faces betraying neither unease in their exertions nor in their nakedness. A second card depicted a nubile girl bending over as a hunched satyr inserted himself. Soon Macdonald held a clutch of postcards in his hand. A fan of compliant attitudes, professional and amateur poses, easily flaunted flesh. And he felt a terrible, lustful sadness. The shock of empty desire for its cold reproduction. The sepia bodies trapped on the surface of the glossy paper like insects in amber.

'For God's sake, man,' he protested.

His instinct was to hide these images, but he didn't know where to put them. So he stuffed them into his jacket pocket. The stallholder began to complain loudly.

'*Mais, vous voulez combien?*' the Beast enquired in an atrocious accent.

The man continued to argue with Crowley who replied with a self-confident inarticulacy. It was soon clear to Macdonald that the Beast knew little of the language. Macdonald's French was far better. He had served in the Egyptian Army where it was expected that all officers could speak it adequately. And Crowley appeared to have no real idea of the sum he was being asked for. He flourished a note grandly. Macdonald noticed that it was ten francs. As the stallholder started to explain that he would give him change Crowley took this to be some further barter and gave a dismissive wave with his hand. The stallholder shrugged and the Beast looked triumphant.

'See?' he declared to Macdonald. 'It's easy when you know how.'

'What?'

'To be free. You can be free here.'

'I don't understand. What am I to do?'

'There is another way, you know,' the Beast declared.

Macdonald started at these words. Each one cut into him. They had been said to him only two days before. *There is another way, you know.*

'What do you mean?' he demanded.

'We will find a way,' Crowley reassured him. 'There are plans to be laid. Fate has decreed our meeting. We must join forces and fight the good fight together. Now, there are things that I must attend to. I will call on you later. Shall we say, seven?'

'Fine,' Macdonald muttered, exhausted by it all.

'Very well then. Adieu.'

The stallholder was staring at Macdonald. He muttered some obscenity and Macdonald looked away to gaze across the Seine, where the Louvre loomed over the river.

'Wait,' he said, and turned around.

But Crowley was nowhere to be seen. He had vanished.

III

BACK AT THE HOTEL REGINA, Macdonald went through the routine of checking the newspapers left out on the side table in the foyer. There was nothing about him in the late editions of the international press. No letters for him at reception. He went up to his room and sat on the edge of his bed.

There is another way, you know.

He shuddered as he remembered the other occasion those words were said to him. What was there to do now? The meeting with Crowley had been disquieting but it had provoked all sorts of notions and possibilities that he hadn't considered. His mind was disturbed, but maybe that was a good thing. An opportunity somewhere but what? The fact was, from what the man said, that rumours were spreading and soon the scandal would break.

When that happened he really would need magic to escape his predicament, he thought, remembering the grotesque expression on Crowley's face and the dread sense of recognition it gave him. This was a man sympathetic to his plight and yet it was someone he would despise in normal circumstances. Perhaps it was not too late to revise his opinions about the world. First, he must review his situation. He tried to concentrate on where he had gone wrong. He had played this one very badly indeed. Left himself no room to manoeuvre.

Rushing headlong into it, that had been his mistake. London, that had been a bloody disaster. It had been the Governor's suggestion, to return home on leave and consult with his superiors. Find another posting, another appointment. Then he could leave Ceylon for good and no more need be said on the matter. That was the idea.

But this required a strategy well beyond his scope. He had never been one for grand schemes or complex tactics. For most of his army career he had been in the thick of it, even as an officer. Leading from the front, that was his way. He was still a ranker at heart.

He had no influence, that was his real shortcoming. No well-placed friends, no circle, no clique, no breeding, no politics, no family, no society, absolutely no society at all. He had no idea how to play the game. He had gained promotion by mere merit and that left him at a terrible disadvantage. And at the very moment when he had needed to draw upon his seemingly vast reserves of prestige, he had found himself alone in London at the Army and Navy Club in Pall Mall, with no one to call upon. He was to present himself to Lord Roberts at the War Office. Little Bobs – the diminutive Commander-in-Chief of the Imperial General Staff.

Macdonald had known the Chief a long time but he had never been part of the 'Roberts Ring', his intimate circle of officers. Neither had he been known within Lord Wolseley's 'Ashanti Ring', the clique of Roberts' great rival. He had even found himself excluded from the 'Band of Boys', the group of young sappers in the Egyptian Army that had surrounded Kitchener in the Sudan. These strange cabals and factional loyalties had always been a mystery to him. They were secret societies, impenetrable to the uninitiated. Yet he knew that this was how the officer corps of the army was really organised. It was how you got on. It was how you were protected.

Little Bobs had built his house of war on his knowledge of his officers. He would always have to know who everyone was in every room, in every mess hall. And if, at the racecourse in Calcutta, or riding through the Simla bazaar, he encountered someone whom he thought he ought to know but didn't, he would send his aide-de-camp after him to find out his particulars. The hapless aide might have to track the man for miles, seek out his quarters or run him to ground at his club, but Little

Bobs would want his details to add to his mental trophy case of names and families. Fighting Mac had always remained something of a mystery to him. The cypher of his fame had compensated for his lack of social position. But there were always doubts that he would prove a gentleman.

So Macdonald had walked down to Whitehall only a week ago, in his dark suit and bowler hat, with scarcely a notion of how to ingratiate himself. He was off to see the Chief. To plead with him.

There's a little red-faced man, which is Bobs, rides the tallest 'orse 'e can – our Bobs.

The Chief didn't keep him waiting long. Maybe, hoped Macdonald, the little man might feel some responsibility towards him. Because of all the times they had known each other. All the places they had served together, for the Great March from Kabul to Kandahar at least. He had been something of a protégé to him back then. Their army career like a music-hall song: Little Bobs and Fighting Mac.

They had first met in Kabul at the height of the Afghan campaign in the winter of 1879, when Macdonald was still just a colour-sergeant in the Gordons. It was a god-forsaken place. Freezing cold, filthy and poverty-stricken. A brooding hatred throbbed through the town. A day rarely passed without a public hanging. A military commission had been formed to deal with anyone found complicit in the massacre of the British diplomatic mission earlier that year. Roberts had ordered that 'punishment should be as will be felt and remembered'. Patrols were sent out to capture suspects and to forage. Villages that showed any resistance were burned to the ground. On the surrounding hillsides tribesmen were gathering and the mullahs called for *jihad*, to rid the country of the infidel invaders.

Macdonald had been twice mentioned in dispatches on the march on Kabul from Simla. The first instance was at the Shurtar-garden Pass where there had been an ambush and the whole van of Roberts' column had been pinned down by a thousand Afghan riflemen who had positioned themselves on a steep spur commanding the defile. Macdonald had been in a forward position with eighteen highlanders and forty-four sepoys of the 3rd Sikhs.

He had shown himself an able soldier up to that point. Drill and discipline had become second nature. Through his own diligence and determination he had reached the highest rank he could expect among the non-commissioned. Other aspects of manly duty he was not so certain of. He hardly ever drank and he would avoid the pay-night excursions to the brothels in the Jullunder Cantonment where they had been billeted since 1871. He gained a reputation for fastidiousness, which drew predictable comments in the mess hall, the occasional taunt. He tried to ignore the regular vulgarities of soldier's banter. It meant nothing compared to the deep contentment he felt in belonging to such a fine, well-trained body of men. Among all the banal ribaldry there was the fierce affection of the enlisted. Sometimes the unspoken love that he felt for his comrades was almost overwhelming. He put all his faith in the spirit of the body and ignored the strange fear that nagged at him.

So, in that first moment when he found himself under fire, he knew that he had to prove himself. He would rather have been killed than funk it in front of his fellow men. And the realisation that he might die before he could take another breath gave him a marvellous tranquillity of purpose. It was then that he felt a steadying sense of control; the extreme danger cancelled everything else out. He suddenly gained the lucid clarity of action. He knew what to do and, no officer being present, he took the initiative. He led the small force upwards in order to take advantage of superior cover. The thrill of danger gave him a fantastic energy; he was bold, decisive. Their situation was perilous: they were outnumbered and completely cut off from the main body of the column. They had to wade through a tumbling stream and clamber up a broken hillside as continuous fire rained down on them. Macdonald signalled his men forward, in twos and threes, until they were above the enemy. It was the pleasure of drill, of being bodily possessed by the precision of movement. With death buzzing in the rocks around them, there were no petty distractions, no unmanly doubts in his head. He felt exhilarated, pure. When they had gained their position above the enemy, Macdonald mustered them into line, and they used the rocks and scrub around them as cover. He waited until the tribesmen were in full range then ordered controlled and concentrated fire.

He discovered that it was only in action that the fear completely left him. That little hum of terror he scarcely noticed except when it was silenced. As the fusillade burst around him and the Afghans began to flee below, all was quiet within. It was in these moments that he could vanquish the enemy that lurked inside.

His second mention in dispatches came after an assault on the Charasiah Heights, on the outskirts of Kabul. His platoon had been sent to dislodge a party of snipers. This was a bloody sweat, climbing a bare slope in places so steep that they were on their hands and knees. He was full of fury and frustration as he reached the top, a depth of anger in him that he had never quite given vent to before. He broke into a stumbling charge and a hoarse-throated scream. It was from this time onwards that he began to be known as Fighting Mac.

He was summoned in front of Roberts two months later and offered a commission. One of the many stories told about him when he became famous was that he had been given the choice between promotion and a Victoria Cross. This wasn't true; if it had been he would almost certainly have chosen the decoration. A colour-sergeant with a VC would have been ensured respect and an easy life for the rest of his service. As a second lieutenant, without a private income, from no respectable family, lacking the credentials of a gentleman, with no connections, indeed with no circumstances at all, he would embark on a lonely and precarious career. There would be constant money worries, since an officer's pay would scarcely ever meet the expense of being one. Forever cut off from the camaraderie of the non-commissioned and never fully accepted in the officers' mess, he would always be the clever but clumsy ranker, raised above his station and rarely afforded proper friendship, just supercilious tolerance. Accepting this promotion was his truly reckless act of daring. And he always remembered the euphoria of the moment when he was offered a commission. The prospect of grandeur that he had always been denied. From the bleak rain-sodden croft, the one-room schoolhouse, the stultifying boredom of a drapery apprenticeship in Inverness: he could take his revenge on all that. Here was the sheer glamour of ambition that had drawn him to the colours in the first place. The whole world opened up to him. He felt a lightness as he said yes to it. He was rising up.

Twenty-four years later he had finally come down. Here he was, in front of Roberts again, over a matter of conduct. This time his reputation was on the line. This was the most precarious position he had ever been called on to defend. All he could hope for was a new appointment. A posting out of trouble. A new command and a fresh start. A place for him somewhere.

The Chief looked at him across the desk in his office, his face turned slightly, looking askance at the man in front of him.

'I don't understand,' the Field Marshall began. 'How could you have left your post like this?'

'It was the Governor's idea, sir. That I take extended leave and consult with my superiors in London.'

Roberts' eye twitched.

'Consult, man?' he demanded. 'Good God, what is there to consult about?'

'Given the nature of the accusations against me, sir.'

'The Governor has informed me of their nature, Macdonald. They are terrible charges. Unless you are cleared of them you are in an intolerable situation.'

'Sir.'

'You say you can exonerate yourself from these accusations?'

'Yes, sir.'

'Then we must follow proper procedures.'

'But, sir—'

'I never thought you would let me down like this, Macdonald.'

'Governor Ridgeway's opinion was—'

'Ah yes! Ridgeway wanted you out of the way, didn't he? I suppose that you and the Governor thought that this matter could all be swept under the carpet. A transfer to other duties, a posting far away and out of sight. A quiet way out of this mess. Well, it won't do, Macdonald, it simply won't do. Do you know what I've had on my desk this morning? A report that suggests that sixty per cent of potential recruits for the South Africa War were deemed physically unfit for service. Sixty per cent! The nation is facing severe physical deterioration. And do you know what lies at the heart of it?'

'Sir?'

'Moral degeneracy. Without self-control, discipline, restraint, continence, how can we expect to hold the empire?'

'I agree, sir.'

'We have to lead by example. We must be above suspicion.'

Oh 'e's little but he's wise

'Yes, sir, but—'

'And I have to tell you, Macdonald, in the light of this, and all other considerations of your case, I have to tell you that you cannot remain in the army until you have cleared your name.'

'E's a terror for 'is size

'Please sir, I beg of you . . .'

'And, consequently, it is my opinion that you should return to Ceylon and face a court martial there. I am making this my recommendation to the Prime Minister and the Colonial Secretary.'

An' – 'e – does – not – advertise

'Sir, no, please, anything but that.'

'And to the King of course.'

Do yer, Bobs?

A dreadful groan echoed through the Field Marshall's office. Macdonald had started to sob. It was appalling. He could not control himself. He was crying in front of the Commander-in-Chief of the Imperial General Staff. Fighting Mac was blubbing like a bairn.

'For goodness sake, man,' said Roberts, standing up from his desk, calling out for an adjutant to take the wretched fellow away.

IV

When Crowley arrived back at Gerald Kelly's apartment in Montparnasse his host was emerging from his studio with a young woman. She was short and fine-boned. Kelly's gangling frame craned over her as he escorted her to the door, like some kind of wading bird, his sharp features pecking down. The Beast stooped to catch sight of the face that nestled beneath a huge black bonnet. It was pale and elfin, a snub nose and a tiny pink mouth.

'And who is this delightful creature?' he demanded, beaming at her.

Kelly gave an impatient sigh.

'This is Sibyl,' he replied. 'She is just leaving.'

'Ah!' the Beast gasped loudly, causing the departing girl to jump a little. 'A veritable Sibyl! A prophetess, a seer.'

'She's nothing of the sort. She's a good clean girl from St Germain.'

Kelly ushered his model swiftly to the door and Crowley wandered into the room beyond. He went up to study the canvas on an easel in the middle of the room. It was Sibyl's contemplative profile, rendered in sombre hues against a prussian-blue background. The Beast was a little disappointed.

'Well, it has a certain vibrancy,' he said, when Gerald Kelly returned to the studio. 'But you've hardly done the nymph justice. Sibyl should be trembling with passion.'

'I wanted something more tranquil,' Kelly countered. 'Something that would recall the quiet spirituality of the Spanish masters. Something impressionistic.'

'Hmm,' snorted Crowley. 'The problem is that when the

English turn to Impressionism they are in perilous danger of being dull.'

'Well, it doesn't shout at you, I'll grant you that. There's a simple tonality and delicate composition that, perhaps, requires a certain refinement of appreciation.'

'It's positively timorous! You're all the same. Coming to Paris to paint, to let yourself go, but you can't. You're all afraid of making mistakes. You're all so afraid of being vulgar. You all paint like governesses!'

'Really, Crowley!' Kelly protested.

The Beast stopped and saw the hurt look in his friend's eyes. They had known each other since Cambridge and had always sought to encourage each other in their artistic pursuits. Kelly had shown enthusiastic support for Crowley's poetry and the Beast, in return, had never failed to be openly critical of his comrade's painting.

'I'm sorry, Gerry,' said Crowley, after a moment's awkward silence. 'I have had an extraordinary day and I am filled with a fantastic energy. I am always argumentative when I am like this.'

'Hmm, well,' Kelly muttered, still smarting from the Beast's insult.

'I met a knight today.'

Kelly's eyes suddenly brightened.

'Oh really,' he piped up. 'Who?'

'Really, darling,' the Beast chided him. 'You'll never make it as a bohemian if you continue to be so keen on polite society. Besides, this was not some inbred specimen of effete nobility, this was a real knight. One who has earned his title through martial prowess. A warrior chieftain, and one in great distress. I intend to come to his assistance. And to call upon his power to sow confusion amid my enemies.'

'You mean Mathers?'

'Yes. I have surpassed that old fool. I believe that I am close to my hour of triumph.'

'You really have finally fallen out with him, haven't you?'

'He is no longer fit to lead the Order. He has lost his spiritual authority.'

'Well there was that business of the luggage you left with him when you went to Mexico.'

'Yes. It is symbolic of how degenerate his powers have become.'

Kelly sighed and walked over to the mantelpiece.

'You had better see this,' he said.

Kelly picked up an envelope from the shelf and handed it to him. The Beast snatched it from his hands and tore it open. There was a square card within wrapped in a thin leaf of blue notepaper. He unfolded the missive and squinted at a scrawl of green handwriting.

'"It may interest you to know that Soror Dominabitur Astris has made contact and is due in Paris at any moment",' he read.

'Dominabitur Astris? Isn't that the magical name of that German woman?'

'Fräulein Anna Sprengel, the eminent Rosicrucian adept from Stuttgart, who first revealed to us the Cypher Manuscript containing the secret rituals of the Order.'

'But isn't she supposed to be dead?'

'Perhaps she has been transfigured into another corporeal host. Perhaps the Secret Chiefs are about to reveal themselves.'

'Do you think that's possible?'

'It scarcely matters what is possible. It is what we can believe in. What we can convince others to believe in. That's what matters.'

'You're sure that this note is from Mathers?' Kelly enquired.

The Beast examined the handwriting once more.

'It is his ghastly griffonage, yes. Now this' – the Beast held up the white card that had been wrapped in the notepaper – 'this is proof that the magic battle has commenced.'

He showed it to his friend. Printed on it was a grid of letters arranged in a square.

```
S  A  T  O  R

A  R  E  P  O

T  E  N  E  T

O  P  E  R  A

R  O  T  A  S
```

'What on earth is it?' Kelly demanded.

'It is a spell. See? A magic square. An arrangement of five words that can be read vertically or horizontally, backwards or forwards. It has spirtual properties and it carries an incantation. *Sator, arepo, tenet, opera, rotas. Sator* is the sower, the creator; *arepo*, that is like *arrepe*, to seize or lay hold of. *Tenet*, that is a doctrine, *opera* is a work or operation. *Rotas*, well, that is a circular order of appointment. The meaning is perfectly clear.'

'Is it?'

'Oh yes. Mathers sees himself as the sower. He has seized hold of the doctrine, meaning the Cypher Manuscript, and he is using it to replace the personnel of the Order. Including me. It's all here. *Sator, arepo, tenet, opera, rotas.* See? I, the sower, take hold of the doctrine, and use it to operate a rotation of the membership of the Order. I must prepare a counter-signal.'

'What?'

'A magical signal, if properly decoded, can be reworked and sent back to its point of origin. I believe I can use the power of this square against Mathers himself. Get me something to draw with, Gerry.'

The Beast walked over to the work table and cleared a space on it. Kelly handed him the stub of a pencil. The Beast placed the square on the table and stared at it.

'Mathers is foolhardy to send me a spell in the form of a grid,' the Beast announced. 'He forgets that I was a chess blue at Cambridge. I could have been the greatest player of my generation had I not grown bored of it. It is a tedious game in itself but a good preparation for the casting of runes.'

The Beast gave a little hum and then became quiet and still. Kelly noted the trance of concentration his friend had assumed, absently holding the lead tip against his tongue as he scanned the letters. Suddenly it seemed a small flame leapt up in the Beast's eyes.

'Of course!' he hissed. 'I will deploy my knight.'

He thought of Sir Hector Macdonald once more. Of how apt everything was for a second. A cosmic balance in signs and symbols that he could manipulate.

'Here,' he declared, pressing the point of the pencil against the *o* on the bottom line of the square. 'And move as a knight would move.'

He drew a line across to the *r* on the second line from the bottom.

'Now,' he told his friend. 'Mark these letters down as I call them out.'

Kelly grabbed a scrap of paper and a piece of charcoal. The Beast drew quickly, zigzagging the square with lines until he had reached the *r* on the top right-hand corner of the grid.

'And again.'

This time he started from the *o* on the top line and repeated the operation until he had come to the *r* on the bottom left-hand corner. He held up the square, showing the marks he had made on it:

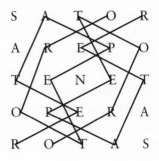

'Now. What do we have?' the Beast demanded.

'I really have no idea, darling.'

'Then read out what is written.'

'Orotepater, orotepater,' Kelly intoned.

'I thought as much,' the Beast said softly, with a smile on his face. 'See? *Oro te pater.* "I beg thee, Father." Repeated. Like an incantation. And the letters left on the square? Go on, read them out too.'

'S, a,' Kelly spelled. 'Er, n, a, s.'

'*Sanas.* Exactly!' He clapped his hands with joy. 'Heal thyself. I think that is quite a perfect instruction for that old fool Mathers. I beg thee, Father,' the Beast intoned with dripping sarcasm. 'I beg thee, Father. Heal thyself!'

'That is quite brilliant, Crowley.'

'I know. Now I must go to his temple immediately. If I can deliver it at once to that sordid little dwelling place the reversal of power will be successful.'

'Darling, you know that you have quite an astonishing mental faculty at times,' remarked Kelly. 'I feel sure that if you concentrated on something mundane you could find an extraordinary success in some field of life.'

'I know, I know.' The Beast sighed heavily. 'But what would be the point? What would be the point when there is so much beyond the world to strive for?'

It was at that moment that Gerald Kelly felt an unexpected sadness for Crowley. For all his overbearing bluster, his awful self-regard that constantly craved attention, for all that he took out on those close to him, at heart he was never quite satisfied with himself. He would never be happy, the painter found himself thinking. His life would be exciting, flamboyant, explosive. It would be lived to the full, that much was certain. But clear and lucid as prophecy came the simple thought: that he would never really be at peace.

'I must prepare myself, Gerry,' the Beast announced.

He went into his room and picked up a small brown bottle from his bedside table. He walked back through the studio.

'This square and my magic potion,' he mused, as if to himself, checking that the cork was secured in the neck of the phial and glancing at the label. *Tincture of Anhalorium*, it read. He smiled as he pocketed it.

'What is that?' the artist enquired.

'Oh, just something I picked up in Mexico. Extract of a rare cactus. It can induce a trance state. The Indians use it in their sacred rituals. Now, I must go. Will you be at Le Chat Blanc tonight, Gerry?'

'Yes. I'm dining with Clive Bell, you know, the art critic.'

'How dreary for you. Never mind,' he declared as he departed. 'I'll spice things up a bit. I promise you a tremendous uproar!'

V

MACDONALD HAD STAGGERED BACK TO the Army and Navy after the terrible meeting with Roberts, his head reeling. The Chief was washing his hands of him. All those years of loyal service were to count for nothing.

Where Roberts had led Macdonald had followed. Soon after his commission, he had been on the move again. There had been dreadful defeats in Helmand province, an entire brigade wiped out by Ayub Khan's army at Maiwand. Roberts assembled his forces for the big push. The Great March from Kabul to Kandahar began. Three hundred miles through deep ravines and immense mountain passes. Ten thousand men at arms and eight thousand followers in a long winding column, lost to the world, sent out to relieve the Kandahar garrison. Across the sterile desert, the biting cold of night, the blistering heat of noon, a huge invertebrate beast undulated forward at a merciless pace of fifteen miles a day. Eighteen thousand became a single myriapod creature with Little Bobs at its head, its tiny and relentless brain. The advance on Kandahar was to make Roberts, give him an immortal name and reputation. But it led Macdonald away from all that he had known. The rest of his life became a great march from himself.

He had to leave behind the simple fraternity of his fellow men. The hardest moment had been with his best friend Kenny Goss, a handsome black-haired lad from Lochaber. They had been lance-corporals together and there had been times when they had shared everything. Pals, that's what they had been. Dear, sweet pals. Kenny had been his other half. But now he was above all that. An officer, a darling of the gods. And so they made a solemn parting, even though they would still be in the same regiment. It was a goodbye to a heartfelt comradeship that could be no more. They shook hands awkwardly, Kenny would be Corporal Kenneth Goss from now on. Macdonald's eyes stung when he had called him pal for the last time. He had to turn away when Kenny had saluted him and addressed him as sir. It was from then on that he experienced a growing yearning for the deep closeness that he had felt among the ranks.

With officers it was a different business. There were often strong ties between fellows that went back to their schooldays. Strange words for things he didn't quite understand. A deeply felt knowledge of what one should say and, more importantly, what one shouldn't. Codes and ways of behaviour, allusions to peculiar things that always seemed just out of his reach.

He had always suspected that he might be different from others, feared it even. It was one of the things that had first attracted him to uniform, that he might fit in somewhere. Now that he was out of the ranks and yet not quite a gentleman, he became a curiosity. Standing out from the crowd, he was always on guard. He took a secret pleasure in the attention. He began to enjoy the image he had acquired for himself far more than his actual being. Fighting Mac, the rugged officer of few words.

And Kandahar opened his eyes to attractions he had scarcely dared dream of. The Great March had led him into temptation. Pretty Pashtun boys, the *halekon*, with their kohl-rimmed eyes, henna-patterned hands, full lips reddened with betel juice, selling themselves in the back streets. They would walk about in groups, languidly draping their arms around each other, reeking of jasmine. Some would perform in the market place, dancing provocatively with belled anklets. There would always be strangely arch comments from fellow officers. *Look at that tart. Oh yes, she's gorgeous.* A knowingness that seemed to treat everything as a huge joke. Things went on, everybody knew that secretly. But it was essential to be discreet. Never to get caught. Not even to think about it too consciously. There was more freedom for the officers but more danger also. Macdonald learned to be very careful and to trust only the darkness.

The 13th Hussars arrived as part of a relief column. They swaggered about the city armed with hog spears and revolvers for protection. There was just as much unrest in Kandahar as there had been in Kabul. There were more public hangings. The insurgents believed that if they killed a British soldier and they were caught and executed they would go straight to paradise.

The Hussars were known for their regimental theatricals and they put on an entertainment one evening in the open air. With their sabres stuck into the ground to mark out a rough stage area they performed Gilbert and Sullivan's latest operetta, *The Pirates of Penzance*. The loudest roar from the crowd came when one of the cast, with an exaggeratedly clipped delivery, launched into 'I am the very model of a modern Major-General, I've information vegetable, animal, and mineral'. It was so obviously a clever parody of Lord Wolseley, the fussy reformist. They jeered him with relish. All those who had been on the Great March were for Roberts, his rival.

Afterwards the officers present were invited to the Hussars' mess for drinks. Late in the evening, one of the cavalry men who had played a female role earlier donned a crinoline and proceeded to entertain the party with songs, dancing and the convincing patter of the persona 'Miss Daisy Bell'. Macdonald was intrigued. A neighbouring Hussar, noticing his curiosity, commented: 'Oh yes, "Bathing-Towel" is famous for his skirt-dancing act.'

All officers seemed to have some jocular nickname. Even in the Gordons, hardly a body of men known for its frivolity, there was a 'Boo', a 'Watty', a 'Grasper', a 'Baldy' and a 'Pouffles'. It seemed part of the public school infantilism that Macdonald was always excluded from. Being saddled with 'Fighting Mac' meant that he was expected to be dour and severe. It marked him out as common, though this could have its advantages. When he spoke with the one called 'Bathing-Towel' that night he found that the man liked him because, rather than in spite, of these qualities.

This subaltern of the Hussars was the first of the few officers that Macdonald could share his secret sense of difference with. The man had an extraordinary capacity for both concealing forbidden passions and finding ways of channelling them creatively. Along with the amateur dramatics, Bathing-Towel had a fine drawing hand and was a good storyteller, contributing to various journals since he found it hard to get by on his army pay. He was of a type: well bred but with little money. Macdonald found that he got on best with this sort; they understood his plight but they did not pity him. Bathing-Towel was allowed the enviable flamboyance permitted in the cavalry. Macdonald would always be poor bloody infantry, drill and simple discipline would be his way of holding himself in check.

Macdonald had found space for himself in the air of rough mystery that hung about him, using the sheer sense of puzzlement that he would inspire in most of his fellow officers as cover. But he sometimes grew tired of his own impersonation. He carried the burden of his self throughout a long and lonely career. Halfway across the world, to the four corners of the great empire and now back to London, where it was all coming to light in dreadful revelation. And London itself held another secret. His foolish mistake. His desperate attempt to escape his own fate. Christina. He would have to see her. Face up to her somehow; he owed her that much. And his son. He must see his son.

VI

THE TEMPLE OF THE BEAST'S former master was a shabby apartment on rue Rivera. Mathers himself was taking an apéritif in a café on the corner when Crowley called. This suited him since it would allow him to deliver the invocation to the rival in his absence, which would prepare the ground for a later meeting. The Beast tacked the reconfigured magic square on the front door of the temple apartment and went back down to the street.

As he took the precaution to look out to see if Mathers was anywhere to be seen he noticed someone across the road, looking up at the building. It was a woman wearing a dark riding cape with the hood up. Her face was almost entirely obscured, only a ghostly chin protruding, slashed with a blood-red mouth. He stepped out on to the pavement and the cowled head lowered slightly, as if in response. He was observed. Could this be some agent of Mathers'? he wondered. Some astral being ordered as a sentinel against him? He began to make his way along the street. The figure crossed over and started to shadow him.

He felt possessed by a furtive thrill at being followed. That it was by a woman, or at least the form of one, aroused a curious excitement, provocative and intimidating. A powerful desire rose up within him to be fugitive. It was not simply a fear of women, though he found that quite intoxicating, it was also a heartfelt resentment that propelled him along as quarry to the chase. A sense of rebellion, of mutiny against his need for their love, for their approbation. This was the brooding influence that they had over him. Even as a child, no matter what physical chastisement or mental torments were devised by men to punish him, it was only his mother who had the power to belittle him. The subtle delectation she took in the way that she chided and ridiculed him. She had been the first to call him the Beast, after all.

There had been times when he had sought to be free of women altogether. Inversion, that had been the nature of the General's scandal. He had had his own experiences of it. Pollitt, he thought, with a gasp of regret. They had met during his last year at Cambridge. He had, at first, merely been intrigued by how Pollitt had captured feminine energy through impersonation and performance. He then became initiated into secret knowledge, tricks of the body he'd scarcely believed were possible. It was his first and purest intimacy, which in the end he had to break free of. But he still regretted their bitter parting and was still burdened with a petulant desire for the opposite sex.

As he fled, he suddenly realised that this was how it should be. It would not be he who would seek their love, no, he would be the one pursued. To be chased, overwhelmed, run to ground and humiliated, this is how it would work for him. As he picked up the pace he considered the exquisite agonies of being preyed upon. Actaeon turned into a stag by Artemis and torn to pieces by his own hounds. The ecstasy of visceral terror. This is what flesh is, after all, he thought. The fearful pleasure of it. To be coursed like a hare. The switch and twist of the body as it tries to slip away from its fate. He began to enjoy his flight, dodging between passers-by, adding a nimble skip to his step, making a dance of it. He was quite agile, after all, despite his size. Whatever weight he might have gained in the past year, he still had a mountaineer's fleet-footedness.

But as he risked a stealthy glance behind, he saw that his pursuer was having trouble keeping up. There was a good chance that he might lose her altogether. He slowed down but she was still a fair way behind. She was not as competent at following him as he had hoped. If she couldn't go a little faster they might be at it all night. She might even give up. By chance he passed a cul-de-sac and took the opportunity to turn into it, making his movements extravagant enough for her to see where he was headed. Then, once he was sure that she was still on his trail, he indulged himself in the drama of the dead-end, the breathless delight of being trapped.

He turned and the woman approached him, her head still covered. As she came up close she threw back the hood in a ceremonial manner, scattering a mass of golden coils that glittered and hissed like snakes against her brow. She drew back the rest of the cape and he saw that her body was trim and athletic. In a close-fitting dress of blue and silver silk, she was as lithe as a huntress. Her eyes were speckled grey and hard as flint. High cheekbones and sharp chin, hawklike. And what a mouth! A merciless scarlet. The lips were full, the edges curled upward. She smiled: it was the snarl of a wild animal.

'I wish to talk to you,' she said.

The voice was deep, the accent harsh, teutonic. The Beast caught his breath. He nodded.

'You are Frater Perdurabo?' she enquired.

How did she know his magical name? He was overcome by wild imaginings. Perhaps she was some vampire succubus sent by Mathers to destroy him. If he contemplated the face of this beautiful Gorgon might he not be drained of all his powers? It was a ridiculous idea that amused him no end.

'Who art thou?' he demanded.

'I am Soror Dominatibur Astris.'

Her teeth bared slightly as she uttered this discordant oath. The timbre was certainly German. Could she really be the mythical Fräulein Sprengel or an embodiment of her? Might he finally make contact with the Secret Chiefs and attain the sacred knowledge of the Everlasting Light? He was utterly transfixed by the creature before him. And he was out of breath.

'Let us find somewhere we can sit down,' he suggested.

VII

From the Army and Navy Club Macdonald had taken a cab to Farringdon Station, then a train to Forest Hill. It would be dark by the time he got to her house, he reasoned. The last of the sun simmered on the dimpled water of the Thames as his carriage rattled over Blackfriars Bridge. Christina. He shielded his eyes from the lowering light that strafed at the windows and tried to think what he would say to her.

The Water of Leith. That was where they had first met. When he had been posted back to Scotland after the almighty debacle at Majuba Hill. Ceremonial duty at Edinburgh, guard details and recruiting. He was a full lieutenant by then, with quartermaster duties that gave him a little extra pay. But an officer's life on home service was lonely and expensive. The days were long and the evenings empty. For those with social connections to the gentry of the Lothians or Fife there would be balls and weekend shooting parties, but his spare time was taken up with worrying about how he could make ends meet. On Sundays, after church, he liked to take a solitary walk along that gentle river that twists through the city. That quiet little creek of his thoughts. The Water of Leith.

As he passed by St Bernard's Well he noticed a red-haired girl up ahead, dancing on the banks of the water. It was a strange hopping jig, with lots of expansive arm gestures. She was humming to herself and so self-absorbed that she did not notice his approach. Not wanting to disturb her, he stood a while and watched. Presently she turned and the spell was broken. Her face flushed as she saw him. He gently clapped her performance.

'Who are you?' she demanded sharply, trying to hide her embarrassment.

He laughed.

'Macdonald,' he told her. 'Hector Macdonald.'

'I am Christina Maclouchan Duncan. You may call me Christina.'

'May I indeed?'

'And you may walk with me.'

'I'm honoured,' he replied and they walked along the riverbank together.

'I think Hector is a fine name,' said Christina. 'He was a Greek hero. A brave warrior I think. I will look him up when I get home.'

'Well, I am a soldier.'

Christina stopped and frowned at him. She had obviously been warned about soldiers, thought Macdonald.

'Och, don't worry,' he reassured her with a smile. 'I'm an officer.'

Her green eyes widened.

'An officer!'

'Aye, a lieutenant in the Gordons.'

'The gay and gallant Gordons.'

'The very same.'

'And do you have a sweetheart?'

'No. I do not.'

'Then you can pretend that I am your sweetheart.'

'But you're just a wee lassie.'

'I am not. I am a young lady. I am to be sixteen this year. Here.' She put her arm through his. 'It's only pretend, mind. The brave officer must have a sweetheart. Otherwise people will look and think that you are all alone in the world.'

The red-haired girl was waiting at the same place the following Sunday and they walked along the water together again.

'I've looked up Hector,' she told him. 'He was a Trojan, not a Greek.'

'Aye, well, it's much the same.'

'No, it isn't. Now listen, his wife Andromache begs him not to go to war for her sake and the sake of their son. But he fights and slays Patroclus. This puts Achilles into a rage because he loves Patroclus. He stops sulking in his tent. He rushes out and kills Hector. Then he drags his dead body behind his chariot.'

'How do you know all this, Christina?'

'Papa has a very good library. He's a schoolmaster.'

'Well, you're a very clever girl.'

'I'm a very clever young lady. I found something else. A copy of the *Illustrated London News*. With you in it. You're a real hero, not just a mythical one.'

'Och, it's no more than a lot of blether.'

'But you were at Majuba. It says you fought at the end with your bare hands.'

'Aye,' he said with a bitter laugh. 'We had run out of ammunition.'

Majuba. It had been a bloody disaster. And it was partly his fault they had ever been there at all. After Afghanistan his regiment was back in Cawnpore in India. Ready to be shipped home to Britain when news broke out of trouble in the Transvaal. The Boers had raised a republican flag in the Heidelberg. The junior officers of the 92nd Gordons were spoiling for a fight. Active service meant advancement for them. Macdonald was as keen for this as any of the lieutenants; it was his only real chance for promotion. So he joined in sending a rather provocative cable to Sir Evelyn Wood in South Africa: PERSONAL. FROM SUBALTERNS 92ND HIGHLANDERS. SPLENDID BATTALION EAGER SERVICE MUCH NEARER NATAL THAN ENGLAND TO SEND. The senior staff of the Gordons were not informed of the communication, and God knows what the ordinary rank and file would have made of it, but before they knew it the regiment had arrived at Deolali with new orders for embarkation, on the troopship *Crocodile*, bound for Durban.

Sir George Colley led a column into northern Natal. It was to be a punitive raid against the Boer commandos that had gathered around Laing's Nek. Major-General Sir George Pomeroy Colley was a Wolseley protégé, and among that circle considered one of the most gifted men in the army. An ensign at sixteen, a lieutenant at eighteen, he had completed a two-year Staff College course in ten months with the highest marks ever recorded. He was a professor of military law and administration, had studied Russian, chemistry and political economy. He was even reputed to be a talented artist. An archetypal Wolseley man and a stalwart of the Ashanti Ring. He could have called upon more substantial reinforcements, but with them would come Lord Roberts to supersede him as commander, and that would never do. So, rash to assume battle, he marched out from Pietermaritzburg with only a thousand men.

Majuba Hill overlooked the Boer *laager*, and seemed to present a great strategic advantage if it could be taken. Colley planned a night assault, with three companies of the Gordons, detachments of the 58th and 60th Rifles, and sixty-four men of the Naval Brigade with Gatling guns and rocket tubes. It was a fearful climb in full kit. Colley wore carpet slippers, claiming that they were quieter and better suited for the job than heavy marching boots.

They reached the top just before dawn and found it completely deserted. It seemed that the brilliant Colley had executed a magnificent tactical coup. They overlooked the Boer camp and the undisciplined rabble below had no idea that they were even there yet. Colley was supremely confident. He assumed the nonchalant air of success, the detached but dangerous calm of theoretical victory. By the time he realised the terrible mistakes he had made, it was too late.

Majuba was no ordinary hill. It was an extinct volcano. The summit was a shallow hollow that offered no proper view or advantageous position over the Boers except at its very rim. And there, as one appeared on the skyline, a soldier might present himself as an ideal target for any sharpshooter below. The terraced slopes lower down gave better cover than its peak. And there were no Gatlings or rocket tubes: the Naval Brigade had failed to get them up, as they were too heavy for the drag ropes. So they had no heavy ordnance, just their Martini-Henry rifles.

As the sun came up the Boers soon noticed the red-coated enemy above and began to move cautiously towards the hill, occasionally letting off volleys of fire, testing for their range. Colley was asked if they should start digging in, making entrenchments or throwing up breastworks of defence. He replied calmly that this was not necessary. Instead, he ordered a well to be sunk at the bottom of the crater. Water was found at three feet. Rations were opened. At 9.30 a.m. he sent a heliograph message to field headquarters on Mount Prospect: ALL VERY COMFORTABLE HERE. BOERS WASTING AMMUNITION.

'We could stay here for ever,' he announced cheerfully to his adjutant.

Macdonald and twenty men had taken a position on a thin spur that projected from the west of the hillside, with a similar detachment of Highlanders on his flank. The Gordons could now see large numbers of men below the ridge, climbing up and out of general view. Again permission was requested to entrench and prepare better defences. Again Colley denied it.

'All I ask,' he reasoned patiently, 'is that we hold this hill for three days.'

By noon there seemed a clear danger that they were being encircled. A Highland officer was once more dispatched to Colley for instructions but the Major-General was taking a nap and was not to be disturbed.

Colley's calm was finally shattered in the early afternoon, when Commander Romilly, in charge of the Naval Brigade, in full staff dress and holding a pair of field glasses, peered over the western ridge. He noticed that a Boer scrambling below had suddenly stopped and had brought his rifle up to his shoulder.

'I say,' Romilly declared. 'There's a man down there who

looks as if he's going to shoot at us. What do you think the distance is?' he asked his second-in-command, handing him the binoculars.

'Nine hundred yards I should say,' came the reply, just as Romilly clutched at his neck, blood spilling out through his fingers from a mortal bullet wound.

Chaos held command from then on. Men were falling everywhere. The Boers had completely infiltrated the rocky citadel while for the most part remaining invisible. The main body of Colley's force was concentrated in the hollow of the hill, nestled vulnerably in its shallow cupola. Fire came from all quarters. The British held little ground that could protect them, and could scarce see the enemy to return fire. Colley rushed about, vainly trying to muster some coherence of position, of thought even. In the panic all his once lively genius coalesced into a dull and morbid timidity. The Gordons called for the order to charge. To do something.

'Wait!' he cried. 'Wait!'

Colley stood still. He seemed to be making some desperate calculation in his head. He was last seen walking in a circle, waving his white handkerchief about. Whether this was an attempt to surrender the position, or a signal to withdraw, or some other complex sign or new protocol conjured from the depths of his great intellect, it was hard to determine clearly, as within seconds a Boer round struck him in the head, putting an end to the most promising brain in the British Army. Sir George Colley lay dead, still in his carpet slippers.

There was a general flight, redcoats tumbling down Majuba helter-skelter. Macdonald stayed with his men. His detachment still held their meagre edge of spur. Wreathed in fire and smoke he saw them fall around him. Corporal Goss went down and Macdonald crouched beside him. Kenny died in his arms, his red tunic dark with blood. Macdonald held him as he wheezed his last. He stood up once more, expecting to be hit himself at any moment, roaring out unintelligible orders full of rage at the gross stupidity of their situation. He was the last man standing when the Boers finally overran the position.

'It was awful Christina,' he confided to her. 'Awful.'

'But they say that you didn't give in. That you held your ground while others fled.'

'Aye, well, they said lots of things.'

His actions at Majuba had become another great story and he had quietly revelled in the glory of it all when he had arrived back in Edinburgh. Always consciously playing down his bravery, he let others heap praise upon him, cherishing a furtive thrill in the hero-worship of other men. But here with this young redheaded girl he felt no urge to impress. Her little face dimpled with childlike curiosity as it looked up at him. He found a lonely desire to talk about how he really might have felt. To explain what had actually happened to him. The shock of battle had wiped out most of his memory. He could remember little of the last moments but for an oblivious rage.

'I was angry, ye ken?' he said to her. 'I'd seen a lot of fellows die.'

Part of his fury was that he had survived. Of the twenty he commanded that day, twelve had been killed and eight wounded. He alone had escaped unscathed. Fighting Mac had now become a legend and an object of superstition. Fellow men regarded him with an almost fearful apprehension. Majuba marked out another distance between him and ordinary human contact. The day Kenny was killed. Once his other half, now gone forever.

'I lost ma best pal,' he told her softly.

Christina looked at the stern mask of his face and the soft uncomprehending eyes that stared out at the world. He was like a lost little boy with so much to learn. So much that she could teach him. She put her arm into his.

'Like Achilles,' she suggested, walking him along. 'Like his wrath when Patroclus is killed by Hector.'

'I suppose so.'

'Except that you're Hector.'

'Aye.'

'And Hector is killed by Achilles.'

'Is that right?'

'Because Achilles loved Patroclus.'

'Well,' he reasoned, 'they were fighting a war, too.'

'Always wars for men to fight. And women to be left behind.'

'Well that's the way things are.'

'His wife Andromache hardly gets to say anything. Listen.'

She took her arm from his and stood still for a second, making a plaintive gesture with both hands. She then began to recite in a quavering voice:

> *Too daring prince! ah, whither dost thou run?*
> *Ah, too forgetful of thy wife and son!*
> *And think'st thou not how wretched we shall be,*
> *A widow I, a helpless orphan he?*

She played it as melodrama, throwing her head back and rolling her eyes. Macdonald laughed, she smiled at him for a second, then, raising her arms skyward, assumed a tragic countenance once more.

> *Oh grant me, gods, ere Hector meets his doom,*
> *All I can ask of heaven, an early tomb!'*

Macdonald clapped.

'Did ye learn all that off by heart?'

'It's not that hard. As I said, she doesn't get to say much.'

'What is it? The poem, I mean.'

'It's Alexander Pope's translation of Homer.'

'It's very pretty.'

'Well, it might be good poetry but it's soft.'

Macdonald laughed. 'Soft?'

'Yes. She wants to die if he dies. That's silly.'

'She loves him.'

43

'Yes, but there should be more to her life than just that. It's not as though Hector seems to worry about her too much. Achilles shows more love for Patroclus than Hector does for Andromache. Why are there so many stories where women just cry over men? We should have more to do than that. I want to do lots of things.'

'What sort of things?'

'Well, Papa says that I can train as a schoolmistress when I turn sixteen.'

'Is that so?'

'Yes. I'm to go to the Normal and Sessional School at Moray House.'

'That's good.'

'But I want to do a lot more. I want to see something of the world. I don't want to be like Andromache, weeping over some man off to war.'

'That's a shame.'

'Why?'

'Because I plan to be away from here some time soon.'

'Where?'

'Half the regiment is in Egypt. The rest of us might be called to join them at any time. There's fighting to be done out there. Would you no weep for your daring Hector off to battle?'

She scowled at him playfully.

'I certainly would not,' she insisted.

The train arrived at Forest Hill Station. Office clerks and shop managers were making their way home in the gloom. The gas was being lit in the streetlamps of Lordship Lane as he walked towards Christina's house. Dulwich, a quiet little suburb with neatly trimmed hedges and coal-scented air. Home to everything Macdonald had been fighting for in all these years and yet utterly alien to him. Since he had left Edinburgh he had spent only a matter of months in Britain, usually short periods between foreign postings. What it might be to really come home, he had long since given up thinking about. Where that might be was a forgotten dream. Yet his own blood was here in this dreary south London suburb. Wee Hector.

When he rang the bell and heard the footfalls in the hallway he knew that it would be Christina coming to the door. She could not afford servants or even a maid, though she was technically, if not officially, Lady Macdonald. She would not have the privilege of sending him away without seeing him. No refuge in formality. No time or space for subtle dignities. Not now.

He scarcely recognised her framed in the doorway. Her ginger hair in a tight bun, streaked with grey. Her face was creased with the long years of waiting, the once inquisitive expression now withered into a wrinkled frown. She squinted out at him, her eyes struggling to adjust to the dimness of the suburban night. Then she saw that it was him. Her thin lips twisted into a tight little rictus.

'Oh,' she sighed. 'It's you.'

'Christina.'

'I heard you were back. So you've decided to come to visit at last. Isn't that nice?'

'Please . . .'

'I suppose it makes sense now, doesn't it? With what they've been saying. Maybe now you don't want us to be such a great secret.'

'Christina, please. I just want to talk.'

She sighed again.

'Well, you had better come in then.'

VIII

'So, Frater Perdurabo,' the German woman began when they had settled at a table on a nearby café terrace.

'Please,' the Beast countered. 'Call me Aleister, otherwise our discussion may become a little long-winded. Might we not use our temporal names for the time being?'

'As you wish. I am Astrid.'

'A perfectly charming name.' The Beast grinned at her. 'It means fair and beautiful goddess, I believe. Which order do you serve? Die Goldene Dämmerung?'

'That and many others. Of course, many sects and all traditional orders of Freemasonry do not permit women. We are working to change that. We are forming a new sect, Ordo Templi Orientis.'

The Beast had heard something of this German Order and of the man behind it.

'With Theodor Reuss?' he asked.

'You know of him?'

Crowley nodded. Reuss was well known in occult circles in London. He had also been involved in radical politics as well as singing in the music halls. He had left rather swiftly though, when he had been exposed as an agent of the Prussian secret police, employed to spy on émigré Marxists and anarchists.

'I have been sent by him to contact Mathers.'

'For what purpose?'

'For the mutual benefit of our respective orders. There are many charters, constitutions, ritual manuals, permissions and the like that could be usefully exchanged, provenances of documents that could be confirmed.'

The Beast nodded. Mathers was up to something. He still possessed the sacred Cypher Manuscript of the Golden Dawn. He most certainly could not be trusted with it any more.

'And *have* you made contact with Mathers?' he asked her.

'Not yet. When I have called at his temple he is out or indisposed.'

'Indisposed?'

'Unable to receive visitors. Perhaps in the middle of a magical operation. I went there last night and he was in some sort of trance.'

Drunk more like, thought the Beast.

'So that is why I followed you. You are his foremost acolyte, no?'

'I wouldn't describe myself in such a way,' the Beast replied indignantly.

'Oh. I was hoping that I might be able to make representations to Mathers through you. But if this is not possible . . .'

She pouted, her tiny nostrils flaring a touch. Her bright grey eyes wide and imploring.

'Of course I have the authority to act on his behalf,' the Beast assured her. 'I have attained the degree of Adeptus Major. I am a Lord of the Portal to the Vault of the Adepts.'

He hoped that she would look suitably impressed at this but her bowed eyebrows merely twitched slightly, like antennae. He would have to take advantage of the situation. Find out what Mathers was up to, and in the meantime keep the attentions of this sorceress for himself. He looked directly at her and projected the unfocused stare that he had practised for so long. He tried to exert a magical force at her. But her expression remained impassive, her demeanour inviolate, her eyes hard as polished stone.

'Tell me about your new Order,' he said.

'Ordo Templi Orientis will revive the hidden power of the Knights Templar, the pagan powers hidden within Christianity. It will be a rebirth of the pan-Germanic religion, the elevation of the Chosen Few.'

47

'I see.'

'There is a tradition of Higher Beings from the Tibetans, the ancient Aryans, the Tribes of the North that maintained their purity. The Superior Race must cleanse itself through ritual transformation and ceremonial power. And there is one key that will open up all the Masonic and Hermetic secrets.'

'And what is that?' he asked.

'The invocation of power through sexual ritual,' she replied. 'Sexuality is the key to other realities. The ecstasy of the human orgasm unlocks divine knowledge.'

'Quite,' Crowley croaked. His throat had become quite dry.

She had grown animated. The Beast could not help but notice the movement of her finely muscled thorax beneath the tight silk dress. Her breasts were small and firm. Her neck arched as she tossed back her thick mane of curls. He saw the sharp white teeth flash in her mouth as the deep red lips formed the animal grin once more. He was no longer merely intrigued, he was enchanted.

'And the joining of the flesh,' she went on, 'mirrors the cosmic act of creation. We reject the traditional Christian notion that creation happened at some fixed point in the past. It is continuous, always ready to happen. The world is always waiting to be born. Through sex magic we can enact this moment.'

'Sex magic?'

'Of course.'

'And, er, how?'

'Disciplined ritual. Tantric exercises. Techniques learned through Hatha yoga.'

'Oh yes. I've studied yoga.'

'Really?'

One of her antennae arched.

'Yes. In Ceylon.'

She flattened her lips and nodded in approval at this.

'Then you know of Kundalini energy?'

'Yes.'

48

'Then maybe I can initiate you,' she purred at him.

The Beast swooned within; in his mind he was prostrate before her, enslaved by her power. He was overcome by the combination of terror and joy at the thought of his flesh and spirit subjugated to her will. She clearly had extraordinary powers. Perhaps she had cast some spell on him. He would have to be careful.

'Er, yes,' he said. 'Certainly.'

'We are destined to replace the fallen angels and assume their heavenly thrones. We must create a suprasexual, psychocratic elite.'

'Of course.'

'We must attempt to re-order all the various rites, and construct a new temple, an entire edifice, universally recognised, comprising the highest degrees of membership from every Order.'

'Yes.'

'That is why I must contact Mathers, as the nominal head of the Order of the Golden Dawn.'

'Well . . .'

'When can I do this?' she demanded.

The Beast had to put this off for as long as possible.

'It is very difficult at the moment,' he explained. 'You're absolutely right, he is engaged in an important magical working and he can only be disturbed by me, you understand. I will see him later today.'

He would find out exactly what Mathers was up to.

'Shall I come with you to the temple?' she asked.

'No. I'll meet you this evening.'

'Where?'

The Beast thought for a moment.

'Le Chat Blanc.'

'Le Chat Blanc?'

'A restaurant on rue d'Odessa in Montparnasse. Here, I'll write it down for you.'

He took a card from his pocket and wrote the address on the back with a tortoiseshell fountain pen. He handed it to her.

'"Aleister Crowley",' she read out. '"Laird of Boleskine and Abertarff."'

'One of my temporal titles,' the Beast explained. 'Meet me at Le Chat Blanc tonight at eight and all will be revealed.'

IX

A FTER HECTOR HAD KILLED PATROCLUS, he stripped the corpse of its armour and dressed himself in it. *The rich mail Patroclus lately wore, securely cased the warrior's body o'er*, Christina had read from the heavy volume in her father's study all those years ago. It was this part of the story that intrigued her the most. That when Achilles, full of wrath, confronted Hector, he remembered a chink in the breastplate and knew where to strike to take revenge for his beloved comrade.

Christina had always felt that her own Hector had a weak point but she had been too young to know what it was. There had been something assumed in his demeanour. He presented himself so awkwardly, in a manner so forced that it seemed to have belonged to someone else. Someone else's armour. A lover's armour.

Now he was back in her life after all this time. All the rumours she had heard. It would make sense of it all. He sat in the drawing room and she brought them tea.

'What do you want, Hector?' she demanded.

'I came to see you, Christina. And wee Hector too.'

'He's not so wee these days.'

'Aye.'

'You're in trouble, aren't you?'

'Aye, Christina. There's to be a court martial.'

'What in heaven's name have you done?'

'Och, there have been allegations against me. Slanders.'

'Allegations? Of what?'

'Of misbehaviour.'

Christina nearly laughed out loud at this. *Misbehaviour*: it was hardly a word one would associate with Macdonald. He had always been so well mannered and formal. Sober. Restrained. Except for that one time.

'It's all lies, Christina. You have to believe that.'

'Believe?'

'It's a terrible mess, Christina, I just need—'

'What? For me to believe in you? As your faithful wife. Is that it?'

'Please, Christina.'

'Well?'

He started to say something then stopped. He picked up his teacup and took a sip from it. He swallowed. He looked as lost and lonely as he always did.

The Sunday walk became a regular outing for Christina and Hector. Novelty had soon become habit and after a few weeks it did not seem the least bit peculiar that they should spend this time together. It had all started as a game, so there seemed a reassuring playfulness in how they behaved towards each other. A sense of both innocence and mature detachment was maintained between them. They felt aloof from the awkward couples around them engaged in the clumsy rituals of genuine courtship. That he was nearly twice her age did not seem to matter too much either. The combination of her precociousness and his guileless lack of sophistication more than made up for this discrepancy. They were chaperoned by a childlike curiosity in each other.

Her company eased his loneliness; there were long hours between parades and inspections and although he loved drill he had little affection for ceremonial duty or recruiting drives. He still had a tremor of nerves from Majuba and he longed for active service again, if only to feel in control once more. And he dreaded the anxiety of waiting, the idle thoughts of mischief that haunted him. By thinking of Christina he could steer his mind from thoughts of vice that could not, on home service, be excused as a chance aberration of exotic circumstance. She represented purity for him, an antidote to morose delectation. And their relationship, such as it was, was governed by prudence, any expectations postponed into the distant future.

Hector presented a challenge to Christina. That she might improve him. She saw it as her mission to give him an education and to make a gentleman of him. It would be excellent practice for her teaching and make her own study come alive. He was keen to have better manners, some rudiments of culture and a certain moderation of speech and accent. During the week she would assemble facts for his enlightenment. They had begun with the classics and it seemed reasonable that this was the best grounding for him to have. There were times when it was as if she were showing him a brightness that he had been denied. Moments of illumination like the evening when they climbed Calton Hill and stood at the Parthenon as the sun came down over Princes Street, with all the city glimmering like the Modern Athens it aspired to be.

But Hector much preferred the military history of Greece and Rome to their mythology, poetry and philosophy. Christina was disappointed by this and felt that he would never quite grasp the point of a classical education. She wanted to civilise him. He seemed to want to reduce all ancient culture into a drill book or a manual on tactics.

Despite this, it had seemed back then that the whole world was opening up to her. So much to learn and to teach others. Her playful courtship with the gallant lieutenant was a marvellous game. Her head was full of fanciful notions, dreams. She had been so clever back then. Too clever. She had hardly known anything about the world.

Christina had turned sixteen and started to attend Moray House College. The continuation of her friendship with Lieutenant Hector Macdonald seemed to suit everybody around her. Her father was glad that she had such a polite and considerate escort who would not seek to take advantage. Her new friends at college seemed impressed that she was walking out with such a famous officer. Macdonald himself seemed satisfied with the arrangement. Until he was a captain, he would joke with her, his colonel would never grant permission for him to marry.

She did her best to preen him but Macdonald could be tiresome in his resistance to any behaviour that might seem effete or unmanly. He hid behind his Fighting Mac persona and though there was a swagger in his step, he was a heavy-footed dancer. Christina worked hard at college but had playful longings and felt frustrated that her courtship with Hector lacked any real sense of romance. It was the thought that she might effect some change in him that kept her going. Each time they met she felt sure that she would encounter some great transformation in him, born out of the elaborate fantasies that had begun to occupy her. She would wait by the huge gates of Moray House, watching for him along the Royal Mile, hoping somehow that he would suddenly appear as the dashing officer of her imagination, greeting her with some charming and spontaneous gesture. But he would always be Hector. Never less than courteous and attentive but sadly quite dull.

That they would not have much time with each other at least gave their dalliance a momentum that seemed romantic. Most of his regiment were in Egypt with the Army of Occupation. In the Sudan there had been an uprising. The Mahdi, some charismatic Mohammedan, had started a holy war. General Gordon had been sent to the Sudan and was now besieged in Khartoum. Every day there was an article in the press or a public petition calling for a relief mission to rescue the beleaguered hero.

'You left me behind, all those years ago,' she told him, as he sat despondently in her drawing room. 'I grew old waiting, waiting for this.'

'Christina, I never meant—'

'You never meant anything. You went off to Egypt and I never saw you again.'

'Those were the conditions of service.'

'You never even acknowledged me.'

'Och, Kitchener didn't allow married men in his officer corps, you knew that.'

'Oh yes. Kitchener and the Egyptian Army. No married men allowed. How convenient.'

'Christina—'

'Is it all lies then? All that they have been saying about you?'

Macdonald looked down into his cup, as if trying to divine something. Christina remembered the time that he *had* misbehaved. That terrible afternoon.

It was that Sunday when Hector was very keen that they should go and see some demonstration of young lads performing drill.

'They've asked me along to inspect them,' he told her proudly.

Christina sighed wearily but he did not seem to notice.

It was a new organisation set up by a Sunday school teacher from Glasgow, he explained with enthusiasm. Hector held a pamphlet in his hand.

'"For the advancement of Christ's Kingdom among boys and the promotion of habits of Reverence, Discipline, Self-Respect and all that tends towards Christian manliness",' he read out to her. 'They're calling it the Boys' Brigade.'

'Oh, boys,' she chided him. 'Are you not too old for boy's things now?'

'Och, Christina,' he replied, perplexed. 'I just thought.'

'Have you no interest at all in women or girls?'

'Well, of course, Christina.'

'Is it all just manly things with you? And boys?'

Macdonald flushed and went silent. He swallowed and she noticed how his Adam's apple quivered, betraying something. The flaw in his armour. *Where 'twixt the neck and throat the*

55

jointed plate gave entrance, through that penetrable part. She had touched the weak point.

But she had no clear idea what it was. Not then. It was something to do with how he felt about friendship, she had reasoned. How he had once spoken of his lost friend Kenny with such desperate sadness. She felt excluded from it all, denied. Now she was provoked by his reticence.

'Have you no interest in me at all?' she demanded.

'Of course. I'm very fond of you.'

'Kiss me then.'

He went to peck her on the cheek. She held him back.

'Properly,' she insisted.

In a desperately clumsy motion he kissed her on the mouth. Christina was shocked by the urgency of his embrace. A frighteningly sensuous thrill ran through her. He quivered slightly and it struck her that he might feel as she did. That he might be scared too. Frightened, as she was, of the peculiar tremors of the flesh. This might be his weakness, she had thought and was reassured.

'Come,' he told her.

'So, are we off to see this parade?'

'No,' he replied. His tone suddenly flat and cold. 'We're away to somewhere else.'

He led her quickly along the streets of Edinburgh, through the New Town, towards the sordid outskirts of the city. They walked in silence; he had become sullen. They found themselves on Leith Walk, amid groups of revellers. There were stalls and shooting-alleys on each side, caravans and side-shows. Christina was baffled. It was not a place that he would usually approve of going to.

'Hector,' she caught her breath and pulled at his arm to slow down. 'Wait.'

He seemed in a trance, driven by some insistent motive that she could not comprehend. She felt drawn by her own curiosity. Such a strange and dismal place he was taking her to. In the

56

window of a ruined shop stood a dwarfish waxwork in the costume of a French courtier of the *ancien régime*. Parrots and birds of paradise were perched around the entrance to the Great Show of Curiosities; an old crone crouched sentinel, calling out the entrance fee and a delirious babble of far-fetched description. A monkey tethered by a chain and dressed in a filthy sailor-suit scampered about her feet. Along the Walk were hand-carts and wheelbarrows displaying all kinds of drink and vittles, trinkets and novelties. Hawkers lined the path in gaudy costume. There was much crying out, proud boasts of custom, entreaties for charity, the apocalyptic howl of a pamphleteer, all fighting to be heard above the cacophony of grinding organs, the mournful driddling of fiddles and the drone of the riotous throng passing through.

There were revellers coupling lewdly on the Lower Walk. Garish women paraded above, swaying lasciviously, taking up demonstrative postures. There were signs of drunkenness everywhere. They reached a tavern called the Black Bull and he led her inside. She was baffled. He never went to taverns, he scarcely drank.

They sat at a table drinking port wine. She felt flushed and giddy. She started to laugh.

'What's so funny?' he demanded.

He looked so pompous. Amid all the revelry he still looked ridiculously stiff and upright.

'You,' she slurred. 'You're so funny.'

'Aye,' he muttered and drained his glass.

He called for another bottle and whispered something to the publican. Her glass was filled once more. The wine buzzed on her lips, sweet and aromatic. This was getting drunk, she realised. It was a delirious adventure.

He was helping her up. The saloon bar swayed from side to side, strange oaths and thick laughter exploded about the room. She nearly stumbled as he led her through into the hallway.

'Are we going now?' she asked.

'No. No, not yet.'

He pulled at her arm. He was taking her upstairs. The steps seemed to drop away from her. She felt as though she were falling. Falling upwards.

Suddenly they were in a room. A sordid bedchamber with tattered curtains. He closed the door behind them.

'Hector,' she implored.

He held her to him and kissed her once more. As he pulled away she saw the strained concentration on his face.

'This is it, Christina,' he said. 'This is what it is to be a man, they say. This is what counts. Not duty, nor discipline, nor courage in battle. But this.'

He started to pull at her clothes.

'No,' she protested. 'Please.'

'It'll be all right,' he murmured, his tone coldly plaintive, as if trying to reassure himself.

She sensed that there was no use in struggling. He seemed possessed by a cruel determination, a battlefield order. His face impassive, cold. She became nothing, on her back, on the bed, waiting for it to be over. Her once bright world darkened for ever into awful compliance. She had wanted to close her eyes, become oblivious, but she could not. Fear made her a witness to her own degradation.

Yet despite the pain and the humiliation he had caused her, it was he who had sobbed pitifully afterwards.

'I'm sorry, Christina,' he had whined. 'I'm so, so sorry.'

And she felt it had been her fault, as if she had made him do this dreadful thing. He took her back to her father's house and nothing was said. Life had suddenly become bitter for Christina. All her hopes and dreams seemed childish now.

Three days later he received notification of an imminent posting to Egypt. He had come to the house to see her. Her father let him in, calling to her. She hadn't dared look at him at first, wary that any word or gesture between them might betray the guilt of it all. But he behaved as if nothing had happened. He had become the same old dull and reliable Hector. He spoke to her father, explaining his new orders of duty.

'So, you'll be off to save Gordon?' her father enquired with all the predictable enthusiasm of recent speculation.

'We hope so sir,' Macdonald replied. 'We hope so.'

'Well,' her father turned to Christina. 'I guess you'll want to say goodbye to my young girl here.'

Her father smiled at her, then, seeing the sad look on her face, nodded solemnly.

'I'll leave you two then,' he said. 'The very best of luck, Lieutenant.'

The two men shook hands. Then Christina was left alone with him. Frightened and desolate as she was, she knew that she would have to resolve the matter. Macdonald grinned at her.

'Well, I'm off,' he said.

'But what about . . .'

Macdonald hissed out a sigh. There was a hunted look in his eyes.

'You've not said anything?' he muttered furtively.

'No.'

'Then let's forget it.'

'But what if . . .'

'What?'

'What if there's a bairn?'

He let out another deep breath.

'Oh God,' he groaned.

'And I'm left alone with it? What then?'

'Christina . . .'

She suddenly felt angry. And it gave her courage.

'I want to know that there will be some sort of provision made,' she declared. 'If a child comes.'

'What sort of provision?'

'You know.'

'You mean, marriage? God, Christina, there's no time for that. Not now.'

'Yes. Yes, there is. I don't mean a formal wedding in the kirk or anything like that. We can do it in the old style. The Scottish way, you know, by declaration. *De praesenti*, you know how that works, don't you? We can pledge our troth right here and now. Exchange consent.'

'But what about witnesses?'

'Neither of us wants that, do we? And we don't need them. Just a Bible to swear upon. I just need to know. If there's a bairn.'

'And if not?'

'Then it is only me that has been ruined by this. You can forget me. And I will surely forget you.'

'Christina, please.'

'Never mind that,' she retorted. 'You'll swear?'

He nodded slowly and she went to find the holy book. They did it there and then in her father's study.

There was a child and she called it Hector, to make sure that it would be known who the father was. She had the irregular marriage formalised in a Court of Session, solemnised and made legal. Macdonald did not contest the ruling but he was far away by then. He made provision for her and the child, making regular payments, though he never informed his superiors nor the War Office of his marital status.

Christina moved south to have the baby. She had to leave Edinburgh. Leave the respectable world behind her, give up her studies, spend her life raising a child on her own. Constantly made conscious of her fallen state, bearing the looks and muttered comments, the condescension from people when she explained that her husband was away on foreign service.

All her dreams folded up and forgotten for a life of near drudgery. The bloom of her imagination closed like a flower in the darkness. For a long time she had felt she had failed. Failed to make the life for herself that she had craved. And that she failed to civilise him. He was a brute, after all. Now she realised that it had been that flaw in him that had made him behave like that. His weakness.

She had tried hard not to feel bitter. She had her son, that was something at least. She had made sure that he had a good education, got him into Dulwich College, the very best school she could manage, given her circumstances. All her hopes became narrowly focused on him. Her only child, all that she loved. And that, she reasoned, was what he was back here for.

'So, you'll be wanting to see your son, I suppose?' she asked.

'Please.'

'Do you know what it is like to be a secret? To not really exist?'

Macdonald's eyes suddenly flared up at this.

'Aye, I do,' he declared, nodding grimly. 'I do.'

She looked at his forlorn expression but she could not afford to feel any pity for him. It had all been used up.

'Well,' she told him, 'that's your own burden. The fact is I would have had a better life had I been your widow.'

He tried to make some sort of appeal at that but in standing up she silenced him.

'I'll go and get your son,' she told him.

He heard them in the hallway, arguing. Wee Hector was nearly a man now, but his voice was imploring and childlike. He couldn't make out what they were saying, just the mournful tone of instruction and protest. Christina came through on her own.

'He's shy of you. Scared, to tell the truth.'

'Scared?'

'Oh aye, are you not surprised? To have a father called Fighting Mac? A father he has never seen.'

Macdonald stood up and went to the door. Christina let him pass. He saw the boy standing awkwardly on the landing. His son was tall but slightly stooped, as if not fully grown into the frame of his own body. A mop of black hair fringed wide blue eyes bright with fear.

'Hector?' Macdonald intoned softly.

The lad stood before him nervously but it was Macdonald who felt truly helpless.

'Father?'

He didn't know what to say. He wanted to hold him, make some contact over the empty years. The lost time of service. What could he do? He held out his hand and his son took it, weighing the heavy burden of it in his soft palm. There was a single clumsy handshake then they let go of each other.

'Have you come home, Father?' the boy asked him.

'No. I have to be away again.'

'Why have you come back then?'

'To see you. To see the both of you. Have you been a good boy?'

'Yes, sir.'

'Good. Look after your mother now.'

Young Hector looked at him expectantly but Macdonald could think of nothing else to say. After all this time, all the thoughts that he had had about his own son. There were no words for his feelings, just a terrible longing. The tension of the moment was sickening.

'May I go now, Father?'

'Aye,' agreed Macdonald with a doleful sigh.

Christina came out into the hallway as young Hector thundered up the stairs.

'I'd best be off,' he told her.

'So, we're to be left behind again.'

'I'm sorry, Christina.'

'You know, when I was young, I dreamed of seeing the world.'

'Aye, well, I've seen the worst parts of it.'

'And now? What will happen now?'

'I don't know, Christina. I just don't know.'

'Why did you come here, Hector? Did you want our forgiveness or something?'

'I just—'

'Because it's too late for that, you know.'

She saw him to the door. He turned back one last time.

'Goodbye, Christina,' he said.

'Aye,' she replied. 'And may God be merciful.'

On the way back over the river, Macdonald stared out of the train window, trying to make something out of the night, merely catching sight of his stark reflection. The dim electric lamplight on the glass threw the spectral image of his own face back at him. A hollow mask with a puzzled expression. What would he do now? Go back to his club, try to rest. He would have to make arrangements for his passage to the Continent. He had so little time left now.

It was then that he had remembered something. A scrap of knowledge. A comment he had heard in the dining room of the Army and Navy about the appointment of a new Inspector General of Cavalry. Bathing-Towel would be in London, he realised. Though, of course, no one called him that any more.

X

I SAW A WOMAN SIT upon a scarlet beast, full of names of blasphemy, having seven heads and ten horns, mused Crowley as he strode energetically along the Boulevard St Michel. He took the lines from the Book of Revelation and gave them to the fascinating German creature. Astrid, Fräulein Sprengel, Soror Dominabitur Astris, full of names of blasphemy, just as he was.

He had grown up with his father's hell-fire sermons and the Plymouth Brethren's unwavering assertion that everything in the Bible was God's word. Beneath his mother's vigilant disapproval little Alick, as he was known then, revelled in the descriptions of torments in the holy book and developed an instinctive love of terrors. He had an easier affection for his father, a maniacal evangelist and a leader of men. He loved him just as he had feared him and felt secure in his belief in the coming apocalypse. But when Alick was eleven, Crowley senior developed cancer of the tongue and no amount of prayer by the Brethren could save him. Before he died the great man was struck dumb, his organ of pious eloquence cruelly mutilated. Crowley felt profoundly betrayed. First by the God of Creation who had conceived such a terrible punishment, then by his earthly father who had deserted him for the next world. He had been abandoned with no one to look up to or respect any more. He became difficult, ill-mannered and defiant of discipline. His mother found it hard to control him and they began to share only a brooding resentment. One day she caught him in a shameful act, curled up in her own bed, and it was from that moment she began calling him the Beast. He took the name with all the grace in which it was given. From then on he was intent on rejecting their religion. He would have his revenge on it. The only way to do that, he decided, was to transform it, to make it his own heresy.

He thought of Astrid once more. Perhaps she could be the Scarlet Woman of Revelation. Lady Babylon, the sacred whore, drunk with the blood of the saints and in direct communion with the Hidden Ones. Sex magic, he remembered with a delicious shudder. In Revelation the Scarlet Woman rode the Beast. Yes, this was how it would be. She might be his spiritual consort. *I will tell thee the mystery of the woman and the beast that carrieth her.* To be possessed by her would set him free.

Free of him, he thought with a deadening sense of loss. He had stopped at the corner of boulevard St Germain, transfixed for a moment, entranced by a sudden regret. 'A pure and noble comradeship', he had called it, unwilling or unable to admit what it really was. He knew now that it had been his first love. The meeting with the General had brought this up perhaps. He sighed and started to walk once more, quickening his pace as if to accelerate his purpose.

Ah! The world, the world . . . the failure of the world . . . his footsteps muttered as he turned into St Germain. Once more came the lamented name: Pollitt.

They had first met during Michaelmas term of his last year at Cambridge. He had gone to a Footlights revue in October 1897. The star of the show had been a female impersonator performing a 'Serpentine Dance', channelling the outrageous persona of Diane de Rougy. Jerome Pollitt MA had graduated from Cambridge five years before but still took part in university productions. He was well known among bohemian circles and had a reputation for mischief that fascinated the young Beast.

Crowley himself had been a precocious student, already imagining himself a great poet and boasting of possessing supernatural powers. He had experimented with alchemy and was searching for secret knowledge without much success. He was drawn to Pollitt's protean energy. Here he saw the strange charm of transformation that he longed for, the power of transfiguration. He had told him as much backstage.

'Heavens, darling,' Pollitt had retorted with a louche drawl. 'It's only a bit of skirt-dancing.'

Out of make-up Pollitt was a melancholy spectacle. His face had been made plain by a terrible hunger of the eyes and a bitter sadness of the mouth. He was a slave to beauty. An aesthetic sense was everything to him. All his displays of flippancy masked the deep seriousness he felt about his art. Life was all an act, but that's what he lived for. He wore an insouciant expression that always yearned for a touch of paint or powder. He cared little for the sun; his spirit flourished in artificial illumination. Touched by the limelight, his face would open like a flower. His one great natural attribute was the shock of pale gold hair that framed a bright contrast to his darkling features. Each long filament of this halo seemed to hold a delicate incandescence of its own. Oscar Wilde had once called him 'a sort of gilt sunbeam masquerading in clothes'.

Flattered by a young man's attentions, Pollitt accepted an invitation back to Alick's rooms. They talked into the early hours over a bottle of green Chartreuse. His host, like Pollitt, was more fond of night than of day. He was staying in St John Street, overlooking the chapel. The dark belltower loomed up at the window. Pollitt draped himself languidly over a chaise longue. His eyes hooded and inert, nodding with amused patience as Alick explained his mystic quest.

'Alchemical elements are sexual: sulphur is male, salt is female.'

'Fancy that.'

'They can create a transcendent union with philosophical mercury.'

'Mercury?'

'Mercury is the spirit of flux.'

'It's the only treatment for syphilis, darling. Nasty though. Turned Oscar's teeth quite black.'

'It's a hermaphrodite element.'

'Well, I know all about that, dear.'

'Do you take anything seriously?'

'Oh yes,' Pollitt replied, sonorously.

He stood up and made a plaintive gesture with his hands.

'My performance,' he went on.

'You were very good,' Crowley offered.

'Just my little sacrificial burlesque . . .'

Pollitt swayed slowly, began to dance, his eyes becoming alive once more. He murmured something unintelligible, reaching down to take hold of the young Beast. Alick found himself eagerly submitting to Pollitt's enthusiastic caresses. There was a narcissistic pleasure in being handled as a thing of beauty by such an experienced aesthete and he felt a divine sense of corruption, of alchemical profanity. The bitter taste of salty flesh, the sulphurous incense of the body, the elixir of life that flowed like precious quicksilver. By dawn his mind was numb with forbidden knowledge. They lay together, naked and exhausted as the great grey tower cut clear against the deep blue of morning.

Pollitt became a regular visitor in Lent term when Crowley took new rooms in Trinity Street. Crowley conceived the decoration himself, inspired by his recent initiation. A sickly yellow distemper on the walls and black detailing on the woodwork gave a suitably jaundiced air to the interior. There were Japanese prints and extravagantly bound editions on his bookshelves, the floor was covered with a Persian carpet of peacock blue. Only one corner was free of the influence of his new mentor. Here lay a curious circular mosaic, edged with a band of white marble with an inscription in an unfamiliar language inlaid in vivid red. Two full-length dark mirrors lined the niche. In front of them was placed a small round table supported by an ebony figure of a negro standing on his hands. On its surface was a goat's skull Crowley had found while climbing in Cumberland. The beginnings of an altar. A shrine to something that he didn't yet understand.

The Beast had great ambitions for his poetry and knew that there was still so much to learn from his venerable dandy. Pollitt was a connoisseur, a collector of the works of Aubrey Beardsley, an acquaintance of Oscar Wilde. He could introduce him to a school of art and literature that Crowley had instinctively despised, even while he adored it. His vanity admitted a grudging sense of admiration for something he wanted to transcend. But first he would have to study it. There was an intense refinement of its thought and a blazing brilliance in its technique, a level of artistry as yet beyond his scope. Here were depths to be explored. Pollitt was to be his decadent education.

Pollitt exercised a peculiar influence on the young Beast's desire for expression, compelling him to let go of himself. He also introduced him to Leonard Smithers, art dealer, bookseller, pornographer *par excellence*, who produced various obscure imprints from his shop in Arundel Street near the Strand. Smithers was the most learned erotomane in Europe and the only publisher who dared to issue the works of the disgraced and exiled Oscar Wilde.

'I publish anything the others are scared of,' he boasted over lunch.

Smithers was thickset, loud and impudent. He wore a blue cravat indelicately fastened with a huge diamond tie-pin. His pallid and puffy features Pollitt had likened to the death mask of Nero. He drank champagne from a pint glass. His unapologetic vulgarity was disarming.

'Poets are wrecking my life, you know,' he declared to Crowley.

But he would publish his work. Just as long as costs were met beforehand. This did not matter as the Beast had recently come into his majority. He had a small fortune. They agreed business and Smithers went on to recount that he had once sold a book bound in human skin.

'For a fantastically high price, mind,' he commented blithely. 'Due to the severe prejudices of medical men, it's extremely difficult to obtain portions of dead humanity.'

The Beast was intoxicated by a sense of sinfulness and the atmosphere of dissolution. His muse taunted him with an evil humour and moods of terrible laughter. He conceived a series of poems that would offer a confessional account of the decline of a young man into utter degradation. A progress of diabolism and insanity, the extremes of pleasure, the worst of pain, a chronicle of sodomy, buggery, pederasty, coprophilia, bestiality, impotence and finally necrophilia. It was Pollitt who came up with the sublime title for the work: *White Stains*.

'You must plumb the depths of joy,' he urged him. 'And soar to the heights of despair.'

The Beast completed the cycle of thirty-six poems in three weeks and pseudonymously subtitled the collection: 'The Literary Remains of George Archibald Bishop, a Neuropath of the Second Empire'. Smithers was delighted with *White Stains* and had a hundred copies printed in Amsterdam.

Crowley was exhausted and overcome by the inevitable disappointment that comes with finishing a creative endeavour. He felt empty. He had expected some kind of catharsis that had failed to manifest itself.

'You shouldn't expect salvation, you know,' said Pollitt, trying to console him. 'You'll only be disappointed.'

'You always joke about this. But I want spiritual sensations. Not just physical ones.'

'Oh dear.'

'All acts are sacramental. Perhaps the most repulsive might be the most effective.'

'For what?'

'To invoke something sacred.'

'Now you are being sanctimonious. Your problem Alick, is that you don't enjoy your perversions. You perform them to overcome your horror of them. As for you and your great temple . . .' Pollitt made a dismissive gesture to the corner of the room.

'Decadence isn't enough for me,' the Beast insisted.

'Decadence? Really! Now you are being vulgar. No one talks about decadence any more.'

'I don't want that anyhow,' he protested. 'I want transcendence.'

'Well, how bloody grand. You want to rise above it all.'

'Why not?'

'Aspiration,' Pollitt hissed. 'Spiritual or otherwise, it's so middle-class. Keeping up with everybody.'

'And I suppose you want to drag the whole universe down to your level?'

'Oh, God, yes. If I could. When I want to transcend, a simple glass of champagne will give my soul wings.'

'Your problem, Jerome, is that you are utterly shallow.'

'I always try to be.'

'Do you believe in anything at all?'

'I wonder if you have ever thought of becoming a preacher.'

'Good heavens, no. Why do you ask?'

'I didn't ask, Alick. I merely wondered. You profess rebellion against your evangelical upbringing but are you really free of all that?'

The Beast started to say something then stopped. He frowned at his lover.

'And yes,' Pollitt went on, 'I'm terrified of anything that takes you away from me.'

'Jerome . . .'

Pollitt forced a smile. 'I had lobster salad for luncheon yesterday.'

'What?'

'Lobster salad. And a glass or two of port. It did not give me indigestion but rather an acute sense of remorse.'

'Remorse for having had the luncheon?' Crowley asked.

'No. A yearning remorse for all the ridiculous things I have done, and still mean to do. A feeling indistinct yet overwhelming. But it was just the lobster and the port. You see, food doesn't affect the body; it affects the soul. Sermons, on the other hand, merely make me hungry.'

'I was only trying to say—'

'So please spare me the sermons, Alick. Now, if you'll excuse me, I really need to go and have dinner.'

Pollitt gently padded out of the room. The Beast felt a sense of remission for a few days, then resentment when Pollitt failed to write to him or make any sort of contact. He was dismayed to discover how deeply he had become attached to the man. He brooded with morose indignation, unable to write, his imagination a dismal forcing house of *ennui*. He felt stifled and needed air. He decided that on going down on the Easter vacation, he would spend a week rock-climbing in Cumberland.

He was packing his bags when Pollitt came up to his rooms.

'Alick,' he implored. 'I'm sorry.'

'The fact is Jerome, we're at odds. There's a deep-seated aversion to each others' souls.'

'But not our bodies, I hope.'

Pollitt reached out and touched him. Crowley felt a tremor in his breast.

'Jerome,' he whispered.

'I'm not entirely disenchanted with the universe, you know. I just find it hard to take all this spirit-mongering seriously.'

'But what do you take seriously?'

'Well, that's just it. Not taking things seriously is my vocation. A sense of humour is my religion. Please don't go.'

'I must.'

'But I will be so terribly lonely.'

'Then come with me.'

'Don't be silly.'

'I mean it.'

'You mean stay with you,' – Pollitt shuddered visibly – '*outdoors?*'

'There's a hotel at Wasdale Head. It's very civilised.'

'Well, thank goodness for that.'

They walked over the fells together, the Beast in his climbing boots, Pollitt shrouded in a huge woollen shawl. A clear blue canopy stretched over jagged scree and stern crags frowned down upon Wast Water.

'Isn't it marvellous?' Crowley demanded.

'Well, it's pretty, I suppose. Rather too much nature though.'

The Beast had brought a curious book with him, *The Cloud upon the Sanctuary* by Karl von Eckartshausen. It had been recommended to him by a Cambridge bookseller to whom he had professed an interest in the occult. It was a text of the Illuminati and the Rosicrucians. At first Crowley did not know what to make of it. It appeared to offer the key to divine and angelic intelligence. There was an 'interior and invisible Church' somewhere, a 'society of the Elect'. But where would he find them? The Beast yearned for transformation, metamorphosis.

'I want a new name, Jerome,' he complained. 'I'm sick of being Alick.'

'Why not just call yourself Alice?'

'Jerome . . .'

'I was thinking of calling myself Hippolyta. You see: Pollitt, Hippolyta. Hmm, quite fancy being Queen of the Amazons. As for you, you'll be wanting a *serious* name, now won't you? Well, the whole thing should be cinquesyllabic.'

'Cinquesyllabic?'

'Of course. If you want something grand, that is, and you certainly do. Five syllables. Three followed by two. A dactyl followed by a trochee. You've already got that with Crowley. You don't want to change that, do you?'

'No. But I hate Alick. It's what my mother calls me.'

She calls you the Beast as well, a voice told Crowley. *But you like that, don't you?*

'What about Aleister?' Pollitt suggested. 'It's the Gaelic equivalent of Alexander, after all.'

'Aleister?'

'Yes. And it's like Alastor. You know, the Shelley poem: "Alastor, or the Spirit of Solitude". Seeking strange truths in undiscovered lands.'

'The spirit of solitude. I like that.'

'Yes. I rather thought you would.'

During the days the Beast practised 'bouldering'. Rock-climbing without ropes that concentrated on balance and agility. He was exploring and perfecting techniques that would advance his ability to tackle longer and more arduous routes. Pollitt watched him from a distance.

'You are quite the mountain goat.'

'This is mere practice. I intend to climb a big mountain some day soon. A real expedition.'

'So up you go. Then down you come. Don't you just end up where you started?'

'Well, I don't expect you to understand the mystical power of the experience.'

'Here we go again.'

'I don't give in to despair. No matter what depths I plumb I am determined to rise upwards. To me it's a question of virility.'

'Well, aren't you the big rough girl.'

By the end of the week Crowley had finished *The Cloud upon the Sanctuary*. It finally made sense to him. It was what he had been searching for. Amid its arcane obscurity shone an astonishingly simple fact, something he had always known: that he was destined to become one of the Chosen. But first he would have to choose himself: between the affection and desire he felt for Pollitt and a devotion to the Secret Assembly of the Saints. He tried to explain when they got back to Cambridge.

'But this is ridiculous,' Pollitt retorted. 'You must see that it is all simply ridiculous.'

'I am determined to make myself worthy enough to attract the notice of this mysterious brotherhood.'

'Please, Alick.'

'I'm not Alick any more. I'm Aleister.'

'Yes. Of course you are. An alastor is a tormenting spirit. You know that don't you?'

And with that they had parted. It had been all too soon. He

knew now that he had learned so much from Pollitt. A sense of wit and deprecation necessary to deal with a brutal cosmos. He had been wrong to reject him. Jerome had represented a side to his nature he had always been slightly timid of. But then the Beast had always desired both men and women. He had tried to explain it once.

'I love them both,' he had told Pollitt.

'Yes,' his lover had replied archly. 'But you don't really *like* either very much, do you?'

They only saw each other on two further occasions. The first was shortly after Crowley had gone down from Cambridge. He was staying at a hotel in Maidenhead and trying to finish a long poem. Pollitt had found out where he was and was determined to have it out with him.

'Jerome, I'm working,' the Beast had insisted.

Pollitt picked up a sheet of paper from the writing desk.

'What's this?' he said, reading the page. '*Jezebel*. I suppose this is about me. Well, I'm not flattered.'

'It's not about you,' Crowley lied.

'"And on my cheek the kiss of hell/the hatred of my Jezebel." Come on, that's me, isn't it?'

'It's nothing to do with you.'

'Still the same overwrought style. After all I taught you.'

'Don't you understand? I'm on a different path from you.'

'Oh, Alick, please.'

'I'm on a sacred journey. I need to go on alone.'

'And leave me behind?'

'Yes.'

'Very well then.'

The Beast sat staring at the pages for a long time after Pollitt had left. He began to sob very gently and wrote these lines:

> Then, as a man betrayed, and doomed
> Already, I arose and went
> And wrestled with myself, consumed

With passion for that sacrament
Of shame. From that day unto this
My cheek desires that hideous kiss.

In the autumn he happened to pass Pollitt in Bond Street. He raised a hand and began to utter a salutation but Pollitt had cut him dead and walked on.

The Beast turned right into rue Bonaparte and headed towards the river. He stopped at an elegant confectioner's and bought a box of pink *dragées*. He needed a little comfort. He rolled a sugared almond in his mouth and tried to banish the lingering regret he felt for his lost friendship. His lost love.

He shrugged visibly, as if trying to wrest himself free of the mistakes of the past, and set his mind on the intriguing possibilities of the future. Deep down he had never really been sure what he believed in but right at this moment everything seemed so auspicious. He would try anything from now on, go from decadence to transcendence and back again if need be. He thought of the poor General, waiting for the scandal to break. It was a sign. The power of the secret that could bring the heavens down. Astrid's talk of sex magic, maybe that was the key to it all. The Beast would have to prepare himself. For all this and his inevitable conflict with Mathers.

He reached an eccentric bookshop on the corner, its windows cluttered with strange prints, obscure heraldry and Masonic regalia. *Ésotérisme et curiosités*, read a sign on the door. He pushed at it and went inside.

XI

THE INSPECTOR GENERAL OF CAVALRY had set up a desk in his room and sat scribbling in a ledger. He had been home only a fortnight but he was determined to get started on this new book. There was no clear plan to it, it was a collection of ideas really, but he had finally caught a sudden vision of it. Of what it could mean. It was discursive, confused even, but supremely expansive. It was a great new adventure. It could just be the most wonderful thing that he would ever do.

The battered military dispatch box lay on its side, spilling out the evidence: loose notes he had made in longhand, newspaper cuttings, extracts torn from adventure novels and true crime stories, observations, travel writing, clippings of his own journalism, his drawings and illustrations. The old rattle bag that he had carried around for years. Full of junk, scraps of genius, ready to be transformed. It would have to be playful, that was the key. It would be a ramble but an engaging one. Entertaining, like a fireside yarn.

On the Observation of Insects, he had written as a heading. _Bees: about bees alone whole books have been written – for they have wonderful powers in making their honeycombs, in finding their way for miles – sometimes six miles – to find the right kind of flowers for giving them the sugary juice for making honey, and getting back with it to the hive._ He stopped and chewed at the end of his pencil for a moment, then added: _They are quite a model community, for they respect their Queen and kill their unemployed._

He smiled to himself. A little sting of learning, he mused. The nettle-rash of childhood. Then he felt a sting himself. That the Queen bee was dead. He would never become completely accustomed to the fact that Victoria had gone. Motherless Empire, what a dreadful thought. The Widow of Windsor – all the years she spent in mourning had never quite prepared anyone for her passing.

His own mother still lived and ruled with an iron will. The formidable Henrietta Grace. Here he was, after so many years of foreign service, back at home living with her. Even at forty-five, this was expected. Until he married, of course. And that was her next big plan for him. Now that he had gained fame and a secure station in society. And he would dutifully follow her will. He could not think of her at all without a pang of guilt. 'If only your dear father had lived', she would often say to her children. She had raised them all on her own, made so many plans for their futures. When he once tearfully insisted that her passing would be the worst thing in the world for him, she had replied, 'There is something worse than you losing me; what if I were to lose you?' When he smiled and asked if she meant him dying she gave him a fierce glare and declared, 'No, I mean if I lost you in life, if you were to turn out wrong and bring disgrace upon the family'. There came a light tapping at his door.

'Come,' he intoned.

'There's a gentleman to see you, sir,' said the manservant as he stood by the open door.

For a brief and happy moment he thought that it might be Boy Maclaren, his fellow officer in the Hussars and dearest loving friend. Then he realised that it couldn't be. The Boy was married and in Scotland. Married. So much to get used to.

'Who is it?' he demanded.

'It is Sir Hector Macdonald, sir.'

He started at the name. Him. Back home in disgrace. It was a stark counterpoint to his own triumphant return and he found it hard not to think of it as a dreadful warning. Just as he had come to London victorious, the hero of Mafeking, poor Fighting

Mac had been caught out in Ceylon. Rumours of the scandal had spread like a drop of ink in water. It meant danger for all of them. He knew that he should send him away, inform him politely that he was not at home to visitors. But he felt a melancholy surge of pity for a fellow soldier. And a fearful curiosity for his fate. He gathered up his notes.

'I'll come down,' he told his man.

He saw Macdonald standing stiffly by the mantelpiece as he entered the drawing room. He observed how the wretched man fairly started as he approached him.

'Baden-Powell,' Macdonald mumbled, still clumsily thinking of him after all these years as 'Bathing-Towel'. 'I'm much obliged, sir.'

Baden-Powell made to hold out his hand, then realised that he had his dispatch box under his arm. He pulled it out with one hand to lay it down on a side table. There was a brief dance as Macdonald at first presented his hand, retrieved it a moment, then offered it once more. Amid the awkwardness, Baden-Powell was relieved to find the handshake firm, that he could look the man in the eye. Macdonald's gaze was as steely as ever. How many years since Kandahar? he thought with a shiver. The grizzled face, now so grim and brooding was still handsome. Macdonald broke the stare to glance down at the dispatch box.

'I'm sorry if I've interrupted your work,' he said.

'No, no,' Baden-Powell explained. 'Just some lark of my own. Ideas for a book.'

'A book?'

'Yes. Well, I've been given Inspector of Cavalry. A glorified desk job really. I'll have time for this.' He patted the battered red box affectionately.

'What is it?' Macdonald asked. 'A memoir?'

He remembered the book that had been published about his own life three years before: *Hector Macdonald, or the Private who became a General: A Highland Laddie's Life and Laurels*. His once great fame would now be ground into the dust.

'No, no,' Baden-Powell corrected him. 'Just something to amuse myself really. I wrote a manual on reconnaissance and scouting a while back. Thought I might use some of the ideas for a book for boys. Maybe a handbook for instruction and good citizenship. Something to strengthen the imperial instinct in young lads, but with plenty of games and outdoor exercises.'

'A splendid idea.'

'I've been invited to speak at the annual demonstration of the Boys' Brigade in May.'

'I've always been dead keen on the Boys' Brigade,' Macdonald enthused.

'Indeed,' Baden-Powell replied.

They stared at each other for a moment, not sure of where to go.

'So, they gave you Ceylon.'

'I'm looking for another posting.'

'I'm not sure if I can help you,' replied Baden-Powell tersely.

There was another uncomfortable silence.

'I'm sorry,' he went on.

'Tell me more about this book.'

'Well, scouting seems a perfect metaphor for boyhood. Finding a track through, into the future. The problem with the Boys' Brigade is that it is all drill and discipline. Sorry, I mean no offence.'

'None taken.'

'Of course boys need discipline. There are so many temptations.'

'Yes.'

'Beastliness,' Baden-Powell declared. 'We must find ways of discouraging it. Whatever temptations that we ourselves face. The young must be forewarned. They must be made ready for the travails ahead. They must . . .' He thought for a second. 'They must be prepared, yes, that's it.'

Baden-Powell reached out to the dispatch box. He would have to make a note of that somewhere, he thought. He stared off into the room. Macdonald noticed his features slacken into an absent expression.

'I'm sorry,' Macdonald said. 'I'm keeping you from your work.'

Baden-Powell started a little.

'No, no,' he insisted. 'What were we saying?'

'About scouting.'

'Yes. Excellent exercise. And woodcraft. Games and fireside yarns. The important thing is to make it playful. Boys are full of romance and they love make-believe more than they like to show. We need to put youth back into the heart of the empire. And it is how we should rule. As the sweet, just, boyish master of the world.'

Macdonald smiled.

'It's a charming idea,' he said.

'We should develop the imagination along with the body,' he went on. 'Strengthen the imperial instinct in recreation.'

'You have a point there. But I'm afraid drill is all I know really.'

'Yes,' Baden-Powell sighed.

He looked at the poor man who stood so straight. Loyal and attentive, he presented an easy target. He was an old soldier, with no sense of camouflage.

'There are hidden trails for us to find too,' Baden-Powell went on, now referring to the unspoken, the unspeakable. 'We have to cover our tracks. Learn our own dodges and secret codes.'

And Macdonald knew that he was right. Mere discipline was not enough. It had never been enough.

'It's too late for that now,' he said mournfully.

'Is it? You've seen the Chief?'

'Yes.'

'And?'

'It looks like a court martial.'

Baden-Powell gasped.

'Good God.'

'I'm to return to Ceylon. Try to clear my name.'

'Look, Macdonald, I wish there was something I could do. Really, but . . .'

'I understand.'

'There must be something. When do you leave?'

'I'll get the boat train to Paris at the end of the week.'

'Do you have any friends in Paris?'

Macdonald gave a bitter laugh.

'I don't have any friends anywhere. Not any more.'

'My dear man, I hope you don't think I'm shunning you.'

'I didn't mean—'

'It's just that . . .'

'I know. I know.'

Macdonald held out his hand once more.

'Thank you for seeing me,' he said as they shook again. 'Many wouldn't have.'

Baden-Powell smiled sadly then remembered something.

'You know Edward Stuart-Wortley, don't you?' he asked.

'Aye,' Macdonald replied. 'We were in the Egyptian Army together.'

'I thought so. Well, he's in Paris. Military Attaché to the British Embassy.'

'I'll bear that in mind.'

'You never know.'

'I'd best be off now.'

Macdonald showed himself out. Baden-Powell sat in the drawing room, brooding. There was something he had wanted to make a note of. What was it? He couldn't concentrate, his entire consciousness burdened with the image of the doomed Fighting Mac, that poor friendless man at the mercy of the curious and vengeful. It *was* a warning to him. The world knew too much now. He would have to be careful.

He finally roused himself from that grim reverie and mounted the stairs once more. He heard his mother come to the landing and call down to him.

XII

THE PROPRIETOR OF THE SHOP emerged from the cluttered back room to greet Crowley.

'Good day, your lairdship,' he said, with a grin.

'Good day to you, Blanchot.'

The walls of the shop were covered with cosmological maps and charts, arcane genealogies, garish mandalas, zodiacal etchings and engravings, an ancient woodcut showing the diagram of the Kabbalah. There were ceremonial objects, animist artefacts, items of ritual costume, crystals, incense burners and candelabra, oils and chrisms, Tarot packs, a human skull and a dusty specimen jar that contained what looked like a curled-up lizard. But most of the space in the small shop was taken up with books and manuscripts. There were alchemic texts, *grimoires*, incunables. Shelf headings listed mysticism, spiritualism, astrology. There were books on the occult sciences, the paranormal, hermeticism, ectoplasmic phenomena, spirit photography, levitation and telekinesis. The premises were crammed with a chaos of gnosis, a word-hoard of all types of heretical writing. The Beast had come here often and been a good customer.

'I have something for you,' the owner announced.

'What?'

Blanchot hesitated.

'Wait,' he said with a smile. 'It would certainly be bad for business to let you know if you were looking for something anyway.'

'Just information.'

'All part of the service.' Blanchot sighed jovially.

Blanchot was fat and rubicund, with a genial demeanour that

seemed at odds with his position as proprietor of a shop specialising in the dark arts. He was jocular and playful but he knew as much about matters of the occult as any man in Paris.

'Do you know of Theodor Reuss?' the Beast asked.

Blanchot laughed. 'That scoundrel.'

'I heard that he was a police spy.'

The bookseller waved his hands dismissively.

'Much worse than that. He is notorious in our trade for buying and selling masonic charters. Forgeries mostly. He speculates on the occult market, trading sacred texts and authenticating doctrines of dubious origin.'

'And you don't like the competition?'

'What we do is not merely trade, you know. It is a vocational craft. A mystery to be protected.'

'He has tried to make contact with Mathers.'

'Ah! Your great rival and former master.'

'Good God!' the Beast exclaimed, suddenly realising a terrible possibility. 'Perhaps the old fool is planning to sell the precious Cypher Manuscript of the Golden Dawn to Theodor Reuss! Well, I'm not going to let that happen.'

'Quite,' Blanchot agreed.

Crowley found the shopkeeper's tone rather overly reassuring.

'Wait a minute,' he added, pursuing yet another thought. 'Has he ever approached you about it?'

'The Cypher Manuscript? Look, I'd tell you if he had. Your credit is good enough to give you first refusal. And it would fetch a good price. So, you are still at odds with Mathers?'

The Beast told him about the magic square and demonstrated how he had counteracted it.

'How marvellous!' Blanchot declared. 'It is like the great magical battle between Stanislas de Guaita and Abbé Boullan.'

'Who?'

'Oh, they were infamous in Paris back in the early nineties. Boullan was a renegade priest and self-styled exorcist who performed exotic rites in honour of Melchizedek. Stanislas de

Guaita headed the Cabalistic Order of the Rosy Cross with Sar Peladan. Ah!' He sighed wistfully. 'Those were the days.'

'What happened?'

'Well, Boullan died in '93 and Guaita was accused by many of killing him with some sort of supernatural curse. He was dead himself by '97. Drug overdose.'

'And what were they fighting about?'

'Oh, they had accused each other of devil worship, witchcraft. The usual. Of course the real satanist back then was Abbé van Haecke, chaplain of the Holy Blood at Bruges. He was said to be the wickedest man in Europe.'

'Only Europe? That's a meagre ambition for a satanist.'

'It was rumoured that he had crosses tattooed on the soles of his feet so that he might have the pleasure of continually trampling upon the symbol of the Saviour.'

'Charming.'

'He gave himself body and soul to Satan. Like so many others. Speaking of which . . .' Blanchot looked around furtively. 'I told you I had something for you.'

The Beast was intrigued. He leaned forward.

'What is it?' he asked.

'What you've been hoping to witness for a long time now. You enquired about it weeks ago. Well, now I know of one happening.'

'You mean?'

'Yes,' Blanchot hissed. '*Une messe noire*. Tonight.'

He took out a card from a drawer in his desk and handed it to Crowley. On it was an address and the word ASMODEUS.

'That is the password. You are to be there at midnight. If you're still interested.'

'Thank you,' said the Beast, pocketing the card. 'And the cost?'

'Only your soul. A trifling matter for you.'

'Very funny. But is a payment necessary?'

'Financially? No. Black masses are not that kind of a racket.

84

If you are a priest and you really want to make money, you sell ordinary masses.'

'Really?'

'Oh yes. You know that there's this poor abbé in Languedoc who somehow managed to renovate his church, new tower and everything. Rumours were that he'd found some sort of treasure buried in the crypt. Nothing of the sort, of course. Where did he get the money? I'll tell you where. Mail-order masses.'

'What?'

'Yes. The sin of simony, very lucrative. You advertise in religious periodicals all over the world. There's no end of people who want a proper Roman mass held for them. So thousands of subscriptions come pouring in every month, one franc a mass, over the years it starts to add up.'

'But how is the priest supposed to say all these masses?'

'Well, he doesn't, does he? Just pockets the money. Simple as that. The thing is, the rumours in Languedoc continue, they get wilder. The treasure becomes a parchment rolled up in the hollow of a column revealing a fantastical secret.'

'What sort of secret?'

'Oh, you know, a hidden tradition, a gnostic alternative to orthodox scripture, the secret of the Holy Grail, you name it. But most of all a conspiracy. That's what people want these days: conspiracy. It reassures. It flatters the believer into thinking that they are sophisticated enough to know that they are being fooled. But it also allows them the luxury of impotence, the illusion that there are powers above and beyond that control everything. Conspiracy makes order out of chaos, that's what people want. They make perfect sense, that's the beauty of them. A perfect sense that reality always fails to provide.'

'You know, Blanchot, that's what I've always looked for.'

'Well, if you want a really good conspiracy there's a wonderful manuscript doing the rounds. Called the Protocols. It's in Russian. Another forgery, of course. It's a lovely piece of work though, sets out the plans that the Jews have for taking over the world. Could be very popular, just needs a good translator.'

'I can't help you there, I'm afraid.'

'Too busy searching for your own version of the truth?'

'That's right.'

'Ah well, without forgeries and conspiracies, I'd be out of business.'

'I believe that the only way to deal with such things is to create them for oneself.'

'An admirable plan.'

'I'm working on it.'

'A spiritual path. But where will it lead?'

'I really don't know, Blanchot.' The Beast held up the card that he had been given. 'It looks as if one might descend from lofty mysticism to base satanism in one step.'

Blanchot laughed heartily at this.

'And why not?' he proposed. 'After all, the modern age is certainly a demonic epoch. Now that God is well and truly dead, it is the age of the Devil.'

'That we have made it so?'

'Perhaps. Though I think that he has taken the initiative. Society has become his apprentice.'

'He is a master craftsman then?'

'No, no.' Blanchot shook his head. 'He is an aesthete. A great artist! And this new century will be his canvas.'

XIII

THERE WAS A KNOCK AT the hotel room door. A bell boy with a letter. Macdonald tore it open. It was from the War Office. So, it was official now. A court martial was to be held in Ceylon. Kitchener was to provide the required number of members. That was it then. Kitchener would make sure of it. This was his chance to get rid of Fighting Mac for good.

There is another way, you know, he remembered grimly.

The last appointment he had in London had been unexpected. He had been called to Marlborough House on his final day there. It was obviously considered more discreet than the Palace. This wasn't to be a formal audience, after all. This meeting was certainly not to be recorded. He was quietly ushered in to a room at the back where a portly man stood in half shadow.

'Have a drink, Macdonald,' the man said.

'Your Majesty,' Macdonald replied with a bow. 'I'd rather not.'

'Have a drink, man. You're going to need it.'

Brandy was served and the King bade him sit down. Edward VII was baffled by this pitiful sight. Roberts had informed him of the delicacy of the situation. There had been frantic communications between the War Office and the Colonial Office. It was like the dreadful Cleveland Street business. Macdonald didn't look the type. But then neither had Podge.

A homosexual brothel in Fitzrovia had been raided in 1889 and it was discovered that the clientele had included several very high-ranking members of society, members of the Royal Household even. His own equerry, Sir Arthur Somerset, 'Podge' Somerset, that big and hearty Superintendent of his Stables, had been implicated. He could hardly believe it. Podge was a sport, such a masculine type, the sort of man who would be welcomed at any card table.

In the end it wasn't Podge he had to worry about but his own son. Prince Eddy, well, he was a different matter. Always the delicate one was Eddy. His mother Alix loved him so much, even when he acted like a damn fool. No real surprise when the finger was pointed in that direction. But really, his own son a sodomite. What a ghastly notion. It had to be covered up. So this business had to be covered up. The question was, how to deal with Macdonald?

'You've come a long way,' he told the man.

'Yes, Sire.'

'When we first met at that banquet after Omdurman, I remember you told me that you had done sentry duty outside my tent in Lahore back in '75.'

''76, Sire.'

'That's a steep climb. I've hardly come very far in my career. Just, you know, taking over the family business, what?'

The King looked for a hint of a smile in Macdonald's face. There was none.

'I just hope you understand the responsibilities of such high office, Macdonald.'

'Aye, I mean, yes, Sire.'

Podge had gone to live abroad, of course. Permanent exile, that was the only option for him. But then he had means. He could live anywhere in reasonable comfort and protection. Macdonald would not be able to afford that. It was hard to imagine how he had managed all these years, merely on his army pay.

'If you are unable to answer these charges . . .'

'Your Majesty.'

'If we have another scandal . . .'

Poor Eddy. The Duke of Clarence. He felt that odd stab of guilt that he could not understand. It had broken Alix's heart when Eddy had died of pneumonia. The heir presumptive. There had always been this awful weakness in him. He had not been strong enough when the fever came. His dissipation had killed him. That awful unmanly vice had enfeebled his mind and exhausted his body.

'So, you're on your way back to Ceylon?'

'Yes, Sire.'

'Listen, Macdonald. You're a brave man.'

He would have to tell him. No one else could have such terrible authority. He was the King, after all. The King Emperor.

'There is another way, you know.'

For a fleeting moment Macdonald felt the swooping joy of relief. Of course, that was what this meeting was for. On the highest authority he would be posted somewhere else. Out of harm's way. His face opened up into the ghost of a smile. He looked at His Royal Majesty directly in the eyes for the first time. But the regal countenance was grim, unyielding.

'The decent thing . . .'

Macdonald gasped softly as he realised what was meant.

'Sire.'

'Courage man. Now, if you'll excuse me.'

He didn't know what else to say. Before he knew it, Macdonald was being shown the door. The King Emperor finished his brandy.

'What a bloody business,' he muttered to himself.

He was in a terrible humour. He couldn't bear the thought of going back to the Palace, to his petulant and near deaf Queen. His mood needed lifting. He wondered which of his mistresses he would visit that evening.

Macdonald was escorted to the front door of Marlborough House. He staggered out on to the Mall. It was a beautiful spring evening. A pink sky over St James's Park, flowerbeds in full bloom, blossom falling gently from the trees. He found himself walking down towards the lake. He didn't notice the guardsman, standing in the shadow of an overhanging branch, until he was right up next to him.

'Pleasant evening,' the man commented.

'Quite,' Macdonald replied.

The top two buttons of the soldier's tunic were undone. His bearing was slovenly, the indolent demeanour that comes with too much ceremonial duty. He made a slight pout with his lips and caught Macdonald's eyes with an implicating stare. With a nod of the head he turned and walked into a thicket beyond the path.

Macdonald followed, full of quiet rage. When they reached a hidden clearing, the guardsman turned and waited. The sky had turned a deep crimson. Macdonald came right up to the man and looked him in the face. The guardsman's breath was soft and low, an expectant purring.

Macdonald suddenly barked an order for attention. It echoed into the night like the howl of a wounded animal. The guardsman jumped. With the stamp of one foot his body was vigorously transformed into a parade ground posture. His face became immobile; only the eyes betrayed bewilderment and alarm.

'Sorry, Sarge,' he muttered. 'I mistook you for someone.'

'You mistook me for a gentleman. Is that it?'

'Sarge?'

'How do you know I'm a sergeant? I might be something else.'

Christ, thought the guardsman. Maybe he's a detective. Most of them are ex-NCO after all.

'Who do you think I am?' Macdonald demanded.

'I really don't know, sir.'

'Good. Now, turn around.'

Macdonald ordered him to take his trousers down and pull up his tunic. The guardsman bent over and took hold of the trunk of a tree for support. Macdonald was full of a lustful rage. For once his anger overcame any sense of shame or fear. He could be caught, right here in the middle of it all, but he couldn't care any more.

'Do they give you a guinea or something?' he asked the man afterwards. 'The gentlemen?'

'Something like that,' the guardsman shrugged. He wasn't used to being buggered. It was usually the other way around.

'Do you want a guinea?'

The man frowned and continued to button himself up. Maybe this was another test.

'No,' he said. 'You're all right.'

'Go on then,' Macdonald ordered. 'Off with you.'

He had taken the boat train to Paris that very night.

There is another way, you know.

The decent thing.

Macdonald paced up and down his hotel room. The condemned man in his cell. He looked at his watch. It was a quarter to seven. If all that was left for him to do was shoot himself he was poorly prepared. He had left his service revolver at his staff headquarters in Slave Island. All alone in Paris. No, not quite. He recalled what Baden-Powell had told him. Edward Stuart-Wortley was at the Embassy. Eddie, he thought, with a sudden flicker of hope. The only officer he could really trust in the whole of the British Army was right here in Paris.

Macdonald came down into the lobby of the hotel to find Crowley waiting for him. He had quite forgotten the arrangement they had made earlier.

'I'm sorry,' he said. 'I have another appointment.'

'An appointment?'

'Well . . .' He found it hard to lie. 'Someone I need to see.'

He gestured to a doorman.

'Where are you going?' asked Crowley.

'The British Embassy.'

'Well, it's conveniently near. It's on the Faubourg St-Honoré.'

'Maybe I should get a cab.'

'Nonsense. It's five minutes on foot. I'll walk down there with you.'

They strode down rue de Rivoli together. Macdonald was in a hurry. It was getting late but Stuart-Wortley might still be at his office in the Embassy. Military Attaché, Baden-Powell had said. Macdonald had exhausted all his hopes in the War Office and the Colonial Office, but the Foreign Office, he reasoned, he might find something there.

He had known Eddie since Afghanistan. They had both been on the Great March and had served in the Egyptian Army together. Stuart-Wortley had been with the spearhead party of the Gordon Relief Expedition that had reached Khartoum just as it had fallen. He had made his escape downstream on the Nile in a leaky steamer, with enemies on both banks and his service revolver pressed against the head of a native pilot. Eddie was blue-blood aristocracy, but the type that saw it as a duty to cultivate the common touch and through his long experience of leading irregular troops, he had become a little irregular himself. Over all the years of campaigning Macdonald had found an easy camaraderie with him. They were both lost souls who found refuge in danger.

Stuart-Wortley was a sentimental man who hid all his disquiet at the world behind a jocular expression and a mischievous temperament. He had spent his entire career trying to avoid the embarrassment of being taken seriously. Macdonald seemed to be the only man in the entire army with whom he failed in this endeavour. Perhaps it was that Macdonald was an outsider, and that his so thoroughly sombre demeanour provoked such melancholy thoughts, but Eddie had confided to him that his father was a hopeless drunk, his close family were almost broke, and that he feared that his weak heart would get the better of him. Stuart-Wortley loved action because he feared more than anything that he might die of a heart attack behind a desk somewhere. He would often spend his leave between engagements recovering in spa towns on the Continent rather than allow himself to be consigned to a staff job for the duration.

Quite how Eddie might take the news of the scandal was another thing. But such things had not been entirely uncommon in the Egyptian Army. Macdonald felt that he could trust the man and Eddie just might be able to find him something in the Foreign Service.

But at the Embassy they were told that Lieutenant-Colonel Stuart-Wortley was indisposed.

'Can I leave a message for him?' Macdonald asked.

'Is it an urgent matter, sir?' the reception official enquired warily.

'Yes. Tell him that Major-General Sir Hector Macdonald is in Paris and is staying at the Hotel Regina.'

'Certainly, sir. And you are?'

'I am Sir Hector Macdonald.'

'Oh,' the man replied. 'I'm sorry sir, I didn't realise.'

'Tell him we're dining at Le Chat Blanc in rue d'Odessa,' Crowley added. 'And he is welcome to join us there.'

'Where, sir?'

The Beast took a card from his pocket and, borrowing a pen from the Embassy official, wrote the address on the back of it. He handed the card to the man.

They walked back out into the street. The General muttered a curse under his breath. He felt the foolishness of disappointment.

'Look, Crowley,' he told the Beast. 'I'm not sure about dinner.'

'But I insist. You can't be left all on your own in a foreign city. That would be intolerable.'

Macdonald couldn't help but be touched by this stranger's generosity. It had seemed so long since anyone had shown any kind of hospitality.

'In that case,' said the General, 'thank you.'

Crowley watched as Macdonald's harrowed features broke into a pitifully childlike grin. It was then that the Beast was absolutely certain that it was his mission to save the General. It would, he decided, become an essential component of his Great Work. Everything was coming together: the conflict with Mathers, his meeting with Astrid, the black mass waiting at midnight. Above all he would take up the cause of Sir Hector's deliverance. He would set him free.

Crowley hailed a cab. As a *fiacre* trotted over the Beast reached into a pocket and pulled out the small circular box of *dragées* he had purchased earlier. He opened it and offered one to Macdonald. The General frowned.

'A sugared almond?' Crowley proposed.

'Well . . .'

'Go on.'

The Beast watched surreptitiously as Macdonald picked one out. He willed him to take one of those that he had doctored, wondering idly if he might notice the discolouration where he had applied the Mexican tincture. The General plucked one from the box and popped it in his mouth.

'Hmm.' He winced slightly.

'All right?'

'A little bitter.'

The *fiacre* drew up and they climbed aboard. They headed for Montparnasse. As the cab picked up speed the General turned to the Beast.

'You said, "There is another way,"' he reminded him.

'I'm sorry?'

'Earlier. You said, "there is another way."'

'Oh yes,' Crowley replied even though he couldn't quite remember.

'What did you mean by that?'

'Well,' the Beast replied. 'Your predicament. If you had something to bargain with perhaps.'

'What do you mean, man?'

'I have always tried to make sure that I have some sort of insurance against accusations.'

'What sort of insurance?'

'A while ago I purchased some incriminating correspondence between Prince Eddy, the late Duke of Clarence, and a boy named Morgan. Cost me a pretty penny too. But I see it as my trump card. If anyone were to bring charges against me, well, I could implicate others. After all, if I am to be seen as a corrupter of morals I wouldn't want to leave the job half done. I'm sure you know many people in high places that you could name.'

'But I would never do such a thing.'

'Wouldn't you?'

'God, no. That would be a terrible thing to do.'

The Beast glanced over at the General. He was a vision of splendid strength and stoicism. There was a heart-rending nobility to him.

'You take the concept of honour very seriously, don't you?' Crowley asked.

'Aye, I do. It is everything to me.'

'I sincerely admire you for that.'

'That is why this, this business is so painful to me.'

Macdonald let out a short gasp. The Beast thought that he might break, right there in the back of the hansom. But he set his jaw and held himself upright.

'I don't know why I am confiding in you, sir.'

'Because you can. My absolute lack of discretion allows you to. And the knowledge that whatever you might have done, I am sure to have done worse.'

'Well, you are honest, at least.'

'And one thing I have learned from mountaineering is that descent is usually the most dangerous part of the expedition. So we have to find the safest route down.'

'I can't see any practical way down from where I am.'

'We have to look beyond mere practicalities.'

'What do you mean?'

'The supernatural.'

The General laughed.

'That again. I told you before,' he insisted. 'I'm a Presbyterian.'

'A superstition.'

'Maybe. But I do believe in the Church.'

'A good place to start. But we have to find the Church within.'

'I don't understand you.'

'Well, take the scriptures. The Book of Revelation for instance. You're aware of that?'

'Oh aye. The Free Church is very fond of it.'

'The Plymouth Brethren too. Plenty of hell-fire. The Apocalypse.'

'You believe in it?'

'Oh yes. All the great empires will crumble. Old certainties will be annihilated. Old moralities will become obsolete. We have to break through into a new world.'

'I rather think that I am stuck in the old one.'

'Then you must break free. Self-transformation. That is all that magic is, really. And the greatest revelation of all is self-revelation. That's what people are really terrified of. All this sense of sinfulness about the body. We have to turn things around. And those sermons that preached fear into us as children, they can be used to set us free. Revelation has such great characters, after all. They can become new archetypes: the Great Beast, the Scarlet Woman, the False Prophet.'

'Maybe you are aiming to be some sort of false prophet yourself.'

Crowley laughed out loud.

'Oh, certainly. I think that false prophets are the only interesting ones. The real ones are so predictable.'

Macdonald laughed along with him. He was suddenly feeling light-headed.

'I thought you said that you were a real magician.'

'Oh, I am,' the Beast intoned in a low voice.

Macdonald turned to see those hypnotic eyes peering at him through the gloom of the carriage. A shudder passed through him.

'What is it?' Macdonald hissed.

'Can't you feel it? An aura in the evening.'

'Och, it's just the sunset.'

The General looked out of the window of the cab. The night was streaked with amethyst clouds that throbbed against the sky. A low drone rose up within him. A call to prayer ululating in his head.

'Oh, God,' he gasped.

'We are going on a journey,' the Beast told him.

Now he would liberate the General, unlock his shackles. The scandal could go up like fireworks, an explosion right in the heart of the empire. This too would be sex magic, with the power to transform the world. Yes, thought the Beast, he would save Macdonald. But in order to do that he would first have to damn him.

The General closed his eyes and was back in the desert. A voice wailed in the wilderness. The False Prophet. The Expected One. It had all been written in the sand. He was having a dream. But it wasn't his dream. It was somebody else's. He feared that at any moment he might disappear. He opened his eyes.

'I'm, I'm . . .' he struggled to articulate his peculiar state of mind. 'I'm having visions.'

'That's a good sign. We're on our way then.'

Macdonald leaned back in the bench seat and felt the first chill of evening. The cold air against his brow was soothing. Sombre mansions loomed each side of the boulevard, immense and dismal. A tranquil gloom was descending upon the city. It was strangely reassuring. Crowley was quoting from the Apocalypse.

'"Babylon the great is fallen, fallen."' His velvet voice was now harsh and sonorous. '"And is become the habitation of devils, and the hold of every foul spirit and a cage of every unclean and hateful bird."'

In his head Macdonald heard a young boy sing verses of the Koran so melodiously that it made his eyes sting with tears. A thousand voices spoke of a coming end, a release from torment. The promise of it touched his weary mind like a benediction. The man beside him continued to recite.

'"Babylon is fallen, is fallen, that great city, because she made all nations drink of the wine of her wrath, of her fornication."'

Streetlamps flickered. All the vast buildings were crowned with gaslight, the palaces and theatres, the smoke-filled cafés and scandalous nightclubs, all the spectacles of pleasure lay prostrate before them, as if observed from above.

Even the churches wore tiaras of fire. As they trotted through boulevards, the City of Sin paraded itself shamelessly. Macdonald felt the drumbeat of memory. The Great March of his life: Kabul to Kandahar, Majuba, Omdurman, Paaderburg, Slave Island, now here. His own *fin-de-siècle*, coming to an end in Paris. He closed his eyes and there was wilderness once more. An empty plain with an endless sky as its bleak canopy. The voice of an imam called out to him in Arabic.

'He seemed to come from nowhere, out of the vast unforgiving desert. He wore a patched *jibba*, the simple raiment of poverty and submission. He asked for nothing: the earth was his bed, the sky his dome . . .'

Macdonald opened his eyes. They were crossing the river amid the trembling stars of illumination. The evening had begun its long recessional into darkness. The Great March into the night.

Part Two

STORM IN THE DESERT

XIV

THE IMAM SPOKE ONCE MORE:

'He seemed to come from nowhere, out of the vast unforgiving desert, a traveller with the piercing light of devotion in his eyes. He wore a patched *jibba*, the simple raiment of poverty and submission. He asked for nothing: the earth was his bed, the sky his dome. He spoke softly with sweet words that watered the parched soil of the wilderness.

'Mohammed Ahmed was a boat-builder's son from Dongola; as a child he had studied at a Khartoum madrassa and at eleven years old could recite the entire Koran by heart. As a young man he had joined the Sufi brotherhood of the Sammaniya, learning sacred techniques of trance and recitation. Secrets of the Dervish. Chanting the ninety-nine names of Allah, he mastered the ecstatic communion where breath becomes spirit.

'He had always known that he was special, that his life would follow a divine path. He became a devout man who saw the coming of the Last of Days. He heard the lamentations of prophecy. He was not alone. Voices whispered everywhere, calling out for a leader to free the faithful from oppression. The desert itself sighed wearily for justice. For a chosen one.

'Abdullahi al Ta'aishi had long dreamed of such a man. Abdullahi was a *feki*'s son from Darfur. He had some spiritual powers of his own; his father had taught him how to make protective charms, but he knew that his true way was to be the greatest follower of a greater man. There were stories of a Sufi adept renowned for his gentle charm and devout zeal. Of a certain Mohammed Ahmed whom his followers called *zahed*, meaning one who has renounced earthly pleasures for spiritual glory. When Abdullahi heard of this man he knew he had to find him.

'A long journey by donkey took him to the waters of the White Nile where his own tribe was hated. Abdullahi was not made welcome by the farming people who saw he was a nomad, one not to be trusted by them. But Mohammed Ahmed did not shun him, rather, when he heard that one of the detested Ta'aishi had come, he took specific pains to offer him hospitality, calling for a prayer rug and water to be brought for the stranger. Mohammed Ahmed had fasted for a week in a small hollow on the banks of the Nile. "I am empty," he had declared to the circle of followers who had stood by the mouth of his cave. "I am nothing. But I have received an order from Allah through his Prophet."

'The next day Abdullahi learned that the man he sought was standing high up on a scaffold, supervising the building of a shrine. He waited patiently below until he heard the creak of a ladder. Looking up he saw a figure descend, darkened by the blinding sun above. On the last steps the man reached out to Abdullahi al Ta'aishi, bringing their hands together, their fingers, like their destinies, entwining. Mohammed Ahmed had found the true believer who would become his first Khalifa.

'Abdullahi blinked the sun from his eyes and in the shade of the shrine looked more closely at Mohammed Ahmed. He noted the high forehead, the delicate structure of his face, a significant mole on his right cheek. When the man before him parted his lips to smile and he saw the V-shaped gap in his front teeth, Abdullahi gasped in revelation. All the signs were here, that Mohammed Ahmed was the Chosen Guide. The Redeemer. The Mahdi that had been promised to lead them.

'"Master." Abdullahi caught his breath. "Is it true that you are the Expected One?"

'The followers of Mohammed Ahmed had gathered to him, clamouring for an answer to the stranger's question. He glanced around at them. Beyond the crowd he saw a small child in rags that crawled in the dirt.'

'"Yes," he declared. "I am. He who follows me will be victorious. He who does not believe in me will be purified by the sword."

'A great cry went up. Abdullahi al Ta'aishi kissed the hand of his messiah. A holy revolution had begun.

'Thousands answered the Call. A great dust storm that stirred and hovered. Pilgrims from all over the Sudan joined the Mahdi. He united the nomadic tribes with the farming people of the Nile Valley. The Ja'aliyyin of the north, the fearsome Beja of the east, the wandering Baggara, all made common cause to throw off the yolk of tyranny. Black slave soldiers who had deserted or had been captured from the Egyptian Army were formed into a rifle corps, the *jihadiyya*. The followers of the Mahdi became the *ansar* and wore the motley uniform of the patched *jibba* to show that they were indeed an army of the poor and righteous. *Jihad* was declared against all unbelievers and hypocrites who had strayed from the true path. All the lands occupied became the House of Peace. Everything beyond was now the House of War.

'And they were blessed by heavenly signs and divine portents. A great comet appeared in the sky, so bright that it was visible even in daylight. Grazing the sun in transit, its incandescent tail flared and spluttered, spitting out lucent fragments that broke away from the main body like angry sparks. It seemed clear that the Last of Days was at hand. At Shaykan they faced a column of the Egyptian Army, heavily armed and eleven thousand strong. It was commanded by Hicks Pasha and other white officers of the Inglisi. The *ansar* army lured them into a forest of thorns and massacred them. They had reason now to believe in the invulnerability that had been promised to them. The Mahdi himself had declared that on the day of battle Allah would send forty thousand angels to join them in ruthless prey upon the infidels. Many warriors would later give vivid testimony of the appearance of this terrible winged and vengeful host.'

*

Macdonald's mind had whirled itself into a trance. His eyelids fluttered with visions, his head gently rocking as the carriage picked up a steady trot as they passed Place de la Concorde. The Beast watched the General muttering to himself in Arabic. The drug was taking hold. With one so repressed the effects could be astonishing, he mused. Such an experiment was full of potential, but danger also.

'Where are you?' he asked Macdonald softly.

'I'm in the desert,' the General murmured.

'Excellent.'

'I'm, I'm scared.' The General's voice was scarcely more than a whimper. He had never known fear like it. It was the worst horror of all. He was losing control.

'Don't be afraid,' the Beast implored. 'Here, take my hand. I'll be your spirit guide.'

Macdonald felt Crowley's palm press against his in the darkness of the carriage. As the General clasped hold of it he was suddenly possessed by a sensation of flight. They were soaring over the desert, following the voice of the imam. It took them beyond a range of broken mountains to a labyrinth of fractured spurs and dry ravines. A desolate place, littered with headstones for nature's own graveyard. *Batn al-Hajar* it was called, the Belly of Stones. The Nile cut sharply into the rocks as it curved through a barren headland, then stretched out to form a flat rocky bank for a mile or so. Below, huddled by the river was a village. He knew where he was. He felt a bead of sweat go cold on the back of his neck.

'Firka,' he whispered. 'I'm in Firka.'

'You've been here before?'

'Yes. In '96, at the start of the Dongola Expedition. The beginning of the reconquest of Northern Sudan. We took Firka in June of that year. But, but . . .' He looked down to see that it was different from how he had remembered it. 'This is before then. Before the battle.'

He gripped Crowley's hand tightly as they seemed to swoop

down into the village. Then they were in a crowd called to evening prayers, among black men from the south, Dinka and Shilluk, like the men who served in his own battalions. But these men all wore the *jibba* of the Dervish and loose turbans with one tail hung behind the left ear. He was in the middle of a company of the *jihadiyya*. With the enemy.

His soul had crossed the border.

'We're on the other side!' Macdonald hissed in astonishment.

'Remember!' The imam in front of them raised a finger as he brought his sermon to a close. 'It was the Khalifa Abdullahi al Ta'aishi who was the very first witness of the Expected One. It was the Khalifa who was the very first man that the Mahdi revealed himself to. It is the Khalifa who continues in his holy mission.'

The assembled ranks began to break as it was clear that prayers and instruction had come to an end. A man in front of him turned and Macdonald saw his face. He recognised the gently domed forehead, the high, sharp cheekbones, the jutting purple lips, and was shocked that this noble profile was as beautiful as he had remembered it. It was Bakhit. He tried to call out to him. He could not. As the young man turned and spoke, Macdonald realised that Bakhit could not see them. He was talking to somebody else.

'Salim,' he called softly to his friend.

Salim came and joined him as they walked off together.

'Same old sermon about the Mahdi,' Bakhit complained under his breath. 'But the Mahdi has been dead for ten years.'

'Careful, Bakhit.'

Salim nodded furtively in the direction of the imam. Either side of the holy man were two *ansar* carrying sawn-off Remington rifles and wearing the distinctive two-horned skullcap of the Khalifa's own bodyguard, the *mulazimin*.

'The Mahdi united all the tribes,' Bakhit continued, keeping his voice low. 'He was among us. The Khalifa sits in Omdurman surrounded by his cronies. He gives power only to his own clan.'

There had been a growing sense of foreboding in the garrison. Kitchener's Expeditionary Force had occupied Akasha to the north. A new chief had been appointed to Firka, emir Osman Azraq, a Ta'aishi, like the Khalifa. There were rumours that the Ja'alayin were close to revolt. The loyalty of the *jihadiyya* was in question as well. There had been many desertions.

Salim prodded Bakhit with his elbow as they approached the imam and his guards, but Bakhit continued his criticism, grinding out the words through clenched teeth.

'Khalifa sends men to teach us to be good slaves.'

Salim flared his eyes warily at his friend. Bakhit grinned and turned to the imam, bowing low in a sudden gesture of obsequiousness. Salim nodded quickly at the holy man and hurried them both along.

'You,' came a stern voice behind them.

As they looked back they saw the imam gesture to them, his retinue suddenly alert, ready to move if ordered. Bakhit grinned again, his face wide and radiant. Salim despaired of how charming and playful his friend could appear in the midst of trouble. Trouble that he had almost always been the cause of. Salim could only manage a guilty frown. He shrugged hopefully.

'Yes, you,' the imam went on. 'Both of you. Come here.'

They walked back. Salim glared once more at Bakhit, willing him to shut up for once and let him do the talking.

'You wanted us, sheikh?' he asked compliantly.

The imam ignored Salim and pointed at Bakhit.

'What is that you said about being slaves?' he demanded. 'Is that how you feel?'

'Is that not what we are, sheikh?' Bakhit retorted, still beaming broadly.

The smile was returned flatly, with eyes that were solemn and piercing.

'Really?'

The preacher's face tilted judicially, ready to weigh every word. Bakhit lowered his eyes. One of the *mulazimin* grunted contemptuously.

'What my friend means,' Salim interjected quickly. 'He means: "we are all slaves of God." Is that not what the Prophet, peace be upon him, has said?'

The imam turned to Salim with an appraising sneer.

'Indeed? And perhaps this slave of God has become above himself. Perhaps he needs to be taught humility.'

Salim again thought swiftly, with a pious agility.

'When the slave becomes the master,' he blurted out, 'that is a sign of the coming of the Last of Days.'

The imam laughed.

'You presume to instruct me? Why do you talk of the Last of Days?'

'We must all be ready for it.'

'You are clever. Maybe too clever. The insolence of your friend is honest and simple. Easy to deal with, permissible even. Often a soldier's complaint is what makes him fight. But you,' the imam pointed. 'You use all the words of devotion. But you have the voice of a ringleader.'

'Sheikh—'

'We know that there is dissent among the *jihadiyya*. Many of you were turned from the infidels and would turn back again given the chance. The Sirdar Kitchener has given a proclamation denouncing the Khalifa and offering good wages for those who would change sides.'

'The Sirdar is al-Dajjal!' Salim spat out the words. 'He is the Deceiver.'

The imam laughed again.

'Another sign of the coming hour?'

'Did not the Mahdi promise that the End was at hand?'

'Yes,' the imam declared firmly, catching Salim's eye with a practised stare. 'The Khalifa also. It is not for us to question when or where.'

Salim remembered himself once more. He bowed again gently.

'I am not sure,' pondered the holy man, 'whether to have you whipped or to appoint you as my secretary.'

'Forgive me, sheikh.'

'And as for your friend . . .'

He beckoned to Bakhit to come closer, and as he did so the imam grabbed at the collar of his *jibba*.

'What do you think, Ali?' he asked one of his bodyguards.

Ali looked down at Bakhit who, despite his discomfiture, was attempting an imploring smirk.

'He thinks he is too pretty for the whip,' Ali said with a salacious pout.

'He is a simple pagan, unlike his clever friend.' The imam pushed him off and something came away with his hand. 'But what is this?'

The imam held up a thin lace of leather; a small metal square dangled from it.

'Is this an animist token? You know that the Khalifa has forbidden all godless amulets.'

Bakhit held up his hands. Salim stepped forward once more.

'Please, sheikh, it is not godless. It is a magic square, but it is blessed by a Muslim *feki*. See? There are no unholy images graven on it. Only sacred numbers. Did not the prophet say, peace be upon him, praise the creator who has bestowed upon man the ability to discover the power of numbers.'

'Enough!' The imam threw the talisman into the dust and Bakhit cowered down to retrieve it. 'I'll spare you the whip. But maybe a night on the mountain would be good for both of you. Sentry duty and time to reflect. I want you to think more.' He prodded at the huddled form at his feet, then looked up to catch Salim with a sententious gaze. 'And you to think less.'

At dusk Bakhit and Salim clambered up the granite terraces of Jabal Firka, the mountain that loomed over the village. Their sentry post was a ruin from the time of the Pharoahs, the cracked shell of an ancient watchtower. They propped their rifles against a broken wall and sat down. Passing the water bag between them, they surveyed the curve in the river. The waters of the Nile reddened as a swollen sun sank into the boundless horizon beyond. Salim exhaled a long lamenting breath.

'You should have been known as trouble,' he told Bakhit. 'Not as the lucky one.'

'Lucky and trouble are the same spirit,' Bakhit replied.

'I wish it were not so.'

'I wish . . .' Bakhit sighed.

'What?'

'I wish I had a cigarette.'

They watched in silence for a moment as the last of the sun disappeared from sight.

'Salim,' Bakhit said as the sky began to darken. 'You really think the end of time is coming?'

'We have been waiting since the Mahdi appeared. Now there are new signs.'

'You said that one sign is that the slave will become the master.'

'It is written, yes.'

'Then the end will never come.'

'Bakhit—'

'The Mahdi was meant to set us free. But we are still slaves.' Bakhit held up his left hand where a branded letter marked him as one of the *jihadiyya*. 'It is written here.'

'We are soldiers first,' Salim insisted. 'If we are slaves it is only because of that.'

'Soldiers can change sides just as slaves can change masters.'

'Hush, Bakhit.'

'They cannot hear us.'

'I can hear you.'

'When the time comes we might have to change. Like before.'

'Not this time. This might be the time of times. If it is, I want to be on the side of the righteous. I do not want to chase the Devil's footsteps.'

'Salim—'

'I have faith, Bakhit. I do not just say the words. I have them in my heart.'

It was getting cold. They took a blanket and huddled together in the corner of the tower. They looked up at the vast celestial canopy. Bakhit watched the shimmering constellations, memories flickering amid an immense oblivion. Pulled back by a solemn gravity, the weight of all his dead ancestors, he felt a dim vision of a pastoral life, the lost time before he was taken.

'Salim,' he whispered. 'Remember when we were little our mothers told us that the stars were the cattle-fires of the people who had their herds in the sky?'

Salim laughed.

'A mother's foolishness,' he declared softly. 'The Koran says that the lower heavens are decked with stars to guard against rebellious devils. They are missiles to pelt the devils with. There is a scourge of fire for those who deny their Lord.'

'Shh, Salim. No more about the Devil and the Last Day. No more about the End. I don't want the end. I want the beginning.'

'Maybe they are the same thing.' Salim yawned.

'The imam is right. You are too clever. Go to sleep.'

Bakhit pulled his half of the blanket around his shoulders and curled up. He took one last look up into the darkness. In the village of his childhood it was said that the beginning was as night; that the sky and earth were connected; just as people were joined with their own divinity. When the light came the world was torn apart from heaven.

In his vision, Macdonald stood holding hands with Crowley on the dark slope of Jabal Firka.

'Tell me what you are seeing now,' the Beast whispered in his ear.

'Two boys sleeping. Bakhit and Salim.'

'You know them?'

'I knew Bakhit, yes. But this is the night before I first saw him in reality. The night before the attack.'

'What happened to them?'

'They lost each other. I was partly to blame.'

'Is that the significance of this vision?'

'I don't know.'

'It must be. Concentrate. You say you knew one of them.'

'Bakhit. Yes.'

'Go closer.'

Macdonald peered through the gloom and made out Bakhit, his face beatific with slumber.

'What is he doing?' Crowley demanded.

'Sleeping. Dreaming.'

'Then you can join him there.'

'Can I?' Macdonald murmured plaintively. It was something he had secretly wished for so many times as he had guiltily watched the lad asleep when they had shared quarters together.

'Of course,' the Beast assured him. 'All dreams exist on a higher level.'

But as Macdonald contemplated this, a sense of descent overwhelmed him. He let go of Crowley's hand and fell into fathomless depths, his mind tracing a swooning arc as it dived into the imagined consciousness of his beloved boy.

XV

DARKNESS. THEN ALL AT ONCE Macdonald's mind was assailed by the memory of noise and commotion in the night. It was the time that the slavers came to the village. Bakhit had told him this story, of when he and Salim were just children. They were not even Salim and Bakhit back then. Chol and Ajang were the names their parents gave them. They were too young to have taken their ox-names, the colour-names of cattle that they would have gained in initiation from childhood when they were taken. Now this time was vividly played out in a dream. It was terrifying. The men of the village thought it was a cattle raid at first and rushed to defend the kraal. Then there were gunshots. Slavers killed all those who resisted and set fire to the huts. Then they killed all those that they considered too old or too young and herded the rest away.

The women and girls were taken north, to join a slave trade caravanserai on the Forty Days Road. The men and boys were marched to a *zariba*, a fortified camp with thick thorn bush picketed around its perimeter. The men were trained as soldiers in the slaver's private army, the youngsters became servants or orderlies. One of the traders gave Ajang a numbered square amulet and called him Bakhit, saying that his name meant lucky gift. When the boy tugged at his friend's arm imploringly, the man took him too, and named him Salim. They became his gun boys, carrying his two large and ancient muskets. They learned how to load them for him and followed him on village raids or battles with rival slavers. They served him for five years until one day, confronted by better-armed tax-collectors, their master gave them to the Egyptian government as part of his yearly tribute.

They were enlisted for life in the 1st Sudanese Brigade under Faraj Pasha. It was a unit almost entirely composed of enslaved black Africans from the south. They received proper training, drill and discipline. Salim was attentive to instruction, though always impatient to learn. He began to teach himself how to read, using the Koran that new recruits were given. Bakhit had a tendency to be wilful, but always looked orderly; there was scarcely a soldier in the whole regiment who took more care over his uniform. He loved his new livery: the red tarboosh, dark blue tunic and white pantaloons. There was constant talk in the barracks about the Mahdi uprising, the shocking victories of the Dervish. When the new Inglisi Governor-General Gordon arrived to deal with the crisis, the 1st Sudanese were called to Khartoum.

Faraj Pasha was a hardened veteran with thirty years' service. He had been in Mexico in the 1860s with the corps of Sudanese loaned by the Khedive of Egypt, Muhammed Sa'id Pasha, to Louis Napoleon's French forces fighting for Emperor Maximilian against the Republicans at Veracruz. He was a tough old soldier but he had known some kindness in his youth that had instilled in him a streak of compassion. As a houseboy in Cairo, his master had treated him well, taught him Turkish and French and a little humanity. At Khartoum he befriended Bakhit and Salim, seeing that they were scarcely more than cadets and could benefit from some protection.

They became part of his personal staff, running errands and carrying messages. They were in the Governor-General's palace when Gordon dictated to Faraj Pasha a placatory dispatch to the Mahdi, appointing him to the sultanate of Kordofan. He enclosed the robes of office with this diplomatic offer. Bakhit gasped with pleasure when he saw the scarlet cloak of a vizier, embroidered with gold thread and lined with silk. He watched as the velvet cape was carefully wrapped by the Inglisi general as a gift to his enemy and handed to an attendant messenger.

'He offers the Mahdi Kordofan,' Salim commented later in a

sullen tone. 'He tries to give the Mahdi what the Mahdi already possesses.'

Bakhit was still overwhelmed by the beauty of the proffered garment.

'But the cloak, Salim. If I was the Mahdi,' he said breathlessly, 'I would wear that cloak.'

On another occasion at the palace they were beckoned into the reception room by Gordon himself. The Governor-General was smoking a cigarette fervently, puffing away like a locomotive. His intense blue eyes flickered with evident amusement as he watched Bakhit stare with utter delight at his own reflection in the gilt-framed mirror above the mantelpiece. Gordon came up behind him and shook his head slowly, making an awkward smile with his cracked and sun-dried lips. He tapped Bakhit on the shoulder.

'Now, now,' he declared in a tone that was half-mocking, half-chiding. 'Let me show you a better looking-glass.'

Gordon went over to his desk and picked up a brass-encased telescope that was lying amid a confusion of papers. He slid apart the concentric tubes of the device to the satisfying click of their full extent. He took Bakhit to an open window and, after a brief demonstration, handed the instrument to the puzzled boy.

Bakhit lined the telescope up to one eye, steadied it into focus, and yelped with revelation as he caught the enchanted image of a flattened and magnified landscape. It was a moment of wonder, that the wide world could be trapped into this small tunnel, that his own perception could travel so far.

Gordon laughed.

'Can you see the relief column coming to save us?' he demanded, unable to restrain the bitterness at his own fate.

Salim stood in the corner observing it all. He felt embarrassed by the behaviour of his friend, and conscious that, despite his more diligent demeanour, the Governor-General had paid him scant heed. He consoled himself with the sudden thought that although good behaviour is scarcely ever recognised, its very obscurity is its own virtue.

Gordon stumbled back to his desk and fumbled in an open tin for another cigarette. Bakhit lowered the telescope and, turning around, approached the Governor-General with an imploring gesture. Gordon tutted audibly, then handed Bakhit a smoke, striking a match on the stone floor. They shared the flame, the Governor-General pouting guiltily at the face so beautiful and so close to his own. He held the match a second too long and it burned his fingertips. He wafted the fan of his hand vigorously, the momentary pain bringing him back to his Christian senses. He looked over at Salim whose nose had curled at the brief tang of sulphur in the room. Picking up the cigarette tin, Gordon offered it to Salim who, with the greater pleasure, refused.

With a dismissive gesture, the Governor-General ordered them from his audience chamber and, collapsing on his divan, the cigarette clenched in his mouth, picked up his notebook and began to scribble notes for his journal.

It soon became clear that the Dervish army had completely surrounded Khartoum. A state of siege gripped the whole city. The pitter-patter of sniper fire built into a slow crescendo of bombardment. There came a continuous series of hopeful declarations from the palace. The endless propaganda of the possibility of relief. Then the telegraph wire connecting Khartoum to Cairo was cut, and the city grew hungry and desperate. Salim and Bakhit were at the palace with Faraj Pasha when a package arrived from the Mahdi. It was the long-awaited reply to Gordon's offer of a sultanate.

They watched as the Governor-General unwrapped the bundle. It too contained the robes of appointment. But it was of a lowly and humble office. It was a patched *jibba*. Faraj Pasha read out the message that accompanied it:

'This is the clothing of those who have given up this world and its vanities, and who look for the world to come, for everlasting happiness in Paradise. If you truly desire to come to

God and seek to live a godly life, you must at once wear this raiment, and come out to accept your everlasting good fortune.'

Salim and Bakhit watched as Gordon threw the garment across the room, picked up his telescope, and went up to the roof to survey his wretched circumstance.

In the evening of that day Salim found a cold relish in the opportunity to make his reply to what Bakhit had said about the sultan's beautiful cloak:

'If I was Gordon,' he declared. 'I would wear that *jibba*.'

Though the Governor-General was a devout man who applied promises towards his soul and curses towards his body, it now appeared that his great humility would be content with nothing but the sacrament of martyrdom. In this he would surpass his nemesis as a mystic, just as the holy leader of the Dervish would prove the better military tactician. The Mahdi held Khartoum in the palm of his hand.

As Gordon prepared to depart his long-detested self, other inhabitants of the city seemed less keen to follow. With worsening conditions and no sign of the promised relief column of the Inglisi, murmurs of mutiny reverberated around the Sudanese Brigade. But though they had no more love to give Gordon, their devotion to Faraj Pasha, for the most part, remained unwavering. He urged them to stand firm and wait for his order. He promised them safety when the time came.

And he kept his word. When the Dervish assault began he took Bakhit and Salim with him to the Massallamiyya Gate to see the 1st Sudanese turned out and in good order. He told them to hold their fire and divested himself of his tunic of office. His men understood this gesture, and began to take off their uniforms also. A meagre privilege of the unfree is liberty from blame for their own fealty. A slave's loyalty is absolute, but only to whosoever is the master. They had a new master now. Faraj Pasha kissed Bakhit and Salim and gave them both blessings of the true Prophet. Then he ordered the gate opened. He tossed away his tarboosh, wrapped himself in a civilian coat, mounted his horse and rode out to parley with the *ansar*. Faraj Pasha was lost in the sack of the city, but most of his brigade was spared and recruited into the *jihadiyya*.

As their name insisted, they had joined a holy war; the price of their manumission was service in the *jihad* and a brand mark on the left hand. Bakhit did not much like wearing the *jibba* of devout poverty, nor that tobacco was forbidden in this new age of divine justice. But Salim felt the embrace of purity; he had more profound appetites and an urgent desire for righteousness. He studied the *ritab*, the small lithographed book of the Mahdi's sayings handed out by their new officers as they were sworn in under a dark flag illuminated with bright words of holy scripture. Salim became intoxicated with all the proclamations. So much was promised, and in those early days of the Call, all seemed possible.

Then the Mahdi died of fever. Scarcely six months after Gordon, he too exchanged this life for heaven. Until he returned, it was announced amid the great lamentation, Abdullahi al Ta'aisihi would succeed him as Khalifa. Deranged by temporal shifts in power and fortune, Salim's doubts urged him to greater beliefs. The New Khalifate was itself in a state of confusion; it had to astonish in order to make itself real. Action was necessary. Abullahi al Ta'aishsi declared *jihad* on King John of the Abyssinians, the oldest and most venerable of Christians. They claimed descent from Solomon and Sheba, being of the lost tribe of Judah, in possession of the Ark of the Covenant. The Khalifa considered them more powerful as infidels than those crawling, exploring missionaries from the Inglisi Empire.

A terrible army was assembled, fifteen thousand riflemen, fifty thousand spear and the great invasion to the east began. There were swift victories at first: burning, looting, appalling slaughter. Then the Abyssinians launched a counter-attack. They surrounded the Dervish encampment at Gallabat, setting fire to the thorn *zariba* and commencing a massacre of all within. Just when all seemed lost, King John was killed, the Abyssinians lost heart and were routed. But it was a costly triumph with many thousands slain on either side. The war was a disaster for the security of the Khalifate. The ancient Christians remained undefeated and the new ones seemed to grow in strength. All the great victories now seemed in the past. The death of Gordon had shocked and stupefied the Inglisi for a while but now stirred within them thoughts of holy vengeance. And, as time went on, all the old and bitter rivalries between the tribes of the *ansar* were soon unforgotten.

Bakhit and Salim were thoroughly bloodied in the campaign. They witnessed dreadful things in the fray and in its sullen aftermath, where atrocity became routine. Weary of battle, Salim's mood darkened and all his idealism became fixated on the Last of Days, the promised apocalypse. In the end was hope.

Bakhit awoke to the rhythmic throb of drums from the village below. It was the *nuqqara* sounding the call to dawn prayers. He roused himself, his mind still thick with memory. The pink light above had washed away the stars and only a few lingering planets burned at the edge of the firmament. Dreamtime was over. Sky and earth were separate once more, the world harsh and distinct in the first light of the day. Salim was still curled up in slumber, looking so unusually peaceful that Bakhit let him sleep a little longer. He walked around the shattered watchtower, shivering in the cold morning. Looking down on Firka he could see figures assemble in groups according to their standards as the light broke over the village. He turned his gaze in the other direction, at the Nile below, and was suddenly conscious of something vast and awful moving along its banks. The day broke into a thousand whispers and hushed footfalls of the enemy breaking cover. He nearly stumbled in shock as he made out nine columns of infantry advancing across the narrow defile between the river and the mountain. The Inglisi were here. He did not know what to do. He looked up at the bright and empty sky and thought: There are no stars left to pelt the devils with. Then he ran to wake Salim.

Salim told Bakhit to fetch their rifles. They crouched down among the rocks and let off a couple of volleys into the approaching horde, in order to sound the alarm. The mountainside was soon alive with the percussion of returning fire. They scrambled further upward to gain better cover. All at once a series of explosions rolled like thunder along the slopes behind them. Inglisi artillery was finding its range from the other side of the valley. Firka was completely surrounded.

They sat high up, safe in the citadel of the mountain, and watched the pattern of battle before them. Bakhit was overcome with a heady sense of divine audience. They observed in fearful wonder the infidel columns shouldering Jabal Firka, fanning out into one broad insect line that curved and wheeled to encircle the village. Gunfire bloomed like buds of mimosa blossom that drifted and opened, hanging in the air, waiting for the cacophony that echoed across the plain. Salim, with a sudden impulse of guilt, made a move to descend. Bakhit held him back.

'It is lost, Salim,' he implored. 'It is lost.'

When it was all over they clambered down together. Salim was sullen and Bakhit put an arm of comfort around his shoulder.

'Be happy, Salim,' he consoled him. 'For we are spared.'

'We are not,' Salim insisted. 'This is not the end.'

They reached the outskirts of the village, a thin veil of blue smoke shrouding the carnage. A troop of Sudanese was escorting a ragged band of captured *jihadiyya*. As they came closer Bakhit and Salim threw down their rifles and raised their arms in weary supplication. An NCO with Shilluk tribal marks grinned and beckoned them over. They were marched with the others through Firka. The wounded and dying were strewn everywhere, groaning plaintively amid dead shapes, blood-blackened and fizzing with flies. They passed a courtyard piled thick with bodies. Yet as they reached the clearing that had served as their parade ground they heard a clamour of celebration. Soldiers of the Sudanese battalions broke rank to come among the assembled crowd of surrendered *jihadiyya*, as they recognised old comrades and fellow clan members. Bakhit saw Aman al-Abd, whom they had served with in the 1st Brigade, and called out to him.

The man walked towards them with an inquisitive frown.

'It's Bakhit,' Bakhit announced. 'And Salim.'

'God is merciful!' Aman al-Abd exclaimed. 'You boys have grown.'

He embraced them both and then pulled out a packet from his top pocket. Bakhit's eyes flashed with delight as he was handed a cigarette.

'What happens now?' Salim asked, holding up a hand to decline the offer of a smoke.

As Aman al-Abd explained that the Sudanese battalions were recruiting from the *jihadiyya*, Salim looked beyond to the far side of the parade ground. A detachment of *fellahin* from the Egyptian Army was standing over a line of Ta'aishi, squatted in the dirt, chained together.

'Come join the Eleventh,' Aman al-Abd said. 'Good pay. Good rations.'

He struck a match and lit Bakhit's cigarette. Salim watched as his friend drew the fumes hungrily into his lungs. He held the breath a second, then released a blue stream of vapour up into the sky. Bakhit closed his eyes gently, a look of ecstasy on his face. It is all smoke, thought Salim, trying to grasp at his own feelings as they floated in the air around his head.

'What about them?' he asked, gesturing at the shackled men.

Aman al-Abd sucked his teeth dismissively. 'They cannot be trusted.'

'They are still loyal to the Khalifa.'

'They are fools. Railway Battalion for them. Hard labour. That will make them think better.'

'Maybe I am still loyal also,' Salim declared.

Aman al-Abd laughed at this. Bakhit lowered his cigarette and turned to his friend. They both noticed the look of solemn defiance on his face.

'Salim, no,' Bakhit pleaded.

A white sergeant had arrived and began barking orders in bad Arabic. The *jihadiyya* prisoners were being lined up for inspection.

'There is no dishonour, you know that,' Aman al-Abd reasoned.

'It is more than that,' Salim replied.

Aman al-Abd shrugged.

'Then go and join the fools,' he said with a sigh. 'Are you coming, Bakhit?'

Bakhit dropped his cigarette.

'Yes,' he said. 'Salim, come.'

'I will not fight my brothers.'

'But we are your brothers. Over here.'

Salim shook his head. He felt his heart harden into a grim certainty. Belief had given him a sense of purpose in an indifferent world. He could not give that up now. He looked at Bakhit. His friend's eyes were full of tears.

'We stick together,' Bakhit protested. 'That is always the way.'

'I have a different path now.'

'But it will be like before. In the Brigade. We will have soldiers' wages.'

Salim smiled sadly. 'It is written: "No mortal knows what he will earn tomorrow; no mortal knows where he will breathe his last."'

He kissed Bakhit twice, tasting the wet salt on his cheeks.

'Stay safe, Bakhit. Stay lucky.'

With that he turned and walked slowly towards the line of shackled men. Bakhit called out after him but Aman al-Abd ushered him towards the ranks of the *jihadiyya*. He stood in line, wiped his eyes and bit his lip. A harsh order was shouted and the Sudanese troops came to attention. Their commander had arrived to inspect his new recruits. He was an Inglisi, his white face reddened by the sun. He wore the uniform of a *miralai*, a colonel in the Egyptian Army. He stopped as he reached

Bakhit, noticing that the man had been crying. The *miralai* had a heavy mournful face, steel-blue eyes that flashed with curiosity as their gaze fell upon Bakhit.

Macdonald felt the jolt of the carriage and started from his dream as the tremor of recognition quivered through him. He had become part of the vision. It was his own face that he was looking at.

XVI

MACDONALD OPENED HIS EYES. HE touched the back of his neck. The drop of cold sweat was still there. He looked out of the window and saw that it was still twilight; a dying sun still struggled to fire up the clouds. They were just crossing the river. He had only been unconscious for a matter of minutes. Crowley smiled at the bewildered look in the General's eyes.

'I, I saw myself,' Macdonald muttered.

'You have been travelling on an astral plane,' the Beast told him. 'Congratulations. Many adepts spend years of effort and never achieve it.'

Macdonald's mind was a scroll unrolling, spilling out memories of the long years in Egypt and the Sudan. All the secret thoughts and feelings he had hidden were being stripped bare. Bakhit. The one he had loved and lost.

'A touch of malarial fever perhaps,' he reasoned.

'It might feel like delirium,' Crowley countered. 'It is a deeper reality coming to the surface.'

'Have you really put some sort of spell on me?'

'On the contrary. I am trying to break the spell. The spell that has held you in its power all this time.'

'I don't understand.'

'Oh, I think that you do. Now, let us proceed. You were in the desert.'

'Aye. I was there with the Egyptian Army.'

'Of course.'

'But in this dream, I was with the Dervish.'

'How marvellous. A truth is revealing itself to you.'

'What truth?'

'I don't know. But it must be something about the time you were in the Sudan. What happened there?'

Macdonald thought back through all those years.

'After the Gordon Relief Expedition failed,' he told Crowley, 'I stayed on and applied for a transfer to the Egyptian Army. The fall of Khartoum had been a terrible blow, and I knew there'd be action in this part of the world sooner or later. Cairo was full of ambitious officers, jostling for positions, playing their sophisticated games of influence. The EA was being rebuilt by the British, with white officers recruited to retrain native troops. The Egyptian service was a good proposition for career soldiers like myself, those with no private means and few social contacts. Even there it was a struggle to get on, to get yourself noticed. I only knew Edward Stuart-Wortley, you know, the man we went to see at the Embassy. He had been aide-de-camp to the Commander-in-Chief, or Sirdar. I got a recommendation from him. I was looking for a career I could never get back on Home service.'

'You were running away from something.'

'Aye,' the General sighed.

Macdonald had dreaded going back to Edinburgh after what had happened there and it was well known that the Egyptian Army offered a refuge for officers of a certain type. He knew what he was now, or rather what he could never be. He wrote to Christina and promised to provide for her and their son. A small allowance, that was all he could manage and for that he would need promotion. In Egypt there were opportunities for active service and advancement. Married officers were generally ineligible for service so he simply kept quiet about that part of his life.

'I joined as a brevet major, a *bimbashi*,' he told Crowley.

He had a simple skill to offer, and one that was sorely needed: an ability to train and lead infantry. He was given a battalion of Sudanese to knock into shape. A ranker, a rough Highlander suited to drilling the blacks, that's what he knew the louche officer corps in Cairo thought he was good for. He didn't care. He soon acquired an affection for the tall and shadow-dark men he trained.

'You served under Kitchener?' Crowley asked.

'Aye, well, that was later. But he rose fast. He rose above us all.'

This restless officer with the Royal Engineers was only a *bimbashi* himself when Macdonald had joined, but Kitchener was already carving out a reputation for himself. In intelligence, operating in the desert behind enemy lines he had formed a frontier force of Abada tribesmen. By 1886, as acting colonel in charge of the garrison at Suakin, the last British outpost in the Sudan, he was grooming himself as a man of destiny, his mission to avenge the Empire and vanquish the Dervish. Gordon had been an idol to him, a model of stoicism and Christian purity. Kitchener gathered a corps of young, attractive bachelor officers around him. He kept his lavish quarters in Cairo exquisitely laid out and furnished. He had a passion for the art of detail, collecting fine porcelain, even supervising the arrangement of flowers on his dining table. All things decorative filled him with great pleasure. Yet Kitchener was cold and distant in public and often tactless in conversation. He had an awkwardness that Macdonald recognised. He preferred to be misunderstood than suspected of any human weakness, constantly vigilant with rigid self-control.

'I was in Cairo myself six months ago,' said the Beast. 'Stayed at Shepheard's Hotel. Rather wallowed in the fleshpots to be honest.'

'I managed to resist the temptations of that place.'

'Well, I certainly resisted the temptation to go and gawp at the Pyramids. Confound them, I thought. I wasn't going to have forty centuries look down on me.'

'Aye, well, I was never much one for Cairo. Full of gossip and backbiting. I liked to keep out of it. Out on the frontier for the most part. Preferred it out there, to tell you the truth. They liked to keep the Sudanese Brigade out of Cairo, out on the border where the fighting was. The Egyptians didn't like the blacks, didn't like them as soldiers anyway. Servants and waiters, aye, but not as soldiers, that's for sure.'

'You were fond of them though.'

'As soldiers? Oh aye. Pitch-black men from the south they were, the wretched of the earth. As wild as Scotsmen. But the best body of men I ever had the pleasure to lead.'

His face opened into a broad grin.

'I loved them,' he said with an astonished gasp. 'My beautiful black battalions.'

The Beast smiled. The drug was certainly working. The General was really opening up.

'Of course you loved them,' he added.

'Och, many a time I lost my temper wi' them, when I was trying to drill some sense into them. They were the dispossessed, enlisted for life and liable for service wherever they might be found and taken. They fought with quiet rage at the world and with a fierce loyalty few would understand. They loved me back in their own way.'

The General broke into a laugh.

'Aye, there was one time, some minor skirmish when they had lost control and forgotten their training, I bawled them out so harshly that they took my anger for fear, and imagined that I was in a panic. A group of them surrounded me and started to stroke me, as if to quieten me down saying, "Don't be afraid. We are here and we shall protect you." They are a much more physical people, ye ken?'

'Oh yes.'

'But I kept myself in check. I tried to love them all wi' no favourites. Until . . .'

Macdonald let out a breath.

'This is what is coming through in your vision, isn't it?'

'Aye,' the General sighed. 'The one I was particularly fond

of. Bakhit. He joined up along with some other Sudanese prisoners we took at Firka.'

Macdonald fell into brooding once more.

'Tell me about him,' the Beast urged.

XVII

'IKNEW THE LAD WOULD be trouble from the moment I first saw him lined up with the other *jihadiyya* prisoners. Those sullen eyes that sparkled with tears.' Macdonald gave a rueful laugh.

'Aye,' he went on. 'In all my years of service I'd learned long and hard how to decipher men that I was in charge of. You learn how to spot a slacker, or one too keen; the barrack-room politician or platoon entertainer, one who might lose his nerve under fire or another who would be too reckless. So many types of men, you know, and my job to know them all. You have to be ready to reward loyalty or punish disobedience. You become accustomed to interpreting any little sign, always on the lookout for any discontent. But this one was strange and difficult to read. He seemed to mask his true feelings as if hiding some unspoken hurt. There was a treacherous sensitivity about him.'

'Sounds dangerous.'

'Aye. In some strange and stupid way that's what attracted me to him in the first place. Something wild and rebellious about him.'

'That makes sense.'

'Does it? Well, he was a handsome lad as well, that's for sure. I tried to convince myself that my curiosity in him had nothing to do with that. I was concerned with a matter of discipline, I kept telling myself, that was all.

'I knew that the youth was not a habitual malcontent and somewhere beneath his sullen demeanour lurked good humour. Bakhit seemed to me as one possessed of a playful spirit that had been lost. He muttered strange and dark other under his breath. Curses that were not loud, but boy were they deep. His was a resentment more personal and intimate than that of common mutiny and more perilous at that.

'And it was a precarious time for morale in those months after Firka, especially among the new recruits. There was a delay in the movement of the campaign, a lull that made the men listless. Lines of communication had been stretched thin. We had to wait for the new railway to catch up with the army's advance, for the new armoured gunboats to be assembled and for the Nile to rise to a navigable level. The camp at Firka soon became foul and insanitary, ridden with dysentery. We moved to a new base at Kosheh, six miles south along the Nile where there was an improvised dockyard. There we watched the steel-plated steamers being riveted together in segments, like bloody great water beetles.

'Then in July a terrible pestilence struck. An epidemic of cholera broke out, killing hundreds and spreading fear and depression in the ranks. I lost two of my own domestic staff: my Egyptian cook Ibrahim and Zakariyya, my personal orderly. There were grim days of quarantine that took their toll on the men. A hateful terror of contagion. Terrible for morale when you can't even trust to be close to one another. The whole brigade became infected with a sense of fatalism and suspicion. It was the middle of August before the disease finally burned itself out.

'It was then that we were ordered south once more, to occupy forward positions at Absarat. It was a perilous forced march across the desert; we were reliant on reaching water depots left by the Camel Corps. The 2nd Egyptian Brigade, on a similar manoeuvre, got caught in a sandstorm, with nine men dead and eighty cases of heatstroke. A war correspondent had called it "the Death March", which didn't help our confidence any. There was scant goodwill to draw upon from the men. Loyalty was on a knife edge.

'During a break in the march I was walking my charger along

the resting column when I caught the sound of Bakhit's voice whispering harshly to two of his fellows. "Wait," I heard him say. "Wait until the next battle, this slave-driver of a *miralai* will not come out of it alive." The lad lifted his rifle in a kind of vicious pantomime. "I'll shoot him myself!" he said.

'The other two laughed, not realising that the very same *miralai* was sat on his horse right behind them. I shouted an order for them to stand to attention.

'I looked down at them and said, "So, you're to shoot me when we are next fighting, are you?" Only Bakhit met my gaze. The others just dropped their heads. The whole column was hushed, men began to break rank to peer and gesture at what was happening. A sergeant marched up briskly to where the men were standing to attention. I made a sign for him to wait.

'"Well, what are you waiting for?" I said. "Why not shoot me now? You have your rifle, why not use it? Here I am – shoot me!"

'I saw Bakhit's eyes widen in fear and wonder. The whole brigade waited in silence to see what would happen next. I sat calmly on my charger staring the lad out. A shriek of mirth suddenly came from somewhere, which broke the tension into a moment of comedy. I heard laughter ripple along the column, Bakhit lowered his gaze and one of his comrades gave him a shove. He landed on his hands and knees in the sand. I just turned my horse around and trotted back to the head of the line.

'It was noted by everyone that no further action was taken over the matter until the brigade was safely encamped at Absarat. I waited three days before I had him called up in front of me.

'The first thing I did was to make the observation that he appeared to be the best-dressed man in the brigade. The lad looked confused at this. It was true though. Despite his rebellious streak he had taken great care over his uniform. The brigade had been so ill-equipped and badly supplied in the last few months that most of the men's battledress was tatty and threadbare. Yet Bakhit always looked ready for parade.

'I asked him how he managed it. Well, Bakhit didn't know what to say to this. His eyes flickered about, wondering if this was some sort of test. He finally admitted that he always liked to take care of how things looked. And it was then it came to me what to do with him. I needed a new orderly, so I gave him the job. Now, being orderly to the CO was seen by all to be a good duty, with the possibility of many perks and I was concerned that his appointment might be a cause of envy, especially given how short a time he had served. It worried me that some might see it as a reward for insubordination and I knew that there would be some evil talk about the real reason for making this particular young man my batman. But I convinced myself that what was more important was to keep any potential trouble close by, never to lose sight of it. And I was sure too that Bakhit would make a pretty good valet.'

'And did he?'

'Oh aye. And we grew to have a great affection for each other . . .' The General sighed. 'I said I managed to resist the temptations of Cairo, but I found them sure enough, out on the frontier.'

'You fell in love with him.'

Macdonald was shocked by the stark honesty of this remark. It was like being unbuttoned.

'I did,' he admitted. 'Aye. Years of keeping myself in check, well, they all meant nothing when he came along. He was a special one.'

'But you said you lost him.'

'Aye. In the end.'

'What happened?'

'Well, I don't know. The fact is I don't know the whole story.'

'But you are learning more of it tonight?'

'Aye. I suppose I am. But I don't really understand what's happening.'

'There is something of great significance to be revealed.'

'You seem very certain of that.'

'I have some experience of such things.'

'So you say. Look, I don't know what's been going on in my head but I want to know what you are up to.'

'You want to know what my mission is, here in Paris?'

'Aye.'

'Then I should explain how I came to be a magician in the first place.'

XVIII

'I HAD LEFT CAMBRIDGE WITHOUT bothering to take my degree,' Crowley began. 'Trinity College had utterly failed to educate me to their banal standards. I sought greater qualifications than any they had to offer. I wanted adventure.'

'Perhaps you were running away too,' the General suggested.

The Beast sighed and thought of Pollitt once more.

'Yes,' he conceded. 'At college I had been bogged down in a quagmire of decadence. I had fallen into the depths and I needed to rise up out of them. The three great disciplines of my life are magic, poetry and climbing, which all combine in a great vocation of aspiration. It was mountaineering that I intended to develop once I had freed myself from the suffocating confines of university.'

'Mountaineering?' Macdonald retorted incredulously.

'I know you imagine me to be a mere aesthete, Sir Hector, but I can assure you I am an accomplished climber. I am hardly in good shape now, but that is largely due to a technique I developed for a scaling of K2 in the Hindu Kush. One builds up large reserves of body fat before starting an ascent and burns it off by the exertion of the climb. But this method of energy conservation can have the effect that the body, when at rest, becomes accustomed to developing an unwanted corpulence.

'Anyway, I had spent part of the summer on the Schönbühl Glacier practising for a Himalayan expedition. I had gone down to Zermatt to relax for a week when I fell in with some fellow British climbers at a beer hall there. I made some casual remark about my knowledge of alchemy and to my astonishment one of the party revealed himself as an accomplished adept in magical formulae. My destiny was in ambush. Just as I seemed intent on scaling physical heights so I was once more inspired to achieve spiritual altitudes. It was through this chance meeting that I was to learn of the existence of the Order of the Golden Dawn.'

'The Golden Dawn?'

'An arcane order dedicated to the practice of ceremonial magic.'

'A secret society?'

'I'm afraid that makes it sound far more exciting than it really is. Ah yes, it held so much promise for me at first, as if I had stumbled across the Hidden Church of the Holy Grail. I thought I had joined the Elect, only to find that the Order was mostly made up of dreary middle-class people, excited by quaint little rituals held in Clapham or Hammersmith. However, I met two men in the Order, both possessed of luminous minds and actual magical ability, from which I was truly able to learn.

'The first of these was Samuel Liddell Mathers, the nominal head of the Golden Dawn. He claimed to have direct communication with the Secret Chiefs, the Unseen Ones, whose power, it is said, directs and controls the Order. And it was Mathers who had first decoded the Cypher Manuscript, the sacred document that revealed the ritual instructions for ceremonial magic. But there were already signs of a schism in the Order when I joined. Mathers had come to Paris to establish a new temple and, having had no satisfaction in gaining a higher grade within the London chapter, I came here myself, three years ago, and made myself known to Mathers directly. He immediately recognised both my understanding of occult wisdom and my prowess as its practitioner. I was personally initiated by him and he anointed me as his successor. Though I think, even back then, he realised that my powers would one day surpass his.

'The second adept I came to respect fully in the Order was Allan Bennett, once a colleague of Mathers' in matters of the occult, but now quite at odds with him. They had a serious disagreement that Mathers had been vague about to me. It was obvious to me, even then, that the old man was envious of Bennett's transcendental powers. The fact was that Bennett possessed a tormented soul, frail in body but capable of tremendous spiritual force. He rejected the pleasures of living and the consolations of physical love as diabolical illusions devised to trick mankind into accepting the curse of existence. He had an aversion to all sexual matters that amounted to horror. His utter craving for a higher state of being fascinated me. In rented rooms in Chancery Lane we invoked spirits and prepared talismans and there he introduced me to the ancient tradition of the use of drugs in magic ceremony.'

'Drugs?' Macdonald frowned.

The Beast smiled. The General still had no idea that he was in the grip of a sacred narcotic.

'Oh yes,' he went on. 'We experimented with trance states and travel on an astral level. Allan had accustomed himself to consuming quantities of opium, morphine, cocaine and chloroform that would poison most mortals. I partook of that artificial paradise in a more moderate fashion. Despite, or rather because of, this great progress in delirious alchemy, Bennett's health deteriorated badly. Knowing that he needed a more benign climate, and that his rejection of the self bowed in the direction of Buddhism, I procured funds for him to go to Ceylon where I visited him last year. You were there then, weren't you?' Crowley suddenly asked Macdonald.

'What?' murmured the General.

'Ceylon. We must have been there at the same time. We should talk of Ceylon later.'

'Certainly,' Macdonald replied grimly. 'But do go on.'

'Well, suffice to say my fearless quest for arcane wisdom seemed to offend the dreary morality of the London membership of the Golden Dawn. Quite how any of them thought they might attain enlightenment was anybody's guess. The loudest voice in their chorus was that self-styled bard of the Celts, W.B. Yeats.'

'Who?'

'Exactly. A minor poet who was a member of the Order. The man accused me of leading an unspeakable life and said that I should be expelled since a mystical society was not intended to be a reformatory. Jealousy, of course, was at the heart of it. As an occultist Yeats was, at best, a dilettante, and as a writer? Well, I'll grant that he did possess enough literary ability to recognise a greater talent.

'As Yeats's group seemed determined to drag the Order into bourgeois mediocrity, the split in the Order became apparent. Mathers expelled most of them and instructed me to recover the contents of the Vault of the Adepts, a secret chamber concealed in a first-floor flat in Shepherd's Bush. After a couple of attempts, my final assault was blocked by Yeats and a fellow Order member. In their cowardice they called the landlord, a constable and a member of the Trades Protection Association who claimed that I had been blacklisted for bad debts.

'Well, that was quite enough. I could go no further on this wretched little island. I had also heard rumours that the police had been watching the flat in Chancery Lane, that there had been allegations made about sexual misconduct. It was certainly the moment for me to move on. It was time to travel the world. America, Mexico, Hawaii, Japan, China, Singapore, Ceylon of course.

'It was there I met up again with Allan Bennett. I studied yoga with him and learned about the falling out he had with Mathers. He gave me quite a different story than I had heard from the other man. He claimed that Mathers had threatened him with a pistol. It was from then on that I began to have serious doubts about the old fool's leadership of the Order. But there was more travel and exploration to be done. Burma, India, the Himalayas, Egypt. Then back here to Paris. Like you I looked for adventure. But the empire I sought was an empire of the senses.'

'I never looked for adventure.'

'No?'

'No. I never had much choice about what happened to me.'

'Then you have been lucky.'

'Lucky? I've marched a million miles through freezing wastes and burning deserts. I've slept ten years under canvas. I've seen all the horror of dozens of battles, of thousands slaughtered. I'd hardly say I was lucky.'

'But this was all your duty. There was nothing you could do about it. I have been spoiled rotten. I have had every opportunity to make the most ludicrous decisions and yet I have never been satisfied, even with my most spectacular mistakes. There has been no chance of heroism. Any dangers I have encountered, and there have been a few, have all been my own fault. I have had all the good things of life but I no longer enjoy or value them. I embrace hardship and privation with ecstatic delight. I grow delirious to contemplate the delicious horrors that are certain to happen to me. I wish to take pleasure in every possibility of existence.'

'Then you are the lucky one. I'm tired of it all.'

Crowley patted Macdonald gently on the shoulder.

'Take heart, Sir Hector. We will find a way through your tribulations. Our meeting is fortuitous. I can help you escape from your persecutors and in return you can assist me in my quest.'

'What quest?'

'Well, here it is. I came back to Paris and what did I find? My former master had completely lost control of the Golden Dawn. He had promised to strike back at the London chapter but he has done nothing. The drunken old fool has lost all power and rights as leader and must now bow to my succession. The last straw, of course, was my luggage.'

'Your luggage?'

'I left some rather expensive items of luggage in his care before I went travelling. A fifty-guinea dressing-case and a crocodile-skin portmanteau. When I returned I found that he had sold them. I mean: what sort of a gentleman is that? The man is an utter fraud. So we are on our way to his temple now and with your help I mean to take rightful possession of the Cypher Manuscript.'

'With my help? I don't understand.'

'Mathers is obsessed with all things Scottish. He uses "Macgregor" as part of his address, often wears tartan and claims kinship with the Jacobite cause. In all honesty I don't believe he has ever actually been to Scotland. Your appearance as a bona fide Gaelic warrior might help to pacify him sufficiently for me to obtain what I want. You haven't by any chance been intitated into the Ancient Scottish Rite of Freemasonry, have you?'

'No.'

'No matter. The duel between Mathers and myself has already commenced.'

'You mean to fight a duel?'

'A magical one. As I said, it has started. So far there has been an exchange of talismans. Today he sent me a magic square.'

'Really?' Macdonald smiled and felt in his pocket.

'I was able to countersign it and send it back.'

'A magic square, you say?'

The Beast noticed that the General was grinning at him. There was a wolfish look to his face and Crowley felt a sudden fear that he couldn't account for. Macdonald pulled something out of his jacket and held it up to the Beast's face.

'Like this?' the General hissed.

A small silver square glinted from the dim glow of the carriage lamp. The Beast struggled to focus on a series of inscriptions within a grid upon its surface.

'My God!' he called out as he saw what it was.

XIX

٢١ ٢٦ ١٩

٢٠ ٢٢ ٢٤

٢٥ ١٨ ٢٣

'DO YOU KNOW WHAT THIS is?' the Beast demanded.
The General laughed. He had completely wrong-footed Crowley.

'It's my lucky charm,' he said.

'It's a *wafq*. An Islamic magic square inscribed with Arabic numbers. I've heard about them but I've never seen one. May I?'

'Be my guest,' Macdonald said, handing it to him.

'Properly deciphered these things can reveal the hidden name of God. Let me see.' The Beast tried to make some calculations in the lamplight. 'Allah is supposed to have ninety-nine names, you know,' he said.

'Do you want me to tell you what the numbers are? My Arabic isn't bad.'

'There's really no need,' Crowley replied with a petulant squint.

There was not enough light in the carriage for him to read by. He turned to the General.

'Where did you get this?' he asked.

'Bakhit gave it to me. Well, it was an exchange really.'

'What for?'

'A trinket. I'd been given an ornamental biscuit tin commemorating Victoria's Diamond Jubilee. The lad was so taken by the wretched thing I let him have it. He insisted I take this. He told me it would bring me luck. When I said he should keep it he shook his head and explained that if I had good luck so would the whole brigade.'

'How very touching. You know that used correctly this talisman has strong magical powers?'

'Well, that's what they say.'

'You know more of sorcery than you've been letting on.'

'Och, I saw plenty of superstition in Africa.'

'Then you'll know the power of numbers as well as words, of course. Everything becomes symbolic. But it is how symbols are ordered that is essential for the casting of spells. Their grammar, if you like.'

Macdonald laughed, suddenly remembering Christina's impatience when she corrected his speech.

'So you have to speak properly to be a magician?' he demanded.

'You have to think properly,' Crowley replied. 'Magic is the manipulation of language, and how we order thought gives us power. The Cypher Manuscript, this book of ritual instructions I seek, it is known as a *grimoire*, which is an archaic word for grammar. In old Scottish, of course, this becomes *glamour*, which as you must know means enchantment.'

'Aye.'

'This grammar does not follow the conventions of polite society. Oh no. You have to re-order the words in your mind to find a new meaning.'

'A new meaning?'

'A new way of understanding yourself. If you can speak the unspeakable, then you might set yourself free.'

Macdonald thought of the scandal once more, of how he might be called to account for himself at a court martial.

'I, I . . .' the General stammered.

'I know it's hard for you, but we've already come a long way. First you must try to come to terms with your past. You can use this amulet to make contact.'

'Contact. With what?'

'Why, with this Bakhit, of course.'

Macdonald saw the Beast's grin glimmer in a flare of gaslight as he handed the charm back to him.

'At the very least it will help you visualise him,' Crowley suggested.

Macdonald held the square in his fist. There was a distinct tingling in his fingertips.

'You feel something, don't you?' asked the Beast.

'Yes,' Macdonald replied, closing his eyes and travelling back to the desert once more.

He would watch Bakhit as he attended to his duties, flitting about the tent with a nervous grace. The boy was so shockingly handsome, his long-limbed angularity beautifully punctuated with a voluptuous roundness. As he moved the tight camber of his shoulders rolled in gentle counterpoint with the high curve of his buttocks. Macdonald caught sight of the smooth cupola of his forehead, the wide dreaming eyes, the full lips that jutted out, always slightly open.

'Do you see him?' asked the Beast.

'Yes,' the General murmured, his hooded eyes flickering.

This was a more intimate and emotional visitation. Macdonald felt the memory flood through his body.

It was easy to watch Bakhit; he so clearly enjoyed being looked at. He did not overplay his performance though, making lyrical, long-fingered gestures as he went about his fetch and carry routine. Bakhit had a natural charisma, a marvellous attitude of self-possession. Macdonald felt the powerful charm of his presence. Sometimes the lad would offer a smile or a nod and occasionally they would be caught in an instant of hypnotic vacillation. Bakhit would suddenly stop and stare, as if awaiting an unutterable order. Macdonald would hold his gaze and savour for a second the sense of luxuriant anticipation. Then he would gesture for his servant to continue, diffusing the charged air with a sweep of his hand.

They attained the intimacy of domestic routine and settled into a tranquil occupancy. Macdonald felt a wistful longing in watchful unspoken moments. Yet he dreaded anything that might disturb the calm with which they passed the time together. At nights when a tightening in the throat reminded him of his profound instinctive yearning, he would go out and take the cool desert air.

Bakhit was diligent in all his duties. He made sure that his commanding officer's uniform was always clean and pressed, his boots immaculate, his tent in good order. This was what he enjoyed doing, seeing to it that things were nicely turned out. It gave him pleasure and purpose and something like a philosophy. This was, he felt, how the world should be. And he started to feel a quiet and simple affection for the fastidious and sad-faced *miralai*.

Macdonald had never got used to having servants, always finding it hard to get over his sense of awkwardness in their presence. They made him feel like an impostor. He had tried, but never quite managed, to cultivate an indifference to them. But with Bakhit, for the first time, he felt a sense of ease in his own quarters. His previous experience of batmen was that they were either overly intrusive or carelessly inattentive. Bakhit somehow managed to appear when he was wanted and simply vanish when he was not.

Macdonald rarely drank alcohol but he ordered Bakhit to make sure that it was on hand for any occasion. A great many correspondents were following the campaign now that it was gaining momentum. Kitchener had an uneasy time with the press, distrusting them thoroughly. Macdonald had little idea of how to deal with journalists but he knew that it helped to provide them with a drink or two.

And he might allow himself a small Scotch in the evening.

He would sit alone reading before bedtime, working his way through Gibbon's *The Decline and Fall of the Roman Empire* one more time as Bakhit tidied up around him. The interest in antiquity that Christina had first inspired had never left him. He would sit in his folding captain's chair, briefly look up at and smile at the wondrous sense of adornment that his orderly gave to the evening.

He knew that he already tended to be over-familiar with the men. Sirdar Kitchener certainly thought so and disapproved. It was said that in his entire military career Kitchener had never so much as once addressed an enlisted man directly. He had made his way to the top with a deliberate sense of sacrifice; all considerations of comfort, affection, even personality had been subjugated for his superior purpose. Yet beyond the coldness and snobbery Macdonald always felt a fiery glow of resentment emanating from the man. Strange gossip dogged Kitchener. Macdonald suspected that there were also stories about himself doing the rounds in Cairo.

Of course there were forms of fraternisation that were perfectly acceptable. To join in with rifle practice or the occasional football match was considered laudable. Any attachment that veered close to friendship was not. And yet with Bakhit he desired this and beyond with a secret fervour.

Brief exchanges in halting Arabic slowly became embroidered into amicable colloquy. Bakhit could be very amusing. He knew when he could be irreverent, taking great pleasure in mimicking a passing turn of phrase or gesture; he also knew when to be discreet or silent. He had a great curiosity and Macdonald never discouraged him from asking questions, though he knew that he sometimes should. Bakhit spoke of his old commander Faraj Pasha, who had told him about France and Mexico and the world beyond. Macdonald kept hold of copies of *Strand* magazine or the *Illustrated London News* if he came across them, knowing that his orderly loved looking at the pictures.

One evening he called to Bakhit to bring him a second whisky.

A letter had come from Christina, informing him that she had moved to Dulwich and enrolled young Hector into a good school there. She enclosed a summary of fees for a non-boarder.

Bakhit brought out the extra glass of Scotch and saw that his *miralai* was looking even more gloomy than usual. Macdonald looked up from the letter and caught his batman's concerned gaze. He attempted a smile but he knew that it must have looked ghastly.

'News from England,' he muttered, suddenly feeling the need to account for his melancholia.

'You miss England, Bey?'

Macdonald laughed.

'Not at all,' he replied.

Bakhit frowned. Macdonald recalled a glimpse of cold sun on the Black Isle in Easter Ross. He remembered the bitter wind shimmering the water of Cromarty Firth, the purpled moor beyond, the distant peaks of Sutherland smudged with cloud.

'You see, Bakhit,' he explained, 'I am not Inglisi.'

The young man looked even more confused.

'Not Inglisi, Bey?'

'No. I belong to a different tribe.'

'Tribe, Bey?' Bakhit smiled at this. 'Like Dinka?'

'Yes. But a lot more savage.'

Bakhit burst out laughing.

'The Scottish,' Macdonald went on. 'Many clans. One great uncivilised tribe.'

'Ah yes, the Scottish.' Bakhit nodded. 'The Scottish are great friends of the Inglisi.'

'Hmm, not exactly, Bakhit. We fight their battles.'

'Like *jihadiyya*?'

'Very like *jihadiyya*. Slave soldiers of the Inglisi.'

'Yes, but not slaves, Bey. You are above us.'

'We are for now. One day things might be different.'

'Different, Bey?'

'Yes, well, the world gets turned upside down Bakhit. Here I am, a northern savage commanding Africans. But' – he tapped a volume of Gibbon on his reading table – 'I have been reading about a great African leader who went to Scotland, my land, to try to put down the warlike natives there.'

He opened the book at a marked page and read aloud:

'"Septimus Severus, a native of Africa, who, in the gradual ascent of private honours, had concealed his daring ambition which was never diverted from its steady course by allurements of pleasure, the apprehension of danger, or the feelings of humanity . . ." Good Lord,' he muttered to himself. 'That reminds me of me.'

His batman looked on uncomprehending.

'Anyway, Bakhit, this Septimus Severus,' Macdonald explained. 'He was an African soldier in the Roman Army. He rose up through the ranks. He ended up ruling the whole empire.'

'The British Empire?'

'No, no. This was the Roman Empire, not the British one.'

'Roman? What is Roman?'

'Italian.'

'Italian? No, Bey, not Italian. The Italians cannot even beat the Abyssinians!'

Macdonald laughed.

'This was seventeen hundred years ago, Bakhit. An African went to Scotland to put down the savages there. That is history.'

Bakhit tried to think of such a large number.

'History, Bey?'

'The times that have passed.'

'Salim always talked of time. He said that soon time will come to an end.'

'Salim?'

Bakhit made a little gasp, as if he had mentioned something he should not have. His bearing stiffened for a second.

'What's the matter, Bakhit?' Macdonald demanded.

The young man let his shoulders drop and let out a melancholy sigh.

'He was my friend, Bey.'

It was then that Macdonald first learned of Salim. The story that had now come back to him in Paris with such psychotic lucidity. Then Bakhit had told the spare details, of how they were taken as slaves, how they served as soldiers with Faraj Pasha, of Khartoum and Gordon, their years as *jihadiyya* and how they had finally lost each other at Firka. From that moment on Macdonald felt another's presence between them, disturbing their once calm companionship. And he ached for the true and absolute amity Bakhit felt for his friend. Macdonald swallowed hard, feeling the same choke of lust that he had that night. He opened his eyes and was back in the carriage.

XX

'THEY HAD BEEN SEPARATED AT Firka,' the General explained to Crowley. 'Salim had gone with a group of prisoners to the Railway Battalion. They were set to work building the line through the Nubian Desert. That's what had made Bakhit so rebellious in the first place. He said he had almost hoped that his punishment for insubordination would have been transfer to the Railway Battalion so that he could be with Salim once more. He was pretty desperate, I mean it was a harsh detail. Hard labour in the desert.'

'He was obviously very fond of this Salim.'

'Aye. They had a bond. Born in the same village. Taken as slaves together when they were young.'

'You had a sense of pity for Salim because of how Bakhit felt for him?'

'Maybe I liked to think that. The fact was I was enslaved by my baser emotions. I felt, well, I felt jealous of his affection for Salim. I had grown so foolishly infatuated with the lad, and when I saw the sadness in his eyes I knew I could never get that close to him. I worried that he would do something stupid and I might lose him. So I decided to resolve the matter.'

'How?'

'To find Salim. To find out what had happened to him on the Sudan Military Railway. There were terrible stories of what happened to the men made to work on it. Kitchener's great holy war of engineering. Everyone had said that it was impossible, absurd even. Two hundred and fifty miles of it from Wadi Halfa to Abu Hamed. Right through the scorching wilderness. Aye, but then he had a ruthless precision. Everything calculated and brought within budget. He became known as the Sudan Machine.'

'Just as I said earlier. The power of repression, like the power of steam. It's what the empire's built on.'

'Aye, well. Kitchener was a study in it.'

'And Salim was working on the line.'

'Forced labour and the lash. That's how it got built. Despite all the science and modernity.'

Yet so much had become mechanised. The Sudan Machine saw to that. The steamers patrolling the Nile, bristling with four-pounder cannon and new fully automatic machine guns, gunships equipped with every modern improvement: ammunition hoists, telegraphs, searchlights and steam winches. Conquest was forged in the workshops of Wadi Halfa with foundries, lathes, dynamos, steam-hammers, hydraulic presses, cupola furnaces and screw-cutting machines. All the paraphernalia of the future had been assembled to triumph over the past. Kitchener's will was coldly imposed. He was ruthless to the physical world, merciless to his own nature.

'The man was quite a Pharoah,' commented Crowley.

'Oh, he had great plans. He would divide up the whole world given the chance. You know, there was one economy he would not make – instead of the narrow Egyptian gauge, he insisted on a slightly wider track, South African gauge, so that one day his railway could link up all the way down through the continent. From Cairo to the Cape.'

'A visionary of the Forward Policy.'

'Aye. I think he dreamed of a new viceroyalty. Well, it wasn't just his own ambition that made him monstrous. He seemed burdened with other people's dreams as well, driven by a kind of nervous rage. He surrounded himself with a group of young and arrogant sapper officers who became known as the Band of Boys.'

'How intriguing.'

'Aye, well, they were a supercilious lot. Anyway, as I was saying. About Salim.'

'Yes.'

'I went to look for him.'

'Wasn't that a bit reckless?'

'Oh yes. I mean, I managed to convince my own staff that it was an intelligence matter. But I knew it could mean trouble if I had to explain myself to Kitchener or any of his Band of Boys. But, as I said, I was infatuated.'

'It sounds romantic.'

'To you maybe. I was making a fool of myself.'

'I would say it was an honourable thing. What did you do?'

The General laughed.

'Why, I caught a train, didn't I?'

He had found carriage space on a supply locomotive heading for the front. Mile upon mile they skimmed through the haunting, monotonous desert. They stopped to change drivers at a wayside station with a signpost naming it simply: No. 6. There was a rest-house shanty of board and galvanised iron, with pictures from the illustrated papers tacked on the bare walls; a group of English railwaymen huddled in the shade, smoking. Then the train started up again, leaving behind this purgatorial suburb.

Towards nightfall, sparse clumps of shrub and dots of mimosa began to gather around the embankment as the track veered closer to the Nile, then a white-tented township emerged out of the gloom as they approached Railhead.

'I saw a swarm of prisoners, still in their *jibbas*, digging out the footings for the next length of track,' explained Macdonald. 'A group of Egyptians overseeing, and somewhere in the distance a white subaltern with a spirit-level. I told the officer I was looking for a *jihadiyya* captured at Firka, that I needed to interrogate him.'

'But you had no luck?'

'A *fellahin* NCO recognised the name and the description. He spat on the ground and said the man was a troublemaker. He also said that he had gone missing.'

'Missing?'

'Well, you can imagine the cost in human life of such an enterprise. Kitchener joked that he had used Dervish gallows as sleepers and, aye, there were rumours of hangings and harsh punishments. A lot of fellows were simply worked to death. All kept quiet, of course, but there were a lot of nameless mounds that marked the ever advancing site of Railhead Town.'

'What did you tell Bakhit?'

'It's hard enough to lie in a foreign language and with Bakhit so much of our communication was in looks and gestures. I think he saw the truth in my eyes even before I could make up something to say to him.'

'He took it badly?'

'He wept so softly, with a whimpering sound like a wee puppy. Great fat pearls of grief rolling down his beautiful face. It was pitiful.'

The General gasped. The Beast reached out and rested a hand on the crook of the man's elbow.

'The thing is' – Macdonald gave a dry sob – 'I never planned it to happen that way but it was that night, when I consoled him . . .'

He remembered that night in the tent. He had given him whisky though he knew he shouldn't, and told him his own tale of lost friendship. Of how Kenny Goss had died in his arms at Majuba. They had cried together and Macdonald slyly put a comforting arm around Bakhit and poured him out another dram. In the darkness he had pressed his maddened head against the boy's, and tasted the spirit, sharp and sweet, on those ripe, forbidden lips. They found a deep hunger in that kiss, mouthing loneliness and lostness. Full of forsaken passion, with no one else in the world, Bakhit gave himself to his commander.

The General took another sharp breath.

'It's terrible but maybe secretly, deep down inside, I had wanted Salim to be dead so that I could have Bakhit all for myself.'

'I don't believe you. That's just guilt you have for your own true feelings.'

'But why did he turn on me?'

'I don't understand. When did that happen?'

'Oh, much later. After Omdurman, for God's sake. When all was safe. He deserted.'

'Well, maybe you can find out now. You have the charm. Perhaps it might reveal the truth.'

Macdonald looked down and opened his hand. The magic square shimmered in his palm.

'We've established that the thing works as a talisman of great power, haven't we?' the Beast went on.

'Aye.'

'And we might have a chance to test it out again soon. For another purpose.'

'What do you mean?'

'We've arrived at our first destination.'

Crowley rapped on the roof of the carriage and called out to the driver to stop.

XXI

THE LEADER OF THE GOLDEN Dawn greeted Crowley and Macdonald at the door of his apartment wearing an inspired combination of ceremonial dress. Mathers' top half was shrouded in a white linen gown gathered at the waist by a wide belt engraved with astrological symbols. A leopard skin was draped casually over one shoulder. His lower quarters were covered by a kilt woven in the hunting tartan of the Macgregor clan and a pair of gartered stockings, one of which bristled with the hilts of several knives. He wore dancing pumps on his feet.

'I've been waiting for you, Crowley,' he growled, showing a set of bloodstained teeth.

'Indeed,' the Beast retorted. 'I see you are quite prepared.'

'I feel like a walking flame. Strong is the power within me.'

'Strong is the liquor, that's for certain.'

'Don't be so impertinent. Remember, I am still your master. Your superior in matters of ceremonial magic.'

'Not for much longer. Thank you for the magic square. I returned it to you, properly amended. *Oro te pater, sanas.*'

'Yes, I was able to decipher your fatuous interpretation.'

'The sentiment is quite sincere, I assure you. I beg thee, father, heal thyself.'

'Very clever, I'm sure.'

'It's been quite a day for magic squares.' The Beast turned to Macdonald. 'Why don't you show him?'

The General held up the metal token. Mathers squinted at it.

'Good lord,' he muttered.

'You know what it is, don't you?'

'Of course I know what it is. It's a *wafq*, an African mathematical talisman, probably Sudanese. It has the power to charm or to curse. It's habitually used by natives to take away the pain of childbirth.' Mathers peered up from the magic square and looked at Macdonald. He frowned.

'It is yours?'

'Yes.'

'And who might you be, sir?'

'I think now is the time for formal introductions,' the Beast interjected. 'This is Major-General Sir Hector Macdonald.'

Mathers' face widened in shock. He gave a short intake of breath.

'Mac . . . Macdonald?'

'At your service, sir.'

'But what? What?'

Macdonald pocketed the amulet and held out his hand.

'You are a great warrior, sir,' Mathers said, with a frenetic shake of the proffered hand. 'I followed your command of action at Omdurman. An extraordinary manoeuvre, sir.'

'Won't you let us in?' the Beast asked with a smile.

'Well, er, of course,' Mathers replied.

He led them through into his drawing room. A wood fire spluttered in the grate, shadows throbbing into the corners of the room.

'What brings you to Paris, Sir Hector?' their host enquired.

Macdonald coughed nervously.

'Why he's an old friend of mine of course,' the Beast cut in.

Macdonald gave Crowley a quizzical look. The Beast smiled and replied with a sly wink. Mathers seemed completely thrown off guard by the appearance of the Major-General. He bade them sit and offered them both a drink.

'I'm afraid there's no Scotch,' Mathers apologised, producing a cheap bottle of cognac. 'It's a great honour to meet you, sir. My two passions in life are magic and the art of war. I was in the infantry myself, you know. The 1st Hampshire.'

'Is that so?' replied Macdonald with an indulgent smile.

'Only the volunteers, mind.'

'No shame in being in the volunteers. That's how I started off.'

'And my first book was on military tactics. I translated a French military manual for use by the British Army.'

'That sounds most interesting,' Macdonald rejoined.

The Beast felt sure that he now had the advantage. His former mentor appeared almost completely disarmed.

'Well,' the old magician announced, holding up his glass. '*Slàinte*.'

Repeating the toast, they each took a sip of brandy. Mathers let out a satisfied sigh.

'The General has expressed a great interest in the Order,' the Beast declared.

'I have?' Macdonald retorted, then, catching Crowley's eye again, went along with the subterfuge once more. 'Yes, I have.'

'He is, himself,' the Beast continued, 'quite familiar with the Ancient Scottish Rite of Freemasonry.'

'Really?' Mathers grinned. 'Of course I'm an ardent follower of James the Fourth. The Wizard King. Are you a mystical Jacobite yourself?'

'Well . . .'

'Mathers,' the Beast interjected. 'With the fortuitous appearance of the great General in our midst, it is time, don't you think, to call a truce?'

'You will promise to obey me from now on?'

'I mean that I'm quite prepared to negotiate terms.'

'Terms? I'm not sure about that.'

'First of all.' Crowley nodded at a loosely bound volume resting on a table by the fireplace. It was cased in worn morocco, with an arcane seal stamped on it and faded alchemical engravings tooled along its edges. 'I see that you have the Cypher Manuscript out.'

Mathers patted it affectionately. 'I have been consulting it, yes,' he replied.

'Well, it is no longer safe in your temple,' the Beast declared.

154

'What are you suggesting?'

'That you hand it over to me for safe-keeping.'

'Never!' he insisted, his right hand clawing at the battered *grimoire*.

'Mathers, you said in your note that there is someone claiming to be Dominabitur Astris in Paris.'

'An envoy of Theodor Reuss and Ordo Templi Orientis.'

'Yes. You've met her?'

'No.'

'Well, I have.'

'Have you entered into some kind of negotiation with this woman?'

'No. Why, are you planning to?'

'What do you mean?' Mathers demanded.

'That maybe you were thinking of selling the Cypher Manuscript to the Germans.'

'That is just the sort of low trick you would pull.'

'You forget, Mathers. I have no need to sell anything. I have independent means. Whereas yourself—'

'How dare you, sir!'

'You have scarcely any means of support, Mathers. Now that the London temples have broken contact. So perhaps if an offer for the Cypher Manuscript came your way . . .'

'I would never dream of such a thing.'

'Really? You are hardly trustworthy in matters of possession. For instance: my luggage.'

'Your luggage?'

'Yes, Mathers. Remember when I departed for Mexico I left in your care two rather precious items. The dressing-case and the crocodile-skin portmanteau.'

'They were mislaid.'

'I heard that you sold them.'

'Well . . .'

'Not that their value concerns me. As you know, money means nothing to me, whereas for you—'

'Yes, yes,' Mathers broke in impatiently. 'I sold them, damn you. I needed funds for the temple.'

'But don't you see how vulnerable the temple is now, given that sort of behaviour?'

'You presume to lecture me on morality? You're a degenerate!'

'The fact is, Mathers, I have surpassed you in spiritual authority.'

Macdonald observed the two men gaze intently at each other. He noticed that Crowley was attempting to hold his rival in that strange unfocused stare that he had seen him use before. Mathers glowered back and with a rasp from the back of his throat spluttered out flecks of blood and sputum.

'You are still merely my apprentice, Crowley!'

'Oh no. My hour of triumph is near. I demand direct access to the Secret Chiefs of the Order. Those of whom I have heard so much and seen so little.'

'You are unworthy.'

'You know that I am the rightful leader, you have forfeited your position. An Equinox of the Gods is at hand! A New Aeon!'

'Nonsense!'

'I have been all over the world. The signs are all there. A new epoch. The Great Work now is to formulate the link between the new cosmological forces and mankind. The earth has been turning while you've been crouching in your filthy temple.'

'So, you've done a bit of sightseeing.'

'I have gone beyond your imaginings. I have seen the truth.'

'The truth?'

'Yes. Of many things. Even of you.'

'What are you talking about?'

'I saw Bennett in Ceylon.'

'So?'

'His account of your falling out was quite different to the one you gave me.'

'Well, there are always different points of view, subjectively speaking.'

'You told me that you had disagreed on a point of theology thus formulating the accursed Dyad and enabling the Abramelin demons to assume material form.'

'I was being a little metaphorical, perhaps.'

'Bennett told me that you argued about Shiva.'

'Oh, God, yes. Shiva. The Great Destroyer. Allan was always going on about him. You know how nihilistic he was back then? Out of his mind on drugs. He believed that if you repeated the name often enough, Shiva would open his eye and destroy the whole universe. Well, you know how much he *loved* that idea.'

'He says you threatened him.'

'I tried to remonstrate with him but he just kept repeating: Shiva, Shiva, Shiva. Sitting there in some ludicrous yoga position, oblivious, intoning his blessed mantra: Shiva, Shiva, Shiva. Well, I'd had enough.'

'So I hear.'

'He was deliberately taunting me, Crowley. I couldn't take any more.'

'And you felt you had to stop him?'

'Yes!' Mathers hissed, his eyes rolling upwards.

'He says that you pulled a pistol on him.'

The old magician grimaced, baring his blood-reddened teeth once more. He nodded slowly.

'I did, yes,' he declared. 'This one.'

Mathers had swiftly pulled a small pistol from inside his ceremonial gown and was pointing it at Crowley. The Beast moved forward from his chair into a crouching position. Mathers stood up slowly, all the time training the gun on his former acolyte. With his free hand he grabbed the Cypher Manuscript.

'You'll not get this!' he screeched. 'Now get out!'

Crowley had frozen in a stooped posture. His upper body was grotesquely hunched, the bull neck gibbous at the green velvet collar, his eyes bulging. Mathers stood over him, with a deranged stare of triumph in his eyes, a shock of grey hair crowning his lunatic regalia. Firelight pulsed behind them.

Macdonald sat entranced by this delirious tableau and for a second or two he fancied what he saw might merely be another strange vision of the evening. The pistol was real, he reasoned, small calibre, a pearl-handled revolver. A delicate but deadly enough mechanism. Just the thing if you wanted to kill yourself. It gave him an idea.

Mathers looked to be on the very edge of hysteria as he aimed the gun at his former pupil. Crowley's face was bright with terror, his lower lip trembling. A fat bead of sweat rolled down his quivering jowls.

'M-M-Mathers, old man,' he pleaded. 'Now don't do anything hasty.'

'You're an ungrateful wretch, Crowley!'

Mathers cocked the hammer of the revolver. The Beast gave out a little gasp of terror.

'Now, gentlemen,' the General announced in a soft and authoritative tone.

They both turned to look at him.

'I think you should put that thing down,' he told Mathers.

'You see that he is trying to steal from me?' Mathers implored.

'I really don't care,' the General went on. 'But you will put the gun down.'

Mathers moved his upper body around to face Macdonald. The pistol was now pointing in that direction. The General reached out a hand.

'It is loaded,' Mathers told him.

'Please be careful, Sir Hector!'

The General laughed.

'Careful? Nae, lad, that's not my way. Don't worry, I'm used tae this. My men regularly threatened to shoot me.'

He now found himself looking into the barrel of the gun. He wondered idly if one shot would be enough. He couldn't be sure unless it went right into the heart. Macdonald reached into his own pocket. Mathers jerked back in nervous vigilance as the General pulled something out and held it up. It was Bakhit's magic square.

XXII

THE GENERAL BROKE INTO A loud cackle as they walked out into the cold night air.

'You had the shite scared out o' you back there,' he declared to Crowley.

'Well, I . . .'

'Just as well I kept ma nerve.'

Macdonald let out another salvo of laughter. The Beast noted that the effects of the drug had now inspired a euphoric state in the General. As they began to walk along the pavement looking out for a cab to hail, Macdonald abruptly picked up his step into a brisk infantry pace, whistling 'Cock o' the North', the marching tune of the Gordon Highlanders. Swinging his arms like a bandmaster, he skipped along the kerb, singing:

> *Ma Aunty Mary, had a canary,*
> *Up the leg o' her drawers,*
> *She pulled a string, to make it sing,*
> *And doon came Santy Claus.*

The General stopped and turned around, his face flushed red, blue eyes gleaming, teeth clenched into a gurning grin.

'So it seems I have magical powers,' he said.

'You certainly have an aptitude for influence,' Crowley agreed.

'Aye, then that's what it is. Mesmerism or something. I was able to control the mind o' that wee madman back there.'

'I can assure you that that man was, and is still in some ways, quite a genius. A scholar and a magus of considerable eminence.' The Beast sighed regretfully. 'It's a shame to see him brought down, but it had to be done.'

'You got what you wanted.'

'Yes. The Cypher Manuscript is in safe hands.'

They had come to the end of the street. A group of men sat huddled around a table outside a café drinking beer. Crowley spotted a *fiacre* approaching and stepped out into the gutter to wave it down.

'Where are we going now?' asked Macdonald.

'Why, to dinner of course.'

The cab driver reined his horse back to trot up to the corner. The Beast and the General walked up to it.

'Le Chat Blanc!' Crowley called up to the coachman. 'Rue d'Odessa.'

They climbed into the back and started off again.

'So this casting of spells,' Macdonald went on. 'It's some sort of hypnotism.'

'Magic is a matter of the will. You demonstrated that yourself.' The Beast laughed. 'You were quite astonishing, sir.'

'Aye. Getting into people's heads, is that it?'

'Or getting into one's own head, having power over one's own mind. You've witnessed yourself the potency of your own imagination.'

'I suppose I have.'

'It's through that that we can commune with spirits beyond. You've further to go in your journey, Sir Hector. To find out what happened.'

'Aye?'

'Yes. To the other side. To everything you have repressed. You have to listen to the voices of those you conquered. The dispossessed.'

'The dispossessed?'

'Yes. Because you have become one of them now. It is their voices you have been hearing tonight, isn't it? The voices of the damned.'

The General sighed and took hold of the talisman. He closed his eyes and felt a pounding in his ears, the roar of blood as his pulse quickened. The crash and clatter of a percussive rhythm built up in his head. He was on the train once more as it thundered across the unsurveyed wilderness. A steel-blue sky darkening over the desert, Kitchener on the footplate with the eyes of a demon calling: *Go like hell!* The face of the juggernaut. The will of the machine urging its fury relentlessly on to Railhead. The engine's whistle shrieked in terror and beneath the steam's breath Macdonald heard the word that Bakhit muttered in his sleep. Pistons hissed the whispered name: *Salim, Salim, Salim, Salim . . .*

'And he will have an ass which he will ride, whose two ears will be forty yards apart!' Salim mutters a hadith, one of the sayings of the Prophet, as they are marched out into the desert in the darkness.

'That is how we will know al-Dajjal,' he implores his comrades. 'The train, you see? The train is the ass of al-Dajjal!'

He speaks of al-Dajjal, the Anti-Messiah. It is two hours before dawn. A line of Dervish prisoners are set to work with the bank-laying gang on the Sudan Military Railway. They file out of Railhead Camp, picks and shovels shouldered. The Egyptian Army escort lead them to where the survey team have pegged out the lines for this day's digging. They are ordered along briskly with harsh oaths, threat and gesture. They move to the sluggish bidding of the whip hand.

'And Sirdar Kitchener is al-Dajjal!' Salim hisses along the line.

A horse-crop whispers back, catching his shoulders. Salim lets out a dry rasp at its sting. A *fellahin* corporal grunts at him to be quiet and he holds his tongue. He will stay silent but not for long. He has found his voice here, down among the prisoners.

They are mostly Ta'aishi and once they would have looked down on a black southerner like himself. A *jihadiyya*, an *aswad abed*, a slave. But they are all slaves now. And the lash, the chain and hard labour have kept them pure and fervent. They are Salim's brothers and they heed what he has to say.

Still dressed in the *jibba* of the Dervish, they are kept apart from the rest of the workforce, treated as pariahs, put to work at the most arduous tasks in the building of the railway. One day ahead of the rest of the gangs that would follow, it is they who break the earth of the desert, following the bare markings of the survey crew. They are the edge of the spade, building up the embankments or hacking out the cuttings. They labour on foot, shovelling sand throughout the fierce heat of the day. At dawn the other gangs arrive, moving back and forth on the material train that unloads its cargo of sleepers, rails, bolts and fishplates. The platelayers, the rail gang, the spiking crews, the straighteners, the lifters, the fillers-in, all take their turn to glide along the track on flatbed trucks, like *djinns* floating across the wilderness. The Dervish prisoners walk all day and toil until sunset. Worked to death by whip, theodolite and spirit-level.

The prisoners shuffle along in the dirt, forced to slouch before the great eighty-ton locomotives. Made to labour in the construction of the very power designed to crush their faith. Their defiance is to be broken. Any emirs or obvious ringleaders among the Dervish have already been taken to Cairo for close confinement and interrogation. The *ratib*, the lithographed tract of the Mahdi, has been confiscated from them. They have lost everything except the flicker of resistance. The glow that needs breath to give it flame. A voice. Salim has the words, and a wise tongue to use them. He speaks of a world that they can understand and gives them hope of salvation. He promises miracles to match those that the infidel can conjure. He tells them that all this progress of the Inglisi is just a greater swiftness towards the Last of Days. And he tells them that Sirdar Kitchener himself is al-Dajjal.

Al-Dajjal is the Great Deceiver. He is to come after the death of the Mahdi and before the End of Time. His red face has but one eye and he rides an ass forty yards long. Salim has heard, from those who have caught sight of him at Railhead Camp, of the ruddy sunburned features of the Sirdar and a cast in his left eye, seemingly sightless and dead.

Salim preaches his message quietly among his brothers as they are marched out to work. It gives them strength to accept the privations of captivity, to renounce this world and choose the next. It is the revelation that the Sirdar is the False Prophet, that the nations of the west are Gog and Magog, that all the gleaming machinery of the enemy will merely hurry them faster to their own doom. As they reach the place where they are to build a new embankment, he speaks of al-Dajjal once more.

'The earth will be rolled up for him; he will hold the cloud in his right hand and overreach the sun at its setting place; the sea will be ankle-deep for him; before him will be a mountain of smoke.'

'Be quiet!' the guard shouts at him once more.

'I am praying!' Salim shouts back.

The *fellahin* raises his whip to thrash him again but Salim does not cower. There are mutters of protest among the prisoners. The guard hesitates. The sergeant of the escort comes over, his right hand resting on the holstered revolver at his hip.

'What's this?' he demands.

'They were talking too much.'

'We were praying, effendi,' Salim interjects with a gentle nod. 'This is the most blessed hour, is it not? To give glory to the Lord before sunrise?'

The escort leader grunts in assent, suddenly embarrassed at the prospect of appearing impious.

'Allow us a short prayer, effendi. We beseech you,' Salim continues.

'Very well,' he agrees and the Dervish kneel down in the dust.

Salim recites from the Koran: *sura* 27: verse 80:

'"On the day when the Doom overtakes them, We will bring out from the earth a beast that shall speak to them. Truly men have no faith in Our revelations. On that day We shall gather from each community a multitude of those who disbelieved Our revelations. They shall be led in separate bands, and, when they come, He will say: 'You denied My revelations although you knew nothing of them. What was it you were doing?' The Doom will smite them in their sins, and they shall be dumbfounded.'"

It is a small victory for the prisoners. One small prayer of defiance. Then they are made to dig. The desert sky is still cold and fathomless. A blood-red tint on the rim of the horizon. Soon the furnace of the day will come. Heat and sweat and dust and toil until sunset, beneath the whips and curses of their overseers. Just one brief chant of liberation at dawn. It is not enough for Salim. He knows that this railway must be destroyed. Somehow he must warn the Khalifa.

He has planned his flight carefully. They are not chained or kept locked up at night. The desert is prison enough. They sleep under canvas at Railhead Camp. Two guards watch each end of their compound. Salim knows that he can crawl out from under his tent unseen.

The survey team's camp is pitched far out ahead of Railhead. Two Inglisi sapper officers, one NCO and a dozen or so Egyptians. All fast asleep by midnight. And they have camels. If Salim can steal a dromedary and enough water he can take flight and disappear into the wilderness.

Beyond there are patrols by camel-men of the Abada, a tribe friendly to the Inglisi whose warriors have sworn a blood oath to Kitchener. Salim's *jibba* will mark him out as an enemy. If he comes within their range they will kill him on sight. He will probably die of thirst anyway. But if he can make it to the river somehow he might find a way upstream to Omdurman.

The General stiffened abruptly, letting out a gasp as he came back to the surface.

'He didn't die at Railhead, after all,' he told Crowley in a shocked whisper.

'No?'

'No. He escaped! He escaped Kitchener's railway.'

'Well, that's a good thing, isn't it?'

'I don't know.' Macdonald frowned.

The brief joy he had felt at the vision of Salim's survival and liberty was tempered by a sense of foreboding. A darkening mood that something worse was to come. His mind shadowed with a creeping sense of doom.

Part Three
LE CHAT BLANC

XXIII

IT WAS HALF PAST EIGHT and Le Chat Blanc was already beginning to get crowded. The narrow and sparely furnished upstairs dining room on rue d'Odessa droned with a low chorus of English and American colloquy. The exiles of Montparnasse arranged themselves around the bare tables that lined the three walls that faced the entrance to the room. The space between allowed a meagre stage, where one might make a calculated entrance into the empty traverse between the diners. Le Chat Blanc catered for expatriate artists, sculptors, writers, and their hangers-on. They had all come to the Parnassus of their dreams – to study, to work, to escape from convention. They were here to paint, sculpt, write, philosophise and have adventures. And to talk loudly about themselves and their aspirations to anyone who would listen.

The dining club provided a haven from the lonely evenings of banishment where émigrés might seek out their own and find camaraderie only slightly tainted with envy and disappointment. There was a fragile humour to the place and a grudging system of barter in conversation. Everybody seemed to crave the opportunity to hold the floor. The air hissed with a glossolalia of Impressionism, post-Impressionism, Symbolism, Synthesism, but intellectual discourse scarcely ever made any mark on the room. A witty comment might work, especially if made at the expense of a fellow expat. A shocking declaration could have an immediate effect, but once uttered the interlocutor risked merely becoming a target of scorn and derision. In the talking shop of Le Chat Blanc there was only one hard and universally recognised currency guaranteed to gain attention: gossip, and the crueller the better.

Astrid had been seated at the right-hand corner of the top table. She sipped a glass of muscat and looked across the room. The man she was waiting for was now over half an hour late. On her left were two Englishmen who had nervously introduced themselves as Gerry the artist and Clive the writer. The door swung open and Astrid looked up hopefully. But it was not Crowley. Instead a thin, debonair man stood puffing a cigarette, immaculately turned out in dinner jacket and red cummerbund. He scanned the room with a bemused frown, clearly thinking that he must have come to the wrong place.

She watched the stranger as he glanced around Le Chat Blanc. She had known haunts like this in Berlin. Cafés and restaurants that promised a bohemian ambience of free-thinking, of political radicals and rebel artists. The place must seem strange and exotic to this well-dressed man, she mused, but it was familiar and predictable to her. She had been singing in just such a dining club in Berlin on the night that she had met Theodor Reuss.

She had been waiting tables at the Jupiter, a dilapidated café on Friedrichstrasse that attracted a disparate circle of anarchists and social revolutionaries. Its rueful owner had been inspired to host an evening of political cabaret on the idealistic grounds that it might draw in a bit of solid business. He allowed Astrid to sing, having heard the raw, strong voice that she would break into when stacking the chairs at the end of the night. In between poetry readings and a comedian who made jokes against the rich and heavily veiled references to the Kaiser, she would give renditions of the macabre and peculiar lyrics she had composed to the folk tunes she had learned as a child.

It was the night she was trying out a new song, 'The Uncle Killer', when she noticed the elegant man in an astrakhan coat enter and sit at a table near the modest platform that served as a stage. There were grey flecks in his slicked-back hair, a princely squint about his eyes, the hint of a smile framed by a neatly trimmed goatee. His avuncular presence suddenly impelled Astrid to direct the song towards him. The words told of a girl tempting her uncle into revealing his stash of money, then ruthlessly killing him for it. As Astrid involved this distinguished stranger in the gruesome *songspiel*, the audience erupted into laughter. The man took it with good grace, with a grin and a nod, a slight turn of his head to show the room that he shared the joke.

After the show, as the regulars gathered to sit around the tables and talk politics, the man in the astrakhan introduced himself to Astrid as Theodor Reuss.

'You have to learn to breathe, my dear,' he told her.

'Sorry?'

'From here.'

He patted his thick lower abdomen.

'Take it from an old professional. You have a strong voice but you will lose it if you are not careful.'

'You're a singer?' Astrid asked him.

'Was. I was in the chorus of the first production of *Parzival* at Bayreuth. Well' – he shrugged – 'that's over now. But if you want to learn, I have many secrets to pass on.'

'You give singing lessons?'

'Yes. And techniques of yoga. But most of all I teach magic.'

'Magic?' she asked, intrigued.

'Yes, my dear.' He gave her a smile and a playful wink. 'Magic.'

With the deftness of a mountebank he slipped his card into her hand.

'Heh, heh. Come and see me. Might be just what you're looking for.'

He went and sat down with the others. He had a quiet charisma that allowed him to appear to hold court without actually saying anything. He waited until all the usual arguments about the coming revolution were near exhaustion and then he began. He had a sonorous voice that filled the room without effort. Astrid saw at once that he was right about respiration. He enunciated with a rich timbre that came from deep within. His manner of delivery had a grandiloquence that matched the curious nature of his ideas. He insisted that he had gone beyond mere political understanding and glimpsed something more astonishing than their meagre utopias.

'Of course, of course,' he retorted, to various objections. 'It's clear that change is necessary. New ideas, new principles. A new religion perhaps? Yes, yes, I know, you want to do without it altogether. But you also know, in your heart of hearts, comrades, that this is not possible. So we need a new faith, free of original sin, free of sexual guilt. It is the false religion that inhabits the Churches that have oppressed us all. Oppressed our true natures as men. And even more so women.' Reuss looked over at Astrid as he said this. 'We need to revive the ancient rites that will set us free. We need to unleash the godlike power that resides in all of us.'

She found herself fascinated by his compelling air of mysticism. She usually became quickly bored by the radical talk at the Jupiter. It had introduced her to political notions of liberty and equality but she had always held her own instinctive ideas. Even as a young girl it had been her great desire to be free, and her deep rancour that in being born female this would always be denied her. Down the ages it had seemed to her that any powerful woman might be denounced as a witch or sorceress. But if only this ancient curse could be reversed and its potency harnessed in the service of women. This became her secret wish. A solitary game from childhood that she possessed hidden powers that would one day manifest themselves.

She learned many things about Theodor Reuss from the regulars at the Jupiter. They muttered darkly that he was a police spy. But it was this very sense of intrigue that truly intrigued her. He had indeed sung for Wagner in the chorus at Bayreuth and spent some time in London, performing in the music halls. It was at this time that he joined the Socialist League, which eventually expelled him, forcing him to return to Germany. He now worked variously as a journalist and an impresario and was writing a book on the occult. It was said that he was attempting to revive the Order of the Illuminati. The rumours that he had been employed by the Prussian secret police to spy on Eleanor Marx when he was in London were almost certainly true. But this did not disturb Astrid as it did the would-be revolutionaries of the Jupiter. Indeed, it was this prowess for subterfuge as much as anything else that attracted her to him.

However it was only the offer of singing lessons that occasioned the visit she made to his house in Belle Alliancestrasse. He assented with a nod and showed her through to his music room.

'Breath, my dear, it is all about breath,' he began, as if simply taking up the brief conversation they had had the week before. 'What does inspiration mean? An intake of breath. Take it in. Hmm,' he demonstrated. 'The life-force. The energy of the universe. And aspiration? The outbreath. Our voice calling out through the vast and empty cosmos.'

All at once he broke into a booming *basso profundo*, lifting his arms in a gesture of invocation and bursting forth with a forceful aria. *Schwules gedunst schwebt in der Luft; lästig ist mir der trübe Druck!* The room shuddered as he sang of a sultry haze hanging in the air, its dull weight oppressive. *Das bleiche Gewölk samml'ich zu blitzendem Wetter, das fegt den Himmel mir hell!* He would summon pale clouds into a lightning storm to clear the fetid sky. He held the last note for a few seconds, then let his hands drop. He dabbed at his reddened face with a silk handkerchief.

'Donner,' he elucidated with a pant. 'The thunder god in *Das Rheingold*. My greatest role.'

He took her through a series of fundamental breathing techniques and showed her some elementary yogic exercises that he claimed could enhance her voice and improve her posture. They seemed to work. As she went through a major scale she felt something lift within her. Reuss had an easy manner. He talked softly, in a confiding tone, casually revealing his thoughts on the great hidden wisdom of the universe, all the time urging her to relax, to let go of her voice. He told her of the occult connections between the mysteries of the east and the pagan gods of the north, of the runic symbols they shared and the great Aryan race they had both engendered. He spoke of the Ancient Ones and the Hermetic tradition. Of a secret history of sacred knowledge, passed on by the Knights Templar, the Freemasons and the Illuminati. There was an Elect of the Unseen that guided things. The power of the goddess was about to be revived, he claimed; Isis would soon be unveiled.

'It is all about breath,' he insisted once more, in a stage whisper. 'That is, after all, the meaning of the word to conspire: to breathe with. Come. Breathe with me.'

Later, as she intoned an ascending scale in a curious minor key, what he said to her became comprehensible in marvellous illumination. She had somehow known it all along: that there was a world within the world. A special place where she would truly belong. Women had been kept out of Masonic orders, Reuss complained. He was working to change all that. He had known Madame Blavatsky, the legendary clairvoyant who had made psychic contact with the Hidden Mahatmas of Tibet. He could testify to the spiritual power of the female. It was the very fact that they possessed a greater supernatural potential than men, he reasoned, that explained why women had been oppressed through the centuries. It would be the liberation of this craft that would lead to true emancipation.

He told her of all the orders he belonged to, showing her some of the insignia he was permitted to wear in ceremony. Reuss was obsessed with degrees of initiation, ritual costume and regalia, secret signs and tokens, handshakes and passwords. He was an avid collector of all kinds of Masonic paraphernalia and he seemed to be in the business of trading and authenticating documents. He quietly divulged to her his plan to create an altogether new form of secret society. One that would admit women and embark on an astonishing new quest.

'I'm looking for a high priestess,' he told her with a softly imploring voice. 'Our new order will possess the key that will open up all Masonic and Hermetic doctrines, reveal all the secrets of nature, the symbolism of religion, namely, the teaching of sexual magic.'

Astrid gasped.

'Illustrious Sister,' he assured her when she had made her protestations. 'I have no interest in rutting with you like a base animal. I seek no violation.'

She did not understand. He explained it to her gently. He would watch and worship. He would not touch her. Only himself.

'I only wish to create the sacred elixir.'

It was quite simple really. It was something she had done on her own, in the darkness of her own bed. He knelt before her, looking up and praying as she stood over him, naked. He took his pleasure in submission. This was one of the great secrets. Of how women could dominate men. She tried to concentrate on making the act a sacrament, sublime and mystical. But it wasn't easy.

As Reuss murmured a low incantation to Baal, Belial, Beelzebub, Astrid tried to summon a sense of power from this perverse ceremony. Bizarre images came to her. A pyramid beneath a blazing sun, a swarm of seraphim darkening the blood-red sky above. A winged bull, a plumed serpent, the rooster-headed god Abraxas. Her perception became a bestiary of harsh deities and degenerate idols, emblazoned with a text of alien hieroglyphs and pictograms. As her body shuddered closer to its moment of consecration she was possessed by a clear and perfect vision: that the whole universe is merely a symbol. The Unseen was visible, here on the edge of consciousness. She felt for a second that all would be revealed to her. Then her mind darkened and surrendered to a void of pleasure.

She became his mistress and was inducted into the Ordo Templi Orientis as an Adeptus Major. She was on her way to discovering the secret magical abilities she had always dreamed of and had found a way of exerting power over men. Reuss requested that she undertake a mission for him. He had recently been in the process of acquiring degrees from irregular Masonic orders in England. He was attempting to build up a comprehensive portfolio of mystical qualifications that would lend weight and authority to his own organisations and certificates of membership. He was dealing in secret deeds, statutes and precedents. He had learned of the schism in the Golden Dawn and that its founding constitution, the Cypher Manuscript, might be on the market. To get hold of this covenant would be a great triumph, its provenance was supposed to be German after all. Astrid would become an incarnation of Soror Dominabitur Astris, an astral form last occupied by a certain Fräulein Anna Sprengel of Stuttgart, and travel to Paris in an attempt to take possession of the sacred book. Reuss was paying her expenses for the expedition and had tutored her in all the occult knowledge she might need. She had been excited at the prospect of this mysterious errand and assuming the identity of a great sorceress had given her a marvellous feeling of power. Already she had been able to use her charm on Crowley. She felt sure that she could use him to get hold of the Cypher Manuscript.

But he was late for their appointment. She watched as the incongruous-looking man in the dinner jacket gestured at the waitress. At her table Gerry, the artist, was attempting to impress his friend by describing a visit he had recently made to Claude Monet's studio. He spoke loudly, hoping that as many people as possible would be able to overhear.

'Of course, he insisting on showing me his garden as well, Clive, even though it was quite grey and overcast. He said to me: "The sun is the ruination of flowers, they look so bright you can't see them, but on a nice grey day like this you can really enjoy the blooms, so come along."'

As the waitress approached the newcomer he spoke to her softly and at great speed. The waitress shook her head at a name he mentioned. Then the gentleman sighed and fished in his pocket. He pulled out a card and showed it to her. At this she laughed, looked him up and down, and then laughed some more. She announced something to him in an encouraging tone, pointed over at Astrid.

'Excuse me madame,' he declared as he came to her table. 'It appears we are both guests of the same gentleman.'

He held up Crowley's card. *Laird of Boleskine and Abertarff* was embossed with a coronet above a gilded *B*, with a tiny inscription in what looked like Sanskrit below.

'Edward Stuart-Wortley, at your service.' He nodded. 'May I?'

'Of course,' she rejoined and he took the chair next to her.

Astrid took a closer look at him, wondering if he was an associate of Crowley's, perhaps another member of the Order. The man sighed as he sat down.

'I'm afraid it's all a bit of a mystery,' he declared.

'A mystery?' Astrid frowned.

'Tonight. I'm sorry, I haven't had the pleasure.'

'Soror Dominatibur Astris is my magical name.'

'How absolutely charming.'

'I'm also known as Astrid.'

'You're German?' he asked, catching her accent.

'Yes.'

'Ah.'

She noticed his face darken for a moment at this, as if he were remembering something. Then he looked up and smiled at her.

'Well, Fräulein Astrid, let's have a drink,' he suggested. 'How about some fizz?'

'Fizz?'

'Champagne.'

He gestured over to the waitress.

'Was in Bad Nauheim five years ago,' he went on. 'Taking the waters. Lovely place.'

'I don't know it.'

'Spa town, north of Frankfurt. Health cure, you know. Bit of a dicky heart.'

He clicked open a gold-plated cigarette case and offered it to her. She declined. He snapped the case shut and tapped out a cigarette vigorously on its lid. He seemed to be hiding something behind his cheery formality. Astrid was becoming impatient. She decided to go for the direct approach.

'Are you an emissary of Crowley's?' she asked him.

'Don't know the man. Just want to find out what's going on.'

'About the Cypher Manuscript?'

'I beg your pardon?'

She knew that occultists would often appear vague about secret knowledge to those that they considered uninitiated. It was time to let him know that she was one of the *cognoscenti*.

'The document containing the encrypted instructions dictated to Fräulein Sprengel by the Secret Chiefs,' she told him.

'I don't know what you mean.'

'I'm sure that you do. Don't worry, I've already spoken to Crowley about it. Is it true that the Secret Chiefs are the very same Hidden Mahatmas of Tibet who contacted Blavatsky?'

Stuart-Wortley's thoughts went from bemused confusion to a suspicious clarity and his instincts as an intelligence officer suddenly on the alert. Hector Macdonald had presented himself at the Embassy with a peculiar fellow called Crowley and here was this beguiling creature, a German to boot. They were the potential enemy now, the battleship race was on and there was even wild speculation about the danger of invasion. He knew that his opposite number at the German Embassy had been up to no good for some time now. He had heard the awful rumours about Mac, the whole of the diplomatic corps were salivating over it. A scandal would make him vulnerable to all kinds of intrigue. Astrid talked of some sort of a codebook and of Tibet. He knew of Curzon's plan for a mission to contact the country's leaders and establish a legation there, but that was top secret. He could not figure out what Macdonald might have got caught up in but it was a curious business indeed.

At that moment the door was flung open and a large figure

in green imposed himself upon the room. Crowley held a battered leather book under his left arm. He took a few steps and looked around at the diners.

'*Mesdames et messieurs,*' he announced. 'Tonight Le Chat Blanc, this modest chamber consecrated informally to the most venerated clique of international artists, writers and philosophers, will act as host to my hour of triumph. You may all, in future times, proudly testify to having been present at the moment of my investiture as rightful prophet of the New Aeon. And I entreat you to give a warm welcome to the honoured guest of this auspicious evening.'

The Beast motioned behind him and it was only then they noticed that there was another man, hanging back, still framed by the doorway. Macdonald shuffled forward looking lost and forlorn. Stuart-Wortley saw that he was dazed, as if in some sort of trance. The room held its breath.

'I present,' Crowley intoned, 'that great warrior and hero of the British Empire, Major-General Sir Hector Macdonald.'

'My God, it really is him,' somebody whispered.

Then the whole of Le Chat Blanc began to purr contentedly as those in the know enlightened the ignorant with all the hateful gossip about the General as Macdonald stood in the space between the tables, staring emptily into the room.

XXIV

'So, this is your mysterious knight,' Gerald Kelly murmured as he greeted the Beast.

'Why, Crowley, this is outrageous.'

'Well, Gerry, I did promise you an uproar.'

The Beast led Macdonald to the corner table where introductions were being made. He gestured for the General to meet them all. Gerald Kelly the artist, Clive Bell the critic and Astrid, a representative of a German mystical society. The Beast frowned at the man in black tie.

'I'm afraid I haven't had the pleasure, sir,' ventured Crowley.

'Edward Stuart-Wortley,' came a cold reply.

'Yes, of course, our Military Attaché.'

'The very same.'

'Then you must forgive the atrociously bohemian protocol. I trust you will be joining us for dinner.'

As Stuart-Wortley nodded his assent, he noted the strangely bound volume Crowley cradled and that Astrid was staring at it intently. He went over to greet his old comrade.

'Mac! Good to see you, old man.'

'Eddie . . .'

They sat down together. The General peered at Stuart-Wortley with enlarged pupils, black and empty as pitted olives.

'How's the wound, Mac?' asked Stuart-Wortley.

'Wound?'

For a moment the question pierced him to his soul. It was as if Eddie knew exactly how he felt, that the whole scandal was like a gaping hole in his heart. Then he realised what he was referring to. Macdonald had taken a bullet in the foot at Paardeburg.

'Oh that,' he murmured. 'Yes, yes, it's fine.'

'Are you all right, Mac? You look ill.'

He felt gloomy. All his earlier euphoria had worn off. There was a growing dread as he contemplated Salim's destiny. And now, meeting his old friend reminded him once more of his own terrible fate.

'I'm in trouble, Eddie. I came to see you.'

'I know, old man. I know.'

'I need another posting. Something in the Foreign Service. Something far away and out of sight.'

'I'll see what I can do.'

'I haven't got much time. They froze me out in London. There's to be a court martial.'

'Good heavens, no.'

'Yes. Kitchener is to preside.'

'Well, K will stick up for you, won't he?'

'I don't think so, Eddie.'

'But he knows you.'

'Exactly. We know each other far too well. We understand each other. That's why he will have to be utterly ruthless. If he were to show the tiniest grain of compassion it might give the game away. Remember that night in Cairo when I nearly had a fight with one of his staff officers?'

'Yes. Someone made a ghastly joke at your expense. That upstart subaltern everyone called the Kid.'

Macdonald had been in Cairo in the summer of 1897 to attend the big parade for the Diamond Jubilee. He had managed to avoid most of the tedious succession of regimental parties but this particular evening he had found himself stuck on his own at a mess function. As he wandered about with an untouched drink in his hand he noticed a coterie of young officers in the corner, making merry. It was the Band of Boys, Kitchener's inner circle, looking very pleased with themselves. The young favourite known as the Kid was holding court, telling a hilarious anecdote.

No one noticed Macdonald approach. They were witnessing a performance. For a moment he wished that he could somehow join in, be as jocular and frivolous as they were.

'So he's dancing with this lady,' the Kid was telling the group. 'Can you imagine anything more priceless? Old Mac dancing.'

And it was then that he realised that the Kid was referring to him. *Old Mac*, that's what they called him. Macdonald was barely in his forties but this was ancient for a white officer in the Egyptian Army at that time. He looked on in horrified fascination.

'And the lady asks him which regiment he is serving in,' the Kid went on. 'And he says: "I'm wi' tha Soonadeese Brigade, madame." To which she declares: "You mean the blacks?" "Och noo, Madame, only our privates are black." "Only your privates are black?" she replies. "How absolutely marvellous!"'

An explosion of laughter stirred up a fury within him. Macdonald rudely broke into the circle of men and made himself known. A hush descended on the room. The crowd of officers took on discreet expressions and gestures; fresh smirks of pleasure oscillated from face to face.

'Ah!' the Kid exclaimed at last. 'Colonel Macdonald. We were just talking about you.'

Macdonald glared at the Kid with a murderous stare. A nervous giggle rippled around the room.

'Come on, old man,' the Kid remonstrated. 'Only a joke.'

He had started to move towards the man. The Kid backed away slightly, a stupid smirk still plastered over his face. It was then that Stuart-Wortley had appeared from nowhere and stepped in between them.

'Steady, Mac,' he had murmured softly.

Then a loud and supercilious drawl broke out across the ballroom.

'What is this dreadful row?'

It was Kitchener. Everyone turned to look at their chief who

184

had been standing in the far corner all this time. Observing quietly with that queer squint of his, the cast left eye staring off-target, with a dull sheen like glazed china. Tall and slender with a huge moustache, with lavish whiskers waxed to sharp points, he appeared absurdly feline.

The crowd parted before him as he approached.

'Well?' he demanded, of nobody in particular.

'I was just telling a funny story, sir,' offered the Kid.

'Shut up!' hissed the Sirdar. 'You evil little boy.'

Kitchener nodded at Macdonald.

'You'll have to excuse us, gentlemen,' Kitchener announced. 'The colonel and myself have matters to attend to.'

'But, sir,' complained another of his apostles. 'We were just about to go in for dinner.'

'Then you'll all have to wait, won't you?'

Kitchener's office was scattered with papers.

'Careful,' he warned Macdonald as he ushered him in. 'You're standing on the Supply returns.'

'I'm sorry, sir.'

'Oh, never mind. Please, do sit down.'

Kitchener cleared a seat of a bundle of forms then clambered around the desk into the swivel chair behind it.

'I detest all that awful mess banter,' he said. 'But one must not allow it to get to one. One can so easily bear a grudge against a fellow. Or cultivate a stupid kind of fondness for one . . .' For a brief moment Kitchener looked wistful. 'One must keep one's mind on higher things.'

'Yes, sir.'

'You're a God-fearing man, aren't you, Macdonald.'

'Aye, I am, sir.'

'Because it is a holy war we are fighting. All the time. Within ourselves as much as anywhere else. When I became a brother of the Guild of the Holy Standard, I made a pledge to be sober, upright, chaste and regular in private prayer. That was the same year that I embarked to Palestine to make a survey of the Holy

Land. I remember a startling image that came to me in all those sacred places. Of the crusaders of old: so fierce in war, so gentle in religion.'

Kitchener's ruddy face shone with a curious passion. One could still see that he had been handsome as a young man, pretty even. Years of hard campaigning had made him grim-visaged, his delicate features marred by sunburn and battle scars. A hooded squint gave him a gorgon's stare, the bright blue orbs long faded to grey. The dead eye glistened with moisture, yet it did not weep. It was as if it held a single tear, caught in surface tension, forever waiting to be shed.

'We are all terribly impressed with your progress with the Sudanese, Macdonald. You seem to inspire a great loyalty among them.'

'I hope so, sir.'

'You mustn't get too close to them though.'

'Yes, sir.'

'I read somewhere recently, a London columnist pointing out that, like the Romans, we rely too much on the martial virtue of our barbarian subjects. Well, he had a point. But we're stuck with that situation for now. And we have to make certain that martial virtue does not get corrupted. I am exceedingly fond of my black troops, as I'm sure you are. We must not, however, indulge them. Nor allow ourselves to be indulged.'

'Sir.'

'Listen Macdonald. Certain vices I can afford to ignore in others. If Major-General Hunter wants to keep an Abyssinian mistress at the Shepheard's Hotel, I do not need to be officially informed. And if some officers are tempted to go whoring in Cairo, there's not much I can do about it. Everyone knows that the best brothels here are owned by the Coptic Patriarch, for goodness sake. But some sins are irredeemable. Do you understand?'

'Yes, sir.'

'The Egyptian Army suffers from a certain reputation. One

186

hears the most hateful gossip. I am determined to ensure that there is no such impropriety among my officers, nor a suspicion of it.'

'Of course, sir.'

They looked at each other across the desk. Macdonald saw a morose and lonely man. One who tried desperately to avoid knowing himself fully in the hope that he might appear obscure to others. For a second he could have been looking in the mirror.

And he knew that Kitchener felt the same. Yet despite the sense of recognition, there could be no fellow feeling, just the contempt of dreadful familiarity. It was an awful vigilance, not for any false move but for a true one.

'I hear you made a visit to Railhead,' the Sirdar went on, with an insinuating whine.

'Yes, sir. I was following up an intelligence matter concerning enemy prisoners taken at Firka—'

'Yes, yes,' Kitchener interrupted impatiently. 'But surely all intelligence matters should be cleared through General Wingate.'

'I'm sorry sir, it was a minor matter.'

'So I understand. I do hope you'll follow proper protocol in these matters in the future. It's said that I am very bad at delegating duties, which is true. But then I see every detail, Macdonald. Remember that.'

The Sirdar rested his one-eyed gaze on Macdonald for a moment longer. Then he looked over at a pile of papers on his desk. He coughed and began speaking once more.

'Now, it was Railhead I wanted to talk to you about.'

'Sir?'

'The line has made tremendous progress. But now the time has come to protect its destination. I'm planning a surprise attack on Abu Hamed. A flying column through the desert.'

'With the Sudanese Brigade as infantry support?'

'Yes.'

They began at once to talk eagerly of transport, supply,

ordnance and battalion strengths, both mortally relieved to be returning once more to the preparations of war.

'That night when K ordered me to his office,' Macdonald explained to Stuart-Wortley. 'That's when I knew.'

'But knew what exactly?'

'That he knew about me.'

'I still don't understand, Mac,' said Stuart-Wortley. 'What did he say?'

'It was what was left unsaid that was more significant, Eddie,' Macdonald replied. 'But it's true what they say. It takes one to know one.'

Stuart-Wortley was about to say something at this, but he was distracted. Everybody had now settled around the table and were loudly discussing what to order. Eddie noticed that Crowley and Astrid were in deep discussion. They seemed to be talking about the heavy volume with the strange binding that he was carrying. He strained to listen to what they were saying.

'But it belongs to Die Goldene Dämmerung and the German orders,' Astrid was insisting.

'Perhaps,' Crowley retorted. 'But I'm not sure that I can entrust it to Theodor Reuss. After all, he has a reputation for counterfeiting. And for spying.'

The waitress then started taking orders from the party: *poulet au riz, entrecôte, tête de veau, pommes de terre vapeur, purée de carottes*. Wine was being called for.

'What on earth are you doing with this dubious character, Mac?' muttered Stuart-Wortley with a nod towards Crowley.

'I've had to become less choosy about my friends of late, Eddie.'

'But really, Mac.'

'He's offered to help me. I'm desperate, Eddie. I'm willing to try anything.'

'That's what I'm worried about, Mac.'

'Maybe he can find a way out for me.'

'Is that what he's said to you?'

'Well . . .'

'Can I ask you a question?'

'Of course you can.'

'In all seriousness, old man' – Stuart-Wortley lowered his voice to a whisper – 'is this fellow blackmailing you?'

'Don't be ridiculous, Eddie.'

They were both then distracted by a minor commotion on the other side of the table. Voices were raised with such vehemence that the old soldiers thought that a matter of honour must be at stake. It took a while to realise that a discussion about art had broken out.

'What a painting represents,' Clive Bell was saying, 'is entirely irrelevant to how we might judge its value!'

'Surely not!' Gerald Kelly protested.

'We have to look beyond mere affectation to see the truth,' the critic went on. 'What we need is an aesthetic response. An aesthetic emotion, if you like.'

'Yes,' said the artist. 'But to what?'

'To the form, of course. That is the most important thing in art. Form!'

Macdonald brooded on the conversation, utterly oblivious to what was actually being said. These were the theories of that precious civilisation he was supposed to have been fighting for all these years. Completely meaningless to him. He could understand Kitchener's love of decoration, a desire to collect beautiful things. But this was quite different, he knew that much. When he had first arrived in Paris he had taken a stroll and found himself wandering into a small gallery on the rue de Sèvres. It was full of strange new paintings, canvases daubed and clotted thick with oil. He had looked upon the garish colours and mutilated images with a sickening sense in his stomach. He had left feeling quite depressed.

'I entirely disagree about form,' the Beast interjected.

Clive Bell turned and gave Crowley a supercilious smile.

'And what, pray, would be your argument?' he asked.

189

'Well, for a start,' the Beast began, 'form has no importance in a technical sense.'

'Really?'

'Yes, really. The ability of the artist is in the lucidity of his language. Form only matters in this regard: we must not be revolted by the extravagance of new symbolic systems.'

'Oh, I see!' Bell retorted gleefully. 'A Symbolist! Oh, how very quaint, I thought they were all extinct. Gerry, you must tell your friend here that despite his obvious attempts at being fashionable, he is woefully out of date in matters of art.'

'I have no interest in mere symbolism,' Crowley insisted. 'Art is High Magic and nothing less.'

The General gazed into the space in front of him, watching the way the gaslight caught the water glass on the table. So vivid and pure, like a prism. This night everything had appeared so bright and lucid to him. He raised his eyes and looked once more at the diorama of faces that surrounded him. This strange chatter about how the world might look if one could imagine it; an argument about how people might think if one could peer into their heads. He felt a sudden urge to join in.

'I,' he began, trying to think of something.

'So tell me,' Clive Bell cajoled. 'This High Magic of art, is this black magic or white magic?'

'I can assure you,' the Beast replied, 'that an adept will have a whole palette of colours at his disposal. Many more than all the shades of grey in your dreary Formalism.'

'I did warn you that Crowley could be quite diabolical, Clive,' Kelly commented.

Macdonald tried to muster his thoughts. He remembered when, after his knighthood, he had been invited to a party at the house of Lady Jeune in Wimpole Street. She was a great socialite, fond of collecting prominent members of society. He had enjoyed all the attention lavished upon him but had felt clumsy and awkward. There had been talk of aesthetics then, and he had dreaded being asked an opinion. Now he felt he had something to say. But what?

'Indeed, Gerry,' the Beast went on. 'And why only today I heard a friend of mine, one of the most accomplished occultists in Paris as it happens, declare that the Devil is an artist.'

'Yes, yes, the Devil!' Macdonald called out abruptly.

The table turned its attention upon him. There was an embarrassed pause. The General appeared drunk.

'Ah,' the Beast responded with a light note. 'Sir Hector has an opinion.'

'Oh, shut up for a moment!' the General bellowed at Crowley.

The room fell quiet but for the chime of china and metal.

'I've not seen the Devil,' Macdonald went on in a deep growl. 'But I've seen his paintbrush.'

'Oh, that's very good,' said Kelly.

'I mean it, sir,' Macdonald insisted. 'I've seen the Devil's Paintbrush.'

There was dramatic hush in Le Chat Blanc. Hector Macdonald beheld the expectant faces with the reddened eyes and ashen face of a man possessed. These sort of people always liked to hear something to shock them out of their soft lives. Well, now he had just the thing.

The food appeared as if summoned by the moment. Plates were laid out, bottles opened and wine poured.

'The Devil's Paintbrush?' Clive Bell ventured softly. 'Why, it sounds fascinating.'

'It might well be, yes,' the General murmured.

'But what is it?' Astrid demanded.

'Eddie knows what I'm talking about. Don't you, Eddie?'

'I certainly do, Mac,' Stuart-Wortley confirmed with a cold laugh. 'I certainly do. Now we really are talking about modern painting.'

The last dish was brought to the table and the diners settled for the course but no one proposed a toast, nor a soul wished *bon appétit*, so intent were they all on the doomed Major-General Sir Hector Macdonald, and what he had to say about art.

XXV

'IFIRST SAW THEM UP close some time in the last week of July back in '97. I'd heard all about them, everyone had. Fantastic stories of what they'd done on the Malakand Pass in Afghanistan, and down in Matebeleland. All wrapped up in silk they were. Wound tight in delicate little shrouds. Can you imagine?'

The General's eyes flickered as he spoke.

'I was commanding the Sudanese Brigade. We were mustered at an assembly area at Kassinger, on the north bank of the Nile, just downstream of the fourth cataract. I'd had a briefing with Kitchener in Cairo. Another special mission, another bloody forced march through the desert to attack the Dervish garrison at Abu Hamed. The railway was vulnerable and overstretched. We were to be sent to secure the southern end of it from any possible attack. Out into the Nubian Desert once more, marching in the cold night and struggling to find any kind of shade all through the infernally hot day. Kitchener's blood-kin Abada camel-men to the fore, running reconnaissance; and a telegraph man to our rear, our only contact with headquarters, looping the wire around a donkey's belly and spooling it out behind as we headed out into the burning wilderness.

'Now, I'm not saying my men weren't keen for it. Aye, they were bloody solid. Even when I couldn't tell them outright where I was leading them. A secret mission it was. A flying column to take Abu Hamed by surprise, just like we had done at Firka. But to gain trust you've got to give a bit. And to be honest I had no idea what I might be able to offer by way of credit, if you get my meaning.

'Anyway, we were forming up at Kassinger, ready to set out, when a detachment of Royal Marine Artillery arrived. They were in charge of the rapid-fire guns, such as they were. Now the marines were always dead proud of their machinery. Fond of them they were, you might say. It's said that Caesar's Praetorian Guard had a kind of reverence for the spears they carried. So as for the marines, these deadly engines seemed somehow to be sanctified. The way they looked after them, anointing them with oil, patting them gently as they were assembled or taken to bits.

'I can't say that my riflemen felt the same way. Not at all. A lot of white men have made the foolish mistake of thinking that anything mechanical might inspire superstition in that wild and barren country. They assume that the natives might be overawed by such things. But you look along the banks of the Nile and you can see the Archimedes Screw that they've been using to draw water out of the river since the time of the Pharoahs. Hardly less complicated than a Gatling gun. These people have known technology. And one thing my men knew about machines and machine guns: they jam. They jammed at Abu Klea, they jammed at Tofrik. A lot of my lads had been on the other side in the *jihadiyya* to know what a bloody disaster it is when they do jam. A weapon that fails when it is most needed is worse than useless and simple bad luck. Most of my seasoned veterans wouldn't trust them if we were forming up a square, would protest that it's better to have a solid line of rifle, with bayonets for when the enemy get into close quarters.

'So when the marines in their nice new field grey and white pith roll up to where we were mustered, they looked right proud of their toys, but I tell you the Sudanese weren't exactly impressed. A Gardner and a Nordenfeldt, great clumsy things they were, like barrel organs. Hand-cranked and multi-barrelled, mounted on fixed carriages, so they were impossible to traverse or to adjust the range easily. Eight hundred pounds of solid brass apiece, liable to overheat in the hot sun, and always jamming just at the wrong moment. They had to be carried on a caravan of camels, in sections. Well, they'd been brought along because they were the same calibre as our rifles, and the Sirdar was always keen on saving ammunition.

'But when they got out the Maxims, well, we could see that these little beauties were something different. Wrapped up in silk, as I said, to protect the mechanism. Barely sixty pounds they were, with a single barrel and a brass case around it to hold the cooling water. Sleek and trim they looked, something new and efficient. My boys gathered round to have a closer look. They couldn't see where the crank handle was and they laughed when one of the gunners told them there wasn't one. Just a trigger. It was explained that the recoil and the spent gas of each bullet ejected the spent cartridge and loaded the next round. Automatic, they called it. That was the first time I heard that word. Now, the lads were amazed at this and could hardly believe such a weapon could be. Curious too. Being riflemen, for them smoke and recoil are a curse, they were keen to see how they might be used as an advantage.

'There was a clamour for a chance to see them in action and I felt that a little demonstration might be good for morale before we set off into the bloody desert once more. I'd heard that the inventor of these guns claimed that they could be used to cut down a tree. So we found a dried-up old acacia out on the plain and had one of the Maxims set up against it. To hell with Kitchener and his precious ammunition saving, I thought, my men could do with a show and I would have to square it with the armourer later.

'Well, the chatter of the thing, fast and steady. We live in a constant chatter, don't we? But aye, this was fluent, and not to be argued with. Five bursts it took, to bring the acacia tree down. It split and fell away to a great cheer. Then we all went up to have another good look at the Maxim.

'Bakhit, my orderly, turned to me full of wonder and said: "It catches its own breath." Nice way of putting it, I thought. He then spoke of smoke and the Devil, telling me that when Allah made angels he made them from light; people he formed out of clay; *djinns*, genies that is, were created from flame; but the Devil himself is made out of smoke. Very poetic. I have to say though, that he was, all the while, puffing quite heavily on a Turkish cigarette. Then the gunners had their say, with me translating as they scarcely had any Arabic.

'A lance sergeant quipped that: "It only took a couple of these to slaughter five thousand niggers down in Matebele. Mowed down like grass they were." But then he saw my frown and noticing the colour of my men he quickly added: "Begging your pardon sir, *enemy* niggers, that would be."

'*Diabolical*, I heard one of the marines call them and thought nothing of it at first, knowing it to be a common enough expression in the ranks with no particular reference to the demonic. But it was in that same conversation that the gunners told me that their pet name for the Maxim was the Devil's Paintbrush, because, as one of them put it: "It's like daubing whole rows of oncoming with red, sir."

'And when the time came we got to witness the ruthless art of those guns. Once they got the range they could spray sharp lines, with bursts of colour. Broad strokes, if you like, splish-splash.'

Macdonald looked around the table and curled his lip.

'Impressionism, I believe you call it,' he said.

Clive Bell was about to say something but he thought better of it.

'And there's another reason why they call it the Devil's Paintbrush,' the General went on. 'Because the Maxim can fire six hundred and sixty-six rounds a minute. And as Crowley here will tell you, him being an expert on Revelations and the Apocalypse, that is the Devil's own number.'

At this everyone turned from the bleary-eyed General to look at the Beast, who gave a little nod of acknowledgement, with a twist of a smile on his lips.

XXVI

'WELL, SATAN IS ABROAD IN the modern world,' the Beast declared. 'We ignore his aesthetic tastes at our peril.'

'I suppose,' Gerald Kelly broke in tentatively, 'a certain ruthlessness is bound to be an influence on art as it has been in all other matters. A scientific violence, perhaps.'

'Modernism will be necessarily brutal,' Crowley insisted. 'It will have more to learn from Sir Hector's world than your effete dabblings. It will all be swept away in a great deluge. That is the future.'

'Then it's rather a grim one,' Kelly muttered.

'Come come, Gerry, it'll be a brave new adventure!'

'You hardly strike me as a man of action,' Clive Bell observed.

'Then I must contradict you. I have always seen art and adventure as going hand in hand. Culture must not be allowed to slump into apathy. We must rise up. For me it's simply a matter of virility.'

'Oh, really?' Bell challenged him.

The Beast wiped his mouth with a napkin and dropped the cloth on the table.

'I have myself sought to combine high art with high endeavour,' he continued. 'When I scaled K2 in the Himalayas last year, I took along a small library of poetry books. I believe they saved my life. They certainly preserved my sanity.'

'Oh aye,' rejoined Macdonald with a hoarse laugh. 'Our friend here is quite the accomplished climber, aren't you, Crowley?'

'I have scant equals in the field of mountaineering,' he announced flatly. 'I would cede Oscar Eckenstein, my mentor and climbing partner as a superior exponent, but few others.'

'You suffer from no false modesty,' said Astrid.

'False modesty is a sign of ill-breeding,' Crowley retorted. 'But I wish to recount my exploits merely to illustrate my point. K2, the second peak in the Karakoram range in the Himalayas, to the east of the Hindu Kush, rises majestically out of an isolated paradise and it is thought by some to be the location of Shambhala, the mystical city of the Tibetan Buddhist tradition, home to the Secret Chiefs or Hidden Mahatmas. We were inspired by the unattainable, driven on by the near impossibility of the task ahead.'

The Beast took a second to glance around the table, making sure that he held the room. In that moment he remembered coming across the sulphurous pools of a hot spring in the foothills of the mountain. The banks were laced with crystalline deposits of an incrustation exquisitely white and geometrical. As he trod the jewelled surface, he felt the delicate shattering beneath his feet as the crisp retort of broken sacraments. The sound was a voluptuous flattery, like the murmurous applause of a refined multitude.

'The land was bleak, the wind vicious, the sun hard,' he continued. 'Terrible extremes existed in temperature between night and day, even between light and shade. One could be frozen by shadow on one side of the face, sunburned by fierce glare on the other. We reached the snout of the great Baltoro Glacier, black, greasy and nearly five hundred feet high at its lowest point. Here flowed the source of the holy Indus. A terrible torrent gushed from the vast cavern, dark and unstaunchable, like the blood from an immense, elemental wound. The sight of it filled me with a kind of horror. Here, as we prepared our ascent on to the bright glacier beyond, I had my first and only serious row with Eckenstein, the leader of the expedition. From this point each of our party was to be allowed forty pounds of personal baggage. I insisted that I be allowed to bring my collection of specially bound books of poetry, that intellectual nourishment was as vital as actual food. And I was right, of course. I witnessed much psychological deterioration on the expedition. Cowering in tents for days on end with scant physical comfort, it is the mind that goes first. Some of our party went quite mad.'

'Did you make it to the top?' asked Astrid.

'For over two months we struggled, making camps ever further up the perilous slopes. I myself made investigative climbs and reached a height of some twenty-two thousand feet. But constant bad weather, and intermittent illnesses among our party frustrated our attempts and the summit was denied us. We did, however, break all hitherto records for endurance and I gained the honour of having written poetry at the highest altitude. I believe Shelley claimed to have written a sonnet while climbing in the Alps; well, I certainly surpassed him in the elevation of my circumstance if not in the sublimity of my verse. We may have failed to make the summit but I was driven to greater nirvanas.'

'Through magic?' Clive Bell asked.

'Magic is the synthesis of art and adventure,' the Beast insisted. 'It is the science of the will. But I am not alone here, on this mystical expedition. We are in the presence of another adept, Astrid, Soror Dominabitor Astris from the German lodge of Ordo Templis Orientis.'

The Beast made a casually ceremonial gesture in the direction of Astrid and the group followed the plaintive signal of his hands.

'Do you believe in witchcraft then, Fräulein Astrid?' asked Gerald Kelly with an impish grin.

'Men choose to condemn feminine power as witchcraft,' she retorted. 'In their fear they know that magic truly belongs to us.'

'Then you believe in the equality of the sexes?' Clive Bell suggested.

'No,' said Astrid. 'Spiritually speaking the power on the female side greatly exceeds that of the male. That is how women are to be emancipated. Through transcendence.'

Kelly laughed at this and turned to the Beast.

'What do you think about that, Crowley?'

'I agree completely. But the power of both sexes should be unleashed by ritual ceremony,' the Beast remarked, aiming his own gaze at Astrid. 'The most powerful drive in human nature, what was once thought of as base, is a sacred energy.'

He was thinking of her as his Scarlet Woman once more. She had such great power. He would have to find a way of controlling it.

'This is all rather absurd,' Clive Bell complained.

'Oh yes,' Crowley rejoined. 'I agree. Absurdity will be the only way we can truly understand the modern age. Like the doctrine of *Credo quia absurdum*, from Tertullian, the theologian of the Early Church. I believe because it is absurd. The son of God has died: this is credible because it is ridiculous; buried, he has risen again: this is certain because it is impossible.'

'You put yourself conveniently beyond contradiction,' noted Clive Bell.

'And you fail to make clear what exactly is your theory of magic,' Gerald Kelly added.

'My dear Gerry, you know that I am not concerned with the theory of magic, but rather the practice of it.'

'Then maybe you could perform some for us,' Bell suggested.

'I am not some vulgar conjurer from the music hall. But if you wanted an example of enchantment, I witnessed a remarkable manifestation of unseen power this very evening.'

'I'm sure it's a regular occurrence in your busy schedule,' said Stuart-Wortley.

'Oh, I was not the only witness. The General here was there too. In fact it was he who cast the spell. Why don't you show them your talisman, Sir Hector?'

Macdonald fumbled in his pocket, took out the metal charm and placed it on the table. Everybody leaned forward in their chairs to peer at the small object.

'What is it?' asked Astrid, craning her slender neck to get a better view.

'It's a magic square. One of the oldest methods of divination and a sign from the future when science will be once more put into the service of the supernatural. It is said that in ancient China, a turtle emerged from the Sho River with markings on the segmented sections of its shell that indicated a grid of figures where each row, column and diagonal added up to fifteen, the number of days in each of the twenty-four cycles of the Chinese solar year. This morning I was sent a magic square by a rival magician containing words of a curse which I countersigned and sent back. Gerry can vouch for that, can't you, Gerry? And now this. A magic square of the Mohammedans, given to Sir Hector by one of his native soldiers in the Sudan. The General used it this very evening to disarm a man aiming a pistol at me.'

There was a short gasp at this. The Beast raised a hand in vindication.

'It's true,' he went on. 'This rival I mentioned pulled a gun on me. The General used this talisman's magical power to wrench the weapon from the brute's hand. He might well have saved my life.'

'Well, when someone points a gun,' Macdonald reasoned, 'you've got to keep your nerve. The fact is . . .'

The General looked down at Bakhit's amulet. He reached out to touch it.

'The fact is' – Stuart-Wortley picked up the theme – 'one always carries a lucky charm into battle. It's a matter of nerves. Superstition's a normal thing under fire, isn't it, Mac?'

He turned to his comrade but the General's face was blank. His mind had set off into the desert once more.

'Soldiers' luck,' Stuart-Wortley went on. 'But I could show you something mystical, if you like.'

'What?' asked the Beast.

The Military Attaché gave a cold laugh that unnerved Crowley.

'This,' Stuart-Wortley said, taking something from his pocket and tossing it on to the table.

It was a pendant of mottled turquoise with an inscription in

Arabic carved into it, embedded in a clasp of pale gold filigree, attached to a thin chain.

'It was given to me by a sheikh of the Ja'alayin tribe who served under me at Omdurman. He swore that it would give protection to whoever wore it. When I was billeted below Spion Kop, during the South African War, a Boer shell landed near my tent while I was sleeping. Everything around me was blown apart, the frame and canvas ripped open, all my equipment and belongings destroyed, kit bag, the lot. Shrapnel everywhere, except for an area around my camp bed – completely unscathed. I sat up in bed and looked at all the destruction around me, well, I checked myself, sure that I must have been hit by something, but nothing. Not even a speck of dust on me. And I found that I was wearing that thing. I couldn't even remember putting it on: something must have told me to slip it over my head as I turned in for the night. Now, of course, I carry it everwhere where there might be danger.'

'Then you agree with me as to the power of talismans in the use of magic,' Crowley insisted.

Stuart-Wortley shrugged.

'You must have witnessed many manifestations of the Unseen from all your time in the east and in Africa,' the Beast went on.

Stuart-Wortley laughed once more.

'I've seen enough to recognise a fraud and a charlatan.'

The Beast bridled at this, drawing his considerable frame up out of his chair. It was time, Stuart-Wortley decided, to get Macdonald out of here. He turned to the General.

'Come on, Mac,' he said, 'let's go. It's getting a bit tedious here, don't you think?'

But Macdonald stared out absently at him, his fingers touching the square amulet on the table.

Salim had followed the Nile, travelling at night, tracing the stars far south. He could have been heading for home for all he knew. He was occasionally reminded that he came from the south; he remembered little else as to the whereabouts of his birth. But when he saw the dome of the Mahdi's tomb he knew that he had reached his true destination. The egg-shaped *qubba* glowed ethereally over Omdurman, its delicate silvering catching the morning sun. A blazing sign that the end of his long pilgrimage was finally in sight. He wept with relief and for the first time in many days began to feel afraid.

Across the river, Khartoum was now a ghost town, the ruins of the old capital empty and desolate. It had been over ten years since he had followed Faraj Pasha there, marching out of the Massallimiyya Gate to join the *ansar* and find his destiny. He began to shiver with thirst, fatigue and hunger. And fear. He consoled himself that his fate was in the hands of Allah: the compassionate, the merciful. There was no doubt that his own being in this world was but an image. Yet still he trembled.

When challenged by the armed *mulazimin* at the entrance to the walled city he declared himself to be a loyal soldier with an important message for the Khalifa. He was immediately arrested on suspicion of spying and was marched off to be interrogated by the commander of the guard. But nothing puzzles God. Salim found himself face to face with al Nur Anqara, an old officer of the *jihadiyya*. Al Nur Anqara had served in the 1st Sudanese before changing sides at Khartoum. He had known Salim from the days of the siege.

'How did you survive Firka?' he asked Salim.

'I was taken prisoner, effendi,' Salim replied. 'We were put to work on the railway. That's what I wanted to tell the Khalifa about.'

Al Nur Anqara kept his eyes on Salim as he reached down to his desk and took a cigarette out of a teak box and put it in his mouth. Salim could not help frowning. Al Nur Anqara's recusant behaviour was well known. He drank and smoked quite openly, even though the Khalifa himself made it clear that he deplored this behaviour. On more than one occasion he had been reproached as a profane and godless heathen, but slave soldiers who had achieved high rank were often given a bit of leeway, if only to confirm the prejudices of others. He struck a match and greedily sucked flame into the cigarette. As he let out a plume of blue smoke he broke into a rasping cough. With each spasm he shook out the match in his right hand and tossed it away.

'These things,' he spluttered, reading the disdain that furrowed the face in front of him. 'They bring their own punishment. So, what did you want to tell the Khalifa?'

Salim told him all he knew about the Sirdar's railway. How it was built. How it must be destroyed.

'Without the trains the Inglisi are lost, effendi.'

'But the Inglisi have taken Abu Hamed, to the south of the line. How are we to attack the railway to the north of that?'

'The track runs through miles of empty desert. An Egyptian battalion is posted at regular intervals to guard it. The camel-men of the Abada patrol the surrounding wilderness, but it would be easy for a small raiding party to break through unseen.'

'And what would they do?'

'They would blow it up.'

Al Nur Anqara laughed.

'This is where they are vulnerable,' said Salim. 'This railway feeds the Inglisi army, like an iron throat. We only need to cut it.'

The older man's smile turned into a frown. He finished his cigarette, stubbing it out in an upturned shell filled with ash on his desktop. Salim was clever. Perhaps he was a spy, after all.

'You could be sending men to their deaths,' he challenged him.

'I would lead the assault myself, effendi. I know something of the layout of the line, after all. There could be a series of attacks on all the weak points, not just the track but the water stations and coal depots, even the trains themselves. All it would take would be a handful of dedicated men.'

'You've thought this through, haven't you?'

'I've seen how this great beast of the infidel moves.'

'So, tell me. How was it that you were sent to the Railway Battalion when you were taken prisoner? From what I hear most of the captured *jihadiyya* are now serving in the Sudanese Brigade.'

'I would not fight on their side, effendi.'

'But we fight on both sides, don't we?' said al Nur Aqada with a cunning smile. 'And yet on neither. Are we not merely weapons in the hands of the masters?'

'It is the hand of Allah that guides me.'

'So you wish to be a weapon of God?'

'If He so wishes.'

'A devout slave.'

'He has raised me up from slavery. When I first answered the call of the Mahdi, I was set free.'

Al Nur Anqara picked up another cigarette and looked at Salim once more. The man had an intensity and fervour that was absurdly artless. An unstudied demeanour that would be hard to fake. He struck another match and decided that the poor fool was sincere.

'I wish I had your devotion. Your certainty.' He lit the cigarette, then took it from his mouth and held it up. 'You know, these things are burning away my lungs. The *araqi* I drink each day eats at my liver. But how can I be sure that either have any effect on my soul?'

Al Nur Anqara grinned at Salim who stared back, sullen and impassive.

'A weapon of God, eh?' he went on, taking another drag from the cigarette. 'Then I should take you to the Khalifa. He should be pleased to see one so loyal and simple-hearted. Though I wouldn't bet on it if he's in a bad mood.'

Two days later Salim and al Nur Anqara knelt with their arms crossed in front of their chests on the vast Persian carpet that was laid out in the centre of the inner court of the house of the Khalifa.

Salim stole a glace at the great ruler of the Mahdiyya resting on the sheepskin-covered divan above. The Khalifa Abdullahi wore a *jibba* of fine white cotton with delicately embroidered patches that were sewn into the robe as an exquisite representation of poverty. Doleful eyes peered out of a rotund face pitted with smallpox scars, his shaven head crowned with a red silk skullcap. Al Nur Anqara explained the purpose of their audience and Salim was called upon to give his account. When he finished he let his head bow a little further towards the patterned carpet.

'You say that the Sirdar is red-faced and one-eyed like al-Dajjal?' asked the Khalifa.

'Yes, Your Highness,' Salim replied.

'And this train is like the ass that al-Dajjal rides, rolling up the earth with a mountain of smoke before him?'

'Yes, Your Highness.'

'And you say we should send people to destroy it by stealth, like thieves in the night?'

Salim hesitated.

'Or like a cattle raid, Your Highness,' al Nur Anqara suggested, quickly coming up with a more honourable simile.

The Khalifa sighed. He was so tired. He did not know what to think. He longed for the visions that had guided them in the beginning. He missed his friend and master Mohammed Ahmed. The Mahdi. The great man had been taken too soon and Abdullahi had been left behind. Left behind to try to make sense of it all. Before it had all seemed easy, miraculous. To start a revolution, to found a nation, to change the world: these were simple things; to try to make a new order work, that was the job of the accursed. The Khalifa was an unlettered man with little learning, forever reliant upon other people's reading of scripture. Over the years he had turned in desperation to soothsayers and astrologers, to analysts of alphabets and *fekis*, those who made lucky charms, just like his own father had done. A numerologist had pointed out that as the Mahdi had appeared at the end of the thirteenth Islamic century, and now approached the end of the nineteenth Christian, did not this mark a sign of the Last Day? There had been meetings with emirs who counselled advancing north to occupy the Sabaluka Gorge. His brother Ya'qub advised that they should retreat to the west, to Kordofan and Darfur. His dissolute son Sheikh al Din was full of contemporary ideas and favoured exploiting divisions between the European powers that now fell greedily upon the whole of Africa like a pack of slathering dogs. A delegation had arrived from Abyssinia, suing for peace. They all said the same thing. The Inglisi are coming. The Inglisi are coming. Coming to avenge Gordon in some savage and unceasing blood feud.

'Why should we not let the Inglisi come?' the Khalifa demanded loudly, letting his anxious thoughts fly out into the inner court. 'Let this railway speed him on his way. Let them come faster in their trains and paddle-steamers.'

'Yes, Your Highness,' Salim replied.

'But what do you really think?' pursued the Khalifa. 'Do you think that this machinery of theirs can overwhelm us?'

Salim thought carefully.

'It is the Devil's power, Your Highness,' he ventured.

'Greater than ours?'

'Only God can tell. We should use any means we can to defeat it.'

The Khalifa picked out a date from the brass bowl by his side and put it in his mouth. Perhaps, he wondered, he should be more flexible in his strategy. Mobilisation, that had been their strength in the beginning. He was a nomad, after all, he had never felt at home confined within the walls of this city. But he would leave behind his concentration of treasuries, arsenals and granaries. Most importantly, he would leave behind the tomb of the Mahdi, the great symbol of the state. The still nascent sense of nationhood would be dissipated. He sighed and removed the date-stone from his mouth. He looked around his inner court, at his attendant eunuchs and bodyguards. He spotted a scribe sitting cross-legged in the corner, parchment and cane pen at the ready.

'You!' he boomed, pointing at the man. 'What do you think?'

The scribe looked up.

'Your Highness?'

'Do you think that we should fear the power of the infidel's new devices?'

'No, Your Highness,' the scribe replied swiftly. 'What is the power of all the new machines and weapons in the world when compared to the power of faith? Our faith is greater than theirs, Your Highness.'

The Khalifa made an angry grunt and threw the date-stone in the direction of the scribe.

'You fear me when you should fear God!' he shouted. 'You tell me lies that you think I want to hear.'

He then turned his head to look down at Salim.

'You, on the other hand, you fear God, but you do not fear me. You speak what you think is true despite what I might think. That is good. And as for al Nur Anqara with his unholy ways,' he went on, 'he does not fear me. Does he even fear God?'

The Khalifa gave a playful lilt to his voice to indicate that he had made a joke. Al Nur Anqara himself led the gentle ripple of indulgent laughter that echoed around the inner court. For a moment the Khalifa was happy. Let them come, he decided suddenly with an exultant smile. The Mahdi himself had once prophesied that a large army of infidels would be destroyed on the plains of Kerrari, beyond the city walls to the north of Omdurman. They would lure the Inglisi there, where their lines of communication were stretched to breaking point. The infidel would be tired, afraid, far from home. Then they would strike. Yes, he was sure of it now, Kerrari would be the killing fields of the last great battle. He would fear God and let them come.

'You are a brave man to come and speak to me,' he addressed Salim once more. 'But you will fight here in my *mulazimin*.'

After Friday prayers a great parade was ordered so that the Khalifa could review his mighty army. The great drum had beaten out his call for the whole garrison to present arms. Everybody rallied to their own standard, and on horse or foot hurried to the parade ground, chanting: 'God is Great'. The *jihadiyya* came from their barracks and stood to the far south. To the west were assembled the massed ranks of the Green Standard and the Black Standard. To the north Ya'qub and the other emirs waited on horseback, each with his own personal banner. Then the *ummbaya* was sounded, the massive hollowed-out elephant tusk that let forth a shrill blast to announce that the Khalifa was on his way. The *mulazimin* filed out on each side of him as he entered the field, their rifles shouldered. As Salim marched with them, he felt calm. All the fear he had felt when he had entered the city vanished into the tranquillity of a collective terror. He had fulfilled his purpose, borne witness to the power of the darkness. The Khalifa had blessed him with words as sacred as the prophesies of the Mahdi woven into the standards held aloft in all parts of the parade ground. He let go of his body and it entered the house of realisation, the whirling skies, the many-layered earth, the seventy thousand veils, into the assembled rapture.

Macdonald's mind droned with the dimensions of the spectacle. Rank, file, echelon, a triumph of pattern and colours so beautifully drilled that as the procession passed he was jubilant and oblivious amid the pageant of the enemy. Salim's mind emptied into his and he felt a serenity of righteousness. As fragments of his consciousness mustered back into the room, he heard the chant go up once more. *Allahu Akbar.* Yes, yes, he thought. God is great. How could He be otherwise?

XXVII

'**M**AC?'
    The cavalcade in his mind broke into a charge, cohorts of the Green Standard, the Black Standard, crying out in transcendent lamentation. Then they were gone, swept away by a *haboob*, the dust storm that howled across the plains of Kerari.

'Have some water, old man.'

He felt a blinding flash, a pool of light in the desert that shimmered like quicksilver. Then the mirage receded and he became sentient to the dining room once more. Salim had joined the Khalifa's army. He would be on the other side at the Battle of Omdurman. He might have seen him there, amid the terrible slaughter. He looked up to see Stuart-Wortley standing over him holding up a glass.

'*Bismillahi ar-rahmani ar-rahim*' muttered the General under his breath and took hold of the water glass.

The Beast hovered above him.

'The General has been having visions again,' he declared.

'He's in shock, poor man,' said Stuart-Wortley.

'I'm perfectly all right, Eddie,' he reassured him. 'In fact, everything is becoming clearer to me. I've just got a bit further to go.'

Macdonald took a sip of water. As he swallowed he pondered on the horrors to come.

'What's going on?' asked Stuart-Wortley.

'Sir Hector has been travelling on an astral plane,' claimed the Beast. 'He has been opening up his mind.'

'Ridiculous!'

'No, he's right, Eddie,' Macdonald told him. 'The truth is

coming out and I cannot hide from it any more. I have to find out what happened.'

'What happened? I don't understand.'

'I want to know what happened to my life. Fighting Mac, marching to glory, it was all a bloody farce, Eddie. There was always somebody else inside.'

'Goodness, Mac, you are in a state. Come home with me, old man.'

'I'm sorry, Eddie,' said Macdonald. 'All the rumours about me. They were true. I don't belong in your world any more.'

'Oh, come on, Mac, I know these things happen. For heaven's sake, it wasn't uncommon in the EA. Out in the middle of nowhere with no women.'

'But it wasn't just circumstance, Eddie. I was always like that.'

'Mac, no.'

'Sir Hector has done his duty to the empire,' the Beast interjected. 'Now he has a duty to himself.'

'What on earth do you mean, sir?'

'That one must not violate one's own nature simply to satisfy public opinion or medieval morality. Is that not right, Astrid?'

Crowley had sidled up to where the German woman was sitting.

'Our sexual nature is sacred,' she agreed.

'Quite,' the Beast added, patting her gently on the shoulder. Carefully taking the tincture bottle from his jacket pocket, he shook a few drops into her glass.

'I have to face the music,' said Macdonald.

'No, you mustn't,' the Beast insisted.

'For once this ridiculous fellow is right,' agreed Stuart-Wortley.

'But I am on my way to a court martial.'

'To a martyrdom,' said Crowley. 'Don't go.'

'A martyrdom?' demanded the General, thinking once more of Salim.

'Like Oscar Wilde,' said the Beast. 'He had the chance to escape to France before his trial, but, no, he had to stay and play the victim. Now, here you are, already in Paris. As I've said, there are plenty here like you, living in exile.'

'You can't compare Sir Hector with that Wilde fellow,' Stuart-Wortley contended. 'He made a show of it. Fools and dandies like yourself, that is one thing, but Mac? An indiscreet act here or there, it does not make a man, you know . . .'

He could not bring himself to say the word.

'A sodomite,' the Beast concluded.

Crowley had moved away from Astrid and now approached Stuart-Wortley.

'I have to say I dislike your tone and your manner, sir,' the Military Attaché warned him.

'You have an Englishman's disdain for the truth,' the Beast declared.

Stuart-Wortley stood up and confronted the man.

'You are talking about a dear friend. It is a matter of honour, sir.'

'Indeed? But he loses no honour in being what he is.'

'An officer and a gentleman.'

'Oh yes.' The Beast made a playful smile. 'And a sodomite.'

At this Stuart-Wortley took half a step back and swung his arm to deliver a swift punch to Crowley's jaw. Despite being a good five inches shorter than the Beast and several stone lighter, Stuart-Wortley's well-aimed blow toppled the magician. The waitress ran out to the kitchen, the patron entered and began to shout, and for a moment the whole of Le Chat Blanc was in turmoil. Stuart-Wortley helped Sir Hector Macdonald to his feet and together they made their way to the exit. Astrid noticed that at the last minute the Military Attaché turned around and snatched the Cypher Manuscript from the table and then both men were gone. She drained her glass and stood up. She made her way through the chaos and followed them down the stairs.

Outside, Stuart-Wortley and Macdonald headed uphill on rue d'Odessa.

'There was no need to hit the man, Eddie,' Macdonald complained.

'The ghastly idiot had been asking for it all evening.'

'Listen.' The General tugged Stuart-Wortley's jacket so that he would turn and face him. 'What he said about me is true.'

Stuart-Wortley caught Hector Macdonald's forlorn face peering at him through the gloom of the evening.

'And what are you doing with that book?' Macdonald demanded.

'I've got to check that it's not, you know, sensitive material.'

The General laughed.

'Och, Eddie, don't be so daft.'

'Well, you never know.'

'You really thought that Crowley was blackmailing me? And what, that thing is some sort of codebook?'

'There was a mention of cyphers.'

'That desk job has really got to you, hasn't it, Eddie? What have you been doing all day, reading cheap novels?'

'It is a bit on the dull side, Mac. That's probably why I clobbered that Crowley fellow. I've been itching for a fight since Ladysmith.'

They both laughed.

'God,' said Stuart-Wortley, 'I'd love another command. Anything, just so long as there was a chance for action.'

'Well, I'm sick of fighting, Eddie.' He sighed. 'I'm tired of it all.'

'Didn't have such a good time in the last show, did you?'

'South Africa?'

'Yes, became a bit bloody, didn't it? All blockhouses and barbed wire.'

'After Paaderburg, we ended up burning farms and organising guard duty for concentration camps.'

'Not our world any more, Mac.'

They had reached the top of the road and come to a circus of narrow streets by a walled cemetery.

'Listen, Eddie, I can't very well come back with you, you know.'

'Of course you can.'

At the corner somebody stepped out into the yellow pool of a streetlamp and stood in front of them.

'*Excusez-moi, messieurs,*' announced a figure wearing a navy blue cap, grey suit, yellow shoes and a bright red *foulard* knotted around the neck. A grin revealed discoloured teeth that clenched an unlit cigarette stub. On closer inspection Macdonald could make out a blue spot of Indian ink tattooed beneath the left eye. And that this mark was borne by a wild-eyed young woman.

Two youths abruptly appeared out of the darkness, each taking Macdonald and Stuart-Wortley by the arm while pressing something hard and metallic at their sides.

'*Permettez-moi de nous présenter,*' the girl in front of them proclaimed with a shrill timbre, producing a flick-knife that sprang open with a burlesque flourish. '*Nous, c'est les Apaches!*'

XXVIII

'GOOD HEAVENS, MAC. THE APACHES indeed! We're supposed to have been fighting savages throughout the empire only to find them here, on the doorstep of civilisation.'

The woman jabbed her knife in the direction of the book that Stuart-Wortley was holding, beckoning with her free hand that he should pass it to her.

Astrid watched from a little way off. She had grabbed her cloak at the door of Le Chat Blanc and pursued the men out on to the street. When she caught sight of them being accosted by a group of youths, she stopped to observe the scene. From a distance it appeared a playful spectacle, the streetlight picking out garish colours and silhouetted gesture. There was a curious throbbing behind her eyes and a bitter taste in her mouth. She covered her head with the hood of her cape and, keeping to the shadows, warily made her way up rue d'Odessa.

The girl pointing the dagger at Stuart-Wortley had been christened Juliet but had taken the gang name of Cho-Cho when she had started to run riot with the Apaches in Montmartre. Since then she had taken to wearing a suit and affecting a male demeanour. Cho-Cho had come down to Montparno with a couple of keen young lads she had picked up loitering outside a *bal musette* in rue des Trois Frères. There were rich pickings to be had down here, she had told them. Plenty of bourgeois English and Americans wandering the streets.

'*Tiens!*' she declared opening the strange book to witness mysterious glyphs and symbols that appeared to dance from its pages. '*Ça c'est quoi, alors?*'

'*C'est un livre de magie!*' hissed Astrid, walking slowly towards her, allowing the sickly gaslight to catch her hooded form, illuminating her harsh chin and cheekbones, hollowing out a darkness at her brow.

Cho-cho gasped and let the blade in her right hand clatter to the pavement as she slammed shut the Cypher Manuscript. Astrid felt a delirious thrill run through her, a feeling of power as she conjured up pure fear.

'*Mais, qui êtes-vous?*' Cho-cho stammered.

'*Moi?*' Astrid retorted sharply. '*Moi, je suis sorcière!*'

Terror spread through the gang. Stuart-Wortley and Macdonald sensed the hesitancy of their assailants at the same time. They moved swiftly: the General slammed an elbow into the gut of the boy who held him, causing him to drop his weapon and stagger away with a groan; Stuart-Wortley grabbed the wrist of his attacker, twisting it around until he was disarmed with a mournful yelp. The lads found themselves facing the two grinning gentlemen and wasted no time in turning on their heels and clattering away down the cobblestones of rue d'Odessa.

Astrid reached out and took hold of the *grimoire*, prising it from the feeble grasp of the bewitched Cho-Cho. As Astrid leaned forward her cowl slipped back to reveal golden braids that crowned her forehead, gilded coils that gleamed beneath the lamplight.

'Ah!' Cho-Cho breathed, utterly entranced by this vision. '*C'est la casque d'or!*'

'*Va-t'en!*' Astrid snapped, her mouth curling into a snarl. Cho-Cho hurried away, terrified that these words might be some evil spell. But later, making her way back towards Montmartre, she remembered the hooded face and savoured the malediction as if it were some kind of wanton blessing. A story was already forming in her young and resourceful mind: of the night she met a beautiful blonde vampire by the gates of the Cimetière du Montparnasse.

'Er, good show,' Stuart-Wortley announced to Astrid.

'Yes,' Macdonald added. 'Thank you.'

Both men felt awkward and unsure of exactly what to say. It was not merely that they were embarrassed that a woman had come to their assistance, they simply had no conception of the social protocol for such an occasion. So they quickly changed the subject.

'Look at this, Mac,' Stuart-Wortley said, holding up the peculiar weapon he had taken from his young Apache. 'I wasn't sure if it was a gun or a knife he was holding against me. Turns out it's both, with brass knuckles to boot. See?'

He held up a vicious-looking device that could be folded up and concealed easily in a pocket. It had a knuckleduster handle, a small revolving chamber like a peppermill, and a blade that clicked into place in the front.

'A charming little toy,' said Stuart-Wortley.

'Doesn't have much of a barrel,' the General observed.

'Well, it's for close quarters only. Stab your fellow then discharge a bullet into him.'

'Lovely.'

Astrid ignored them and had her first proper look at the Cypher Manuscript. Its leather binding was stamped with an embossed seal. An embellished pentangle blazoned within a circle, surmounted by a winged beast and ringed by a concentric band that read: ASTAROTH. She opened the book and examined the codex within. The pages were filled with astrological and alchemical emblems inscribed by a broad-nibbed pen on yellowed paper in what looked like brown ink or dried blood. There was every species of sign and symbol; spirals and curlicues that writhed and twisted; hooked crosses that crawled and crept like insects. Everywhere were hieroglyphs and illustrations: the Tree of Sephiroth; a snake that swallowed its own tail; a green lion devouring the sun; the rose of purity, the raven of putrefaction. Holding a page up to the light, macabre blue watermarks glowed like brooding tattoos on diseased flesh. The ink seemed to moisten beneath the burning gas, the serpentine sigils gleaming in the lamplight like bleeding stigmata. Astrid's heart began to quicken. She shut the book yet it seemed to vibrate with energy in her hands. Her head rushed with a sudden flood of meaning. She understood suddenly, not the particular but the universal. Not a single letter of the text but its entire purpose; the chant and rhythm of it; the spatial grammar of its symbolism. Here was the proof of magic she had long dreamed of and she felt possessed by its power. Then she heard a gasp from the man next to her.

'Are you all right, Eddie?' Macdonald asked.

Stuart-Wortley's breath was suddenly laboured.

'Over-exerted myself a bit, that's all. Now look, let's find a cab and get home. Fräulein Astrid, can we drop you off somewhere?'

The Military Attaché gave out another grunt of pain.

'Eddie, it's your heart, isn't it?'

'I'm fine, Mac. Just need to catch my breath. Getting too old for adventures.'

'I'll get you a cab, Eddie. But I'm not coming with you.'

'Mac—'

'Look, I know you want to help, but there's nothing you can do, is there? You can't really find me a posting, I know that.'

'We could try.'

'No, Eddie. I've got to find another way.'

'But I don't understand, Mac. What are you going to do?'

'I'm not completely sure myself. It'll be a new kind of adventure, I suppose.'

Stuart-Wortley held his chest and took a sharp intake of breath. Macdonald put his arm around his comrade and looked out for a cab. Glancing down the road, Astrid spied the hunched figure of Crowley skulking in their direction.

The Beast was in an evil humour as he slouched towards them. Macdonald had seen a *fiacre* and was waving it down. Stuart-Wortley stood wheezing on the corner, steadied by Astrid.

'The gentleman has been taken ill,' she said as Crowley approached.

'Of course,' said the Beast, aiming a malevolent glare at the Military Attaché. 'I have just put a hex on him, you see?'

Astrid nodded. In her current state of mind such a boast made perfect sense. She saw the hateful expression on Crowley's face and for the first time was afraid of him.

'You're a damned fool,' Stuart-Wortley muttered.

'Anyone who harms my person can expect magical retaliation.'

'Let me hit you again and we'll see what happens.'

'Please,' Astrid insisted, turning to Stuart-Wortley and raising a hand, as if to protect him from Crowley.

The cab pulled up beside them and Macdonald helped his friend to climb in.

'Come on, Mac,' Stuart-Wortley implored one last time.

'No, Eddie,' his comrade replied, thinking of Salim and Bakhit once more. 'I'm changing sides. At least for tonight.'

'What?'

'I can't really explain, Eddie. But there is something I have to find out.'

'Come and see me tomorrow then,' the Military Attaché called out as the cab began to pull away.

Crowley turned to Astrid and gestured at the heavy volume that she held.

'The Cypher Manuscript, if you please.'

Astrid felt his pale eyes of blue flame peering right into her. His lip was swollen and bloodied, making his fleshy mouth even more bestially sensual. His manner now seemed utterly transfigured into a morose and sinister intent. The Beast laughed. Astrid's face burned brightly with fearful exuberance. He noted that her pupils had become wildly dilated, as dark and deep as obsidian. It was taking effect, he concluded, his mood on the rise once more. He reached out and took hold of the *grimoire*. She felt the strength drain from her hands and sighed as the precious book slid from her grasp. She would get it back somehow. She would have to find a way.

Macdonald watched as the carriage bearing his old comrade

clattered away into the night, his last vague hope of any official overture he might make to save himself. Now he had chosen a different kind of bargain altogether. He had no idea where this strange path might lead, but he would still have to face his past.

The memory of the desert campaign advanced inexorably in his weary head. The relentless onslaught towards Omdurman. After the strike on Abu Hamed had come the bloody slaughter at Atbara. Kitchener ordering a reckless frontal assault on the Dervish *zariba*, Macdonald's Sudanese right in the centre, bearing the brunt of enemy fire, breaking through the thorned enclosure to engage in barbarous hand-to-hand fighting.

Then the victory procession in Berber, his brigade on parade as the Dervish emir Mahmoud was exhibited in chains like a captured barbarian in a Roman triumph with Sirdar Kitchener as Caesar, leading in front on a white horse. On it went, the Great March into the night towards the final great battle. *Omdurman, Omdurman, Omdurman*, the word ululating in his mind like a mantra.

Another *fiacre* came into view.

'Pray, what time is it?' the Beast asked, waving at the approaching hansom.

Macdonald pulled out a pocket watch and squinted at it. The cab was turning around the circular junction to draw up to where they stood.

'It's twenty-five minutes to midnight,' said the General.

'The most sacred and profane hour approaches,' Crowley told them. 'I have another appointment tonight and you are both welcome to join me as guests.'

The Beast turned to the General.

'I told you tonight would be a journey of revelation. Well, now it is time to break the seventh seal. To finally break the spell that has enslaved you. Will you come?' he implored.

Macdonald looked into Crowley's eyes and remembered the strange premonition he had felt at their first meeting. That this was a man who would understand all his secret fears. Perhaps he was the only one who could lead him through them.

'Where are we going?' he asked Crowley.

'Where do you think?'

'To hell?'

The Beast laughed out loud.

'Of course,' he said. 'You understand now, don't you? That the only way to be saved is to be damned first.'

Macdonald nodded. This night had opened his eyes. All the truths of his life awaited him.

'Well, let's go then,' he said.

'Astrid,' Crowley called to her. 'Will you join us?'

She followed them to the cab, her mind now in a stupor intent only on possessing the Cypher Manuscript once more. The Beast dabbed his mouth with a handkerchief. He tasted blood and savoured the saturnalia of the night. Soon would strike the perfect shadow of the sun's journey through the sky. As they clambered into the carriage and Crowley handed the driver the address that Blanchot had given him earlier in the day, he had a vision of the Devil card in the Tarot. Souls to be damned could only be delivered if they followed willingly. The horned one held two chained figures: one male, one female. But it was clear that the fetters they wore were loose enough to be slipped off. They were led by their own volition.

XXIX

GHOSTLY BLUE LIGHTNING PULSED WITHIN the thick cloud that brooded over Kerrari plain, its glare picking out a vast array of hunched figures, crowded animals, shelters fluttering in the wind. The immensity of Kitchener's assembled forces caught in flickering moments: the dread host bivouacked in a broad arc, sleeping with its back curled up against the Nile. Bakhit brought his *miralai* a mug of lukewarm soup. Macdonald stood squinting into the darkness. The Dervish Army was out there somewhere, maybe fifty thousand strong. A rough *zariba* had been put up and there were slit trenches here and there, but sentry lines were stretched perilously thin across the whole front.

'If they come in the night, we're done for,' he had heard a puppy-faced subaltern of the 25th Lancers mutter. The gunboats on the river charged up their searchlights; harsh beams strafing, probing the darkling plains. The clouds had swallowed the moon and the stars. Hector could just make out a scattering of campfires that embellished the blackened edge of the distant hills, and the glow of a village burning to the south.

They drew up in a quiet side street in front of a large townhouse that appeared completely deserted. A moment of quiet fury possessed the Beast. He supposed that he had been tricked either by the bookseller or the cabman. But as he turned to shout at the driver he noticed a sputtering of lamplight further along the pavement. In the high wall to the side of the house a door was embedded with a square grille emitting a feeble ray. The *fiacre* clattered away and the Crowley crept up to the postern and rapped his knuckles on a heavy wooden panel. The dull outline of a face filled the grating.

'*C'est qui?*' came a guttural demand.

'Asmodeus,' the Beast declared solemnly.

A heavy bolt was pulled back and the door groaned open. An old woman held up a lantern to scrutinise the visitors, then beckoned them to hurry inside. They were led across a small courtyard to a set of stone steps. At the foot of them stood a small chapel, slits of dismal light seeping from its heavily shuttered windows. They could just hear the low chanting of a dirge that throbbed within. The crone pointed at an arched door below them and croaked:

'*Là-bas!*'

Omdurman. Dawn light stole quietly into the sky behind them, the low sun burning at the edges of scudding grey. In the bleakness, the cracked dome of the Mahdi's tomb could be seen, the gilded *qubba* shattered by a bombardment that had killed a hundred women and children sheltering in a nearby mosque. Now the *ansar* waited at the foot of the mountains. The hills returned the call of thousands as the devoted ranks of the Khaliphate knelt to pray.

Bugles had sounded at half past four. Macdonald felt quietly blessed that the night attack had not come as he ordered his men to stand to their arms. They formed up, some of them whiling away the time by etching at their cartridges with a bayonet blade, making cross-shaped notches at the nose of bullets, improvising dum-dums that would flatten on impact and give them more stopping power.

Some time before six a murmur could be heard from below the mountains. Drumbeats and shouts of advancing forces. The Dervish crested the Kerrari Ridge and came into view. Their front was five miles long, rippling with the shimmer of spear points that caught the dim light of morning. White flags and the many-coloured gonfalons of emirs marked out their battle formations, the sacred Black Standard glimmering with the words of God recited by the Holy Prophet floating above, high and ethereal. A single cry went up and was answered by the multitude, roaring like the sea or the rising wind. The tumult of an oncoming storm.

They groped their way through into a murky apse with a low vaulted ceiling and filed in to an empty pew. A gruesome stench hung in the air. Crowley's eyes smarted and he blinked against a smoky fug, trying to accustom his eyes to the gloom. The General sat quietly, once more in a heavy-lidded trance. Astrid, conversely, looked absurdly alert, her eyes bulging and vigilant, shining with tears. Hanging temple lamps of gilded bronze and red glass lit the chapel. By the altar vapid embers of a brazier burned a foul choking incense. Men and women were lolling on the benches groaning or chanting discordantly so that a dismal hum reverberated around the chamber.

Two altar boys skipped up the aisle to light the black candles of sulphur and pitch that surrounded the altar. The front of the chapel then became visible, as did the altar boys themselves, two dwarfish men with grotesquely made-up faces. A crimson cloth had been draped over the altar, with something misshapen seeming to quiver beneath it.

The priest entered, and the altar boys joined him, one carrying a wooden cage that let out a disconsolate squawk, the other swinging a fuming thurible. The Beast sniffed and caught the liquorice fragrance of hemp resin. He stole a glance at the face of their wicked celebrant. The man had bright, dark eyes that darted to and fro, heavy stubble on his chin and a furrowed brow that glistened with sweat.

The procession reached the altar. As the priest raised his hands, his assistants went to either side, taking hold of the blood-red pall.

'In the Name of the Great God Satan,' he intoned. 'Behold the altar of our Infernal Lord.'

The cloth was pulled back. Astrid gasped as the supine form of a naked woman was revealed, her legs apart and hanging over the altar's frontal.

'Thine is the earth, Lord Satan,' the priest continued. 'We honour the preparation of Thy throne in the name of lust, homicide, luxury and battle.'

With his White Standard to the fore, emir Osman Azraq led the assault of ten thousand Dervish right into the mouth of the infidel. At two thousand and eight hundred yards the Inglisi artillery opened up; field batteries and gunboat crews firing the deadly new lyddite explosive in its first engagement; fused shrapnel shells with a bursting power equivalent to eighty pounds of gunpowder; some primed to airburst, raining down death from above; others crashing into the earth, rooting out prey, churning up flesh, debris and billowing clouds of red dust. The gunners had their exact range, judgement now a matter for the infernal machinery. At two thousand yards came the Maxims with yet more lethal precision. The clatter of traversing fire, stitching from left to right; the oncoming Dervishes simply falling in a line as if they had been told to lie down in a row. The nervous stammer of the future. Trigger buttons held in stuttering bursts, a steady stream of brass cartridge-cases tinkling gently to the ground; the hush of cooling water simmering in the barrel casings, whispering of tomorrow. At twelve hundred yards outgoing fire swelled with the roar of nine thousand rifles.

In one last desperate manoeuvre, Osman Azraq mustered five hundred horse and charged straight at a Maxim battery. The warriors rode unfalteringly until all were mown down, faithful to the end as the Devil's Paintbrush dabbed away at them in murderous pointillism.

By eight o'clock in the morning it was certain that the first attack had failed. The field was littered with thousands of dead and wounded Dervishes. Kitchener was now determined to advance on Omdurman. They would move from their encampment in echelon formation, the British brigades leading, Macdonald's Sudanese to the rear. But as the Sirdar rode up and down the ranks to oversee his orders there was still a smattering of fire along the front as the half-dazed troops continued to blast away at the dead and dying of the Dervish, as if to destroy the very image of carnage that lay before them. Kitchener could be heard to call out in frustration, ever attentive to the logistics of annihilation:

'Cease fire! Cease fire! Cease fire! Oh what a dreadful waste of ammunition!'

'O Satan! O Satan! We invoke you and beg your acceptance of this sacrifice!'

The priest had pulled a fluttering cockerel from the cage and held it by the neck over the altar. A chalice was placed beneath it, its base resting on the belly of the naked woman. With one stroke of a knife, the priest slashed through the twitching fowl's neck and dark blood splashed into the cup. The rooster continued to thrash about for a few seconds, flapping its wings in a final convulsion.

'Glory to the Infernal Lord! We praise Thee, we bless Thee, we glorify Thee. We give thanks to Thee for Thy great power, Lord Satan, Infernal King, Almighty Emperor.'

Now Macdonald was flying across the desert once more, his mind soaring across the battlefield. Crossing over the lines. It was a terrible enough thing to see one side in a battle; to witness both, that was truly infernal. His soul swooped down to the far edge of the field, towards Salim. God, thought Macdonald, there he is.

Salim was with Sheikh al-Din's *mulazimin* on the far edge of the field, engaged in an encircling manoeuvre, threatening the right of the Inglisi encampment. They had been pursuing the Camel Corps, which had been sent out to protect the northern flank. As they chased them down towards the river it looked as though the corps would be completely cut off and driven into the Nile. Then in an instant, as they approached the riverbank, a gunship appeared, its pistons hissing malevolently. The steamer seemed to hover over the sparkling water, gliding gently like a bright water *djinn*. An exterminating angel that turned slowly, scanning the shore and lining up its ordnance. Then the fearsome engine blazed at them, wreathing itself in cruel smoke, spitting out cannon and machine-gun fire that tore into the ranks of the *mulazimin*. Somebody grabbed Salim's arm and pulled him down into cover.

The general assault hesitated, and with another gunship coming into view, they withdrew, allowing the Camel Corps to escape. Then word came for the *mulazimin* to join the Green Standard, which was rallying in the Kerrari Hills. The Black Standard had regrouped out of view behind Jabal Surkhab, across the valley. Now a pincer attack was planned against the Inglisi. Kitchener, imagining that his foe had been vanquished in its first assault, was advancing impatiently on Omdurman. The infidel was on the move on a broad open plain, its rearguard isolated and vulnerable. They were in the jaws of a great trap.

'This is Thy body,' the priest intoned, taking a wafer from a silver paten and holding it aloft.

Astrid's mind danced amid the dark shapes and dreary din. She grinned wolfishly, her nostrils quivering, detecting the scent of blood cutting through the heavy reek in the chapel. Held in the throes of the drug's menacing ecstasy, her mood oscillated wildly from euphoric to sepulchral.

The priest lowered the wafer, drawing it down between the breasts of the woman on the altar, across the belly to press it between her legs. The woman groaned theatrically and wriggled about in a pantomime of desire.

'This is *Walpurgisnacht*?' she asked Crowley in a whisper.

'I beg your pardon?'

'A witches' Sabbath.'

'Yes,' the Beast confirmed. 'I rather believe it is.'

The newly consecrated host was placed on the silver paten. The priest now lifted the chalice.

'This is Thy blood.'

Macdonald shifted uneasily, unsure whether he was seated on the bare boards of a church pew or the saddle of his charger. A lull in the battle, a foreboding silence between sacraments. His mind hovered somewhere above, vertiginous, full of dread. Scared of heights, terrified of depths. He tried to catch his breath as the fetid air rasped in his throat. He remembered the sense of disquiet he had felt at that point on the field.

They're going too bloody fast, he had thought as the British Brigades were marching to the fore in triumphal mood, jostling to be the first to enter Omdurman. And as his brigade wheeled wide and assumed the outermost station of the echelon, his vague uneasiness hardened into a sense of real jeopardy. A wide gap had opened up between them and the main column, leaving them miles to the rear and isolated. As they approached the Western edge of Jabal Surkhab they found themselves vulnerable, surrounded by an expanse of hostile ground.

Then through the heat haze, fifteen thousand Dervishes emerged in twenty-three ranks with a score of banners fluttering, the Black Standard like a great raven's wing swaying above them all. The Sudanese Brigade were cut off from the rest of the Expeditionary Force, outnumbered five to one, in the wrong formation and facing the wrong way.

'Lord Satan, receive this host which I, Thy worthy servant, offer to Thee, my True and Living God, for all here present.'

Macdonald sent a galloper off to the Sirdar for instructions. Kitchener could not yet see the attack massing at the rear. His reply was terse and impatient: *Cannot he see we are advancing on Omdurman? Tell him to follow on.* Macdonald was on his own.

Emir Ya'qub, commanding the Black Standard, had plenty of cavalry and spear but few riflemen. His nephew Sheikh al-Din's *mulazimin* were on the other side of the battlefield, maybe joining with the Green Standard, he couldn't tell. He needed fire cover for his assault but he could wait no longer. The infidel were already lining up their artillery and finding their range. He raised his spear and ordered the charge.

Macdonald ran out his cannon and Maxims to the front, and now had to deploy his infantry from column into line. And quickly. All he had drilled into them, every last command to its last detail, would be needed right now. As the Dervish charge grew ever closer he turned out the 11th Battalion, and laughed as he saw six men detach themselves and run out in front, rifles shouldered: company markers taking posts to ensure a precise line of advance, standing to attention at the oncoming enemy. 'Cool as on parade,' he had urged them as he gave his orders, and they took him at his word. But as the ranks formed up facing to the south-west ready to repel the attack on the flank, the Green Standard was observed entering the field from the north, launching another assault from behind.

The priest lifted the paten with the consecrated host in an attitude of supplication. He then lowered it back on to the belly of the woman and raised the cup.

'O Great Lucifer, the Bright One, we offer Thee this chalice of fleshly lust, that it may arise in the sight of Thy majesty for our use and gratification and be pleasing unto Thee.'

A sacring bell was rung and then the grail descended. The priest then took the thurible and censed the altar and its gifts, turning it anticlockwise, then widdershins, raising it up and down. He then bowed and handed the smoking vessel to an altar boy, and raised his arms.

Macdonald drowsily glimpsed the demonic ceremony. All the sacramental movements of ritual; the spatial symbols to all points of the compass; elevation and genuflexion; like Bakhit's magic square everything signalled a continuous movement of sacred geometry.

This was what his great fame rested upon: the rough lines that he had scored in the sand as he gathered his company commanders together when the second attack was spotted; the orders he gave, brisk and exact; 'I want your movements and behaviour to be just as if you were on the training ground,' he had told them. Rifles hushed in an instant on the whistle blast; the companies rapidly threading back and forward, round and round, in and out, as if it were the figure of a dance. They moved as one, taking casualties all the time but never wavering. His brave, beautiful, utterly disciplined corps of men, in the cockpit of battle, between the deadly pincers of the enemy. The whole brigade had divided and re-formed into an entirely new position. Turning the front ninety degrees in a complete semicircle, facing successively south, south-west, west, north-west. His great manoeuvre, a feature of Staff College training for years to come; how he saved the day at Omdurman; how he put Kitchener forever resentfully in his debt. And as the Black Standard's assault began to wane, the Green Standard's offensive waxed and came on at them. *Wait. Hold your fire.*

'Wait,' Macdonald muttered out loud in the chapel.

A familiar figure once more entered his dream. As the Green Standard came on he spotted Salim with them and became one with him once more.

'Jesus Christ, King of slaves, those that wait upon thee shall be confounded. They will put you out of the temples and you shall be afraid of the terror of the night.'

He turned and beckoned the congregation to communion.

'I shall deliver him unto the asp and the basilisk, to the lion and the dragon, to all sin, to sudden and unprovided death, to lightning and tempest, to the scourge of earthquakes, to plague, famine and war. To the everlasting wrath of Satan!'

*

Salim felt bitter tears prick at his eyes as he realised that the *ansar* of the Green Standard had been deployed too late. Sheikh al-Din had wasted precious time in mustering the fire troops of the *mulazimin*, giving the rearguard of the infidel time to regroup and face them. If their offensive had been simultaneous with the Black Standard's then there might have been a chance to engage fully with the enemy. Instead they merely charged towards the end of time. Shrapnel shells and case-shot hailed down upon them, their line thrashed by the pulsating enfilade of machine guns. This was the Hour of the Signs; the Last of Days he had long dreamed of now stretched out endlessly; each second another lifetime, another chance for uncertainty.

He tried to convince himself that the world really was coming to an end, but at the last he could not quite believe it. They were still fixed in time and way behind, as he had feared. They were losing the struggle against the future. In this apocalypse it would be the infidel that would prevail. Today the modern world had triumphantly come into being. The brutal victory of tomorrow over yesterday. All they could hope for was the day after.

As comrades fell all around him he broke out into a crouching run, holding his fully cocked Remington close to his body, determined to get close enough to the enemy to kill at least one of the Inglisi before he too was consumed by the fire and smoke of al-Dajjal. God granted his final wish and he found himself in one piece and well within range of their line.

As he brought up the gun to his shoulder his eyes swam with sweat and tears. They were not charging at the Inglisi but his fellow blacks of the Sudanese Brigade. For a second he thought that he saw Bakhit notched in the sights of his rifle. Perhaps it was just another *jihadiyya* who looked like him. It did not matter. He couldn't shoot. He couldn't fight his brothers after all. On either side. He wept freely now: for his wavering faith, for a lost dream of nationhood, for his own suffering, but mostly for his soul mate of childhood. He dropped his rifle and reached out, glimpsing at the memories of their boyhood together. The roar of the next fusillade cut him down. As time sucked out of him, he thought of something he wanted to tell Bakhit. That his dear friend was right: that the stars are cattle-fires in the sky, not missiles to pelt the devils with.

'We renounce you, Jesus!' the priest called out, handing the chalice to those who had come forward. 'Lord of Disappointment, Prince of Hoaxes. Long centuries we have wept as you tricked the world of its power with your empty promises. Now we proclaim you dead, now we declare you unrisen, now we trample on your image and consign you to obscurity along with your Father the incompetent God of idiotic purity!'

The altar boys pulled the robe off him and he stood naked before them all, bloated, haggard, dripping with sweat. He took the host and despoiled it with his body and trampled it into the ground, then grabbed handfuls of unleavened wafers from a proffered ciborium and scattered them.

'Satan we adore Thee! We call upon Thee to come and rid us of this great impostor. A new century has come that will see the return to the Age of Darkness. We wait for the Antichrist and look for his demonic signs: the Pentangle; the Hammer and the Curved Blade; the Twisted Cross.'

The battle was over before noon. The plains were littered with the dead and dying of the *ansar*. Two long lines of corpses, one starting at Surkhab, the other from Kerrari, converged at the point where the Sudanese Brigade had stood their ground. Thousands of wounded Dervishes crawled and dragged themselves to the Nile in the blistering heat.

As Macdonald mustered his men to follow the advance on the city he noticed that he had lost sight of Bakhit. He pulled up his charger to gallop back to where the dead and wounded were being attended, terrified that his beloved might be among the fallen. There, amid the confusion, he saw his orderly wandering along the lines of carnage, dragging his rifle behind him. The lad was in distress, crying out over the bloody desert. He thought at first that he must be suffering from battle fatigue. He rode up to him and called out for him to stop. Bakhit turned and looked up at his *miralai*, fury and hatred in his eyes.

'You lied, Bey! You lied when you said that he died on the railway!'

'Come back and join the ranks!' he called to him.

'Salim was right,' Bakhit replied. 'Except it is you that is al-Dajjal, the Great Deceiver!'

'Pick up your rifle and fall in, Private Bakhit! That's an order!'

'You lied, and you fooled me. You made me kill him.'

'Bakhit!'

For a moment Bakhit held up his gun and thought about aiming it at his commanding officer, just as he had once threatened to do. Then, staring Macdonald in the face for the last time, he dropped the rifle, turned and walked away. Macdonald called after him, thinking that he was simply raving, his mind crazed by the heat and the fearful holocaust. He imagined that the boy would eventually compose himself and return to him full of apologies. But in the evening, along with an account of the day's casualties came a report with his name clearly listed as a deserter.

Kitchener rode into Omdurman in triumph. The city descended into chaos and filthy corruption. 'Loot like blazes,' came the Sirdar's order. 'I want any quantity of marble stairs, marble pavings, iron railings, looking-glasses and fittings; doors, windows, furniture of all sorts.'

They blew up the broken *qubba* lest it become a focus for a future uprising. Kitchener had the Mahdi's remains thrown in the Nile, keeping the skull in a kerosene tin as a memento. He thanked the Lord of Hosts and wept for his great hero Gordon as the band played 'Abide with Me'. Kitchener became K of K, taking Khartoum as his title when given a peerage. But he would always be reminded that the glory of Omdurman belonged to

Macdonald. The ranker Scotsman and his blacks had saved the day; their brilliant rearguard action had covered his near catastrophic errors. Macdonald was ever conscious of the danger of upstaging such an ambitious man. The two men grew even more wary of each other, and the further Macdonald rose up, the more isolated and alone he became. He had no clique of officers around him, no band of boys to flatter and console. No one to watch his back as he advanced ever onward. Fame was his only companion; it was how the whole world perceived him but for the dark whispers of rumour. Everybody wanted to meet Fighting Mac, the empire hero. A pasha in Egypt, a knight in the homeland. Guest of honour at countless dinners and ceremonial occasions. The tongue-tied trophy at society parties. Honours and titles solidified him into the picture-book warrior; a little god on a cigarette card.

He was suddenly aware of a strange cacophony around him. The ritual was coming to its bizarre conclusion and his mind blazed with an infernal epiphany. Now all his glories seemed as hideous and obscene as this grotesque ceremony. All the terrible slaughter and sacrifice. He thought of Bakhit, walking away from him through the bloody aftermath. He thought of Salim too, whom he had never known, only dreamed of, and began to sob quietly.

'Fornicemur and Gloria Domine Satanus!' the priest called out.

Those of the congregation who had gone up to the altar for communion were undressing, some tearing off the clothes of others. One of the altar boys knelt before the priest, the other cavorted with the woman who had served as the altar and now stood by the tabernacle waving the chalice around.

The Beast glanced at Astrid, trying to gauge her reaction to the ritual, whether or not she was interested in joining in.

'What do you think?' he muttered to her.

'The General!' she exclaimed through the clamour. 'The General. He is crying.'

She put her arms around him in a sudden impulse of compassion and together they led him back out into the cold night air.

'I'm perfectly well,' Macdonald insisted, swiping at his wet face with a handkerchief. 'No, really I am. In fact I feel a great deal better.'

'Did the ritual upset you?' Crowley asked.

'No, no. This, you know, vision.'

'Yes?'

'I know what happened now. At Omdurman. Why Bakhit deserted. He saw Salim die there. I had deceived him. I hadn't meant to but . . .'

'Of course not.'

'But, but . . .' The General struggled for a moment longer. Then it all came out. 'The whole thing's been a bloody lie! Hasn't it?'

Macdonald gave out a nervous laugh, part of himself astonished by what he was saying, what he was thinking. This was mutiny against everything he had believed about honour and duty.

'Something has happened to me,' he muttered.

It was true that he appeared transformed. His expression was relaxed, serene even. All the great horrors had gone through him and out the other side. Macdonald felt the great burden of his soul sink right down through the earth, into the underworld. He no longer felt that he needed to hold himself up. He had been walking on tiptoe all his life and now, at last, he could plant his feet on the ground. He sighed.

'I've been . . .' He thought for a second. 'What would you call it? Yes. Initiated.'

'Really?' Crowley asked, grinning. 'Into what?'

'Well, I'm one of the damned now,' Macdonald declared, with a smile. 'Aren't I?'

'Congratulations,' declared the Beast.

'So tell me,' said the General, his face beaming. 'You surely know after all, where do the damned go at this time of night? For amusement.'

Crowley let out a dark chuckle.

'Hmm, yes,' he pondered. 'I think I know just the place.'

The blue-black sky was sprinkled with starlight, full of great constellations that wheeled above them. Macdonald felt a shiver from the cold air as they made their way towards the glow of the city, towards tomorrow. All seemed quiet and at peace. Yet across the world an insomniac empire stirred.

It is already morning in Bengal and, as a train pulls out of Calcutta, Lord Curzon of Keddleston, Viceroy of all India, dictates a telegram to Secretary of State Lord Hamilton from his viceregal carriage:

KITCHENER CAME TO SEE ME THIS MORNING ABOUT ORGANISING A COURT MARTIAL OF FOUR INDIAN MAJOR-GENERALS TO TRY HECTOR MACDONALD, SHOULD HE PRESENT HIMSELF AGAIN IN CEYLON. KITCHENER, WITH CHARACTERISTIC EMPHASIS, SAID THAT HE WOULD LIKE THE BRUTE — SUPPOSING HIM TO BE GUILTY, OF WHICH WE HEAR FROM CEYLON THAT THERE IS NO DOUBT — TO BE SHOT. I CAN HARDLY BELIEVE, HOWEVER, THAT THE TRIBUNAL WILL EVER ASSEMBLE, SINCE IT IS THE CHARACTERISTIC OF THE DETECTED CATAMITE TO PREFER THE SECURITY OF A CONTINENTAL RETREAT TO THE DUBIOUS AMENITIES OF ONE OF HIS MAJESTY'S GAOLS.

Part Four

THE LEFT-HAND PATH

XXX

THE CINEMATOGRAPH CLATTERED INTO LIFE at the back of the darkened room, throwing out ghostly shadows with a mesmeric pulse. Motes of dust and smoke reeled in the beam of the magic lantern as the screen shimmered and oscillated. A white flame blazed, then darkened, focusing into the image of a moving figure, a dancing woman.

Layers of delicate cloth swirled around her catching the light with the powdery sheen of a moth's wing. A tremulous body was in turn cloaked and unveiled in rippling waves of silk or damask. Then at once the apparel floated free to reveal a figure stark and phosphorant, naked but for a gaudy headdress, twisting provocatively in a serpentine burlesque of exoticism. Astrid shuddered, entranced by the phantasmagoria, feeling her own psyche starkly projected.

'Ah!' the Beast declared. 'Salome. Of course. The dance of the seven veils before Herod.'

He smiled in the darkness, savouring the spectral vision. The flicker of light and dark, of seen and unseen. Occult and gnosis. The veiled sky, the layered earth. He glanced across at his companions. Astrid was transfixed, hypnotised by the quivering form. The General stared impassively, the lunar glow catching his dour features in stony relief. He seemed indifferent to the strobing image but rather perturbed by the soft shuttering noise. Like the awful flapping of a trapped bird. Through clenched teeth he felt the drone, the whisper of automatic fire.

'Yes, yes,' Crowley went on, more to himself than to anybody. 'The unveiling of the goddess. *Isis denudata*.'

The film fluttered to its end and the screen went dark. As the gaslight flared and colour bled back into the room, Astrid was pulled from the surface of a monochrome trance into a voluptuous interior. They were in a salon richly furnished with red velvet, fur and tiger skin and adorned with ormolu fittings, chrome and vitrolite. Crowley had told them that this place was a *maison de fantasie*. The entrance hall was fashioned as a bare stone cave. He had assured them that this house of illusion contained many rooms, all with different themes. Moorish, Hindu, Japanese, the possibilities seemed endless. From the stark pleasures of a medieval dungeon to the soft luxury of a boudoir furnished in the baroque splendour of the *ancien régime*. Here were chambers that replicated a carriage on the Orient Express or a cabin on an ocean liner, each with a mechanism that simulated the motion of travel. There was a hothouse jungle and even an igloo in the Arctic with a built in refrigerating system. The playful charm of the place was, however, undermined for Astrid by her suspicion that the establishment was a very elaborate and expensive brothel. A fear that was confirmed as a line of scarcely dressed women entered, followed by a stout and personable madame.

'*Messieurs, dames, je vous présente mes charmantes jeunes filles*,' she announced with a sweeping gesture.

'Er, *pardonnez-moi madame*,' Crowley blustered. '*Les filles, non.*'

'*Non, monsieur?*' the madame rejoined with a frown.

'*Non.*' The Beast shrugged. '*Au contraire.*'

'*Ah! C'est des garçons que vous cherchez?*'

'*Oui*,' he replied looking over at the General.

'*Pas de problème, messieurs*,' the madame assured them.

'*Et*,' the Beast went on in his faltering French, '*quelque chose exotique.*'

'*D'accord.*' The woman nodded. '*Mais, il faudra du temps.*'
Crowley screwed up his face.

'*Comment?*' he entreated.

'She says that it might take a little time,' the General explained.

'Yes, well, let's have a drink, eh?' the Beast suggested. 'Champagne.'

'*Naturelment, monsieur*,' the madame replied, hustling the girls out of the room.

The General gave a dry laugh.

'*Quelque chose exotique*, indeed,' he repeated derisively.

'Forgive me for being presumptuous. I just thought from what you said about Africa . . .'

'Do you know what was the most exotic thing I ever saw in Africa?' Macdonald demanded.

'What?'

'A white man.'

The Beast laughed.

'No, but really white,' Macdonald went on. 'Damn near albino. Scarcely more than a boy really. Such pale skin with a light down on it, like he was dusted with flour. You know the Boers, the Dutch, they're one of the whitest races on earth. Well, this one was ghostly.'

'This was in South Africa?'

'Aye. In the north of Orange River Colony. We were burning a farm. Scorching the earth, ye ken? Depriving the Boer guerrillas of bases and supply. We'd burn all the crops, slaughter all the livestock. Then set fire to the homesteads and outhouses. The womenfolk would stand there watching, saying nothing. They didn't have to, we surely felt their silent curses on our backs. Free Protestant, they were, like so many in the Highland Brigade; they even called the church "kirk" just like we did. "It's an awfu' thing," a sergeant complained to me, "to fight against such a God-fearing people." And I saw this lad standing with them, blond as blond can be. His skin so pale and delicate. He must have kept well out of the sun, though his hair looked bleached by it. Quite beautiful he was and strange like a wee sprite or cherub. It seemed an omen, a reminder that we were fighting a white man's war. Something we had most feared. And it struck me then how peculiar, how *exotique*, as you would put it, real whiteness is. We'd all gone red in the sun and I suppose, after all my years with the Sudanese who were so black they looked blue sometimes in the daylight, that pure whiteness had become quite alien to me. And the youth stood there staring at me as a dark pall hung over the veldt. At first I thought he was smarting from the smoke, then I realised he was smiling. And I felt a shiver inside. He had seen me looking and he looked right back into me. Into my soul. Like he knew me for what I really was.'

'A white man's war,' Crowley muttered.

'Aye. A terrible business.'

And so it had been. Kitchener had proved a disaster on the battlefield once more. K of K became known as K of Chaos among the field commanders. At Paaderburg he ordered yet another frontal assault on well-entrenched positions. Macdonald had led the Highland Brigade into the slaughter, taking a bullet in the foot and having his charger shot from under him.

Kitchener's real genius had been, as ever, the lethal precision with which he calculated the greater logistics of war. He had a vivid imagination for all its dreadful possibilities and never flinched at the cold horror of its totality. With methodical attrition he ordered the countryside to be laid waste, women and children herded into concentration camps. He subdivided the entire territory with a network of barbed wire and blockhouses. A civilised premonition of the worst that was to come. A dress parade for Armageddon.

'I never lasted the course,' Macdonald murmured.

'I beg your pardon?' asked the Beast.

'South Africa. Kitchener wanted me out. The brigade had been pulled out of the front by then anyway. Got posted back to India. But then Kitchener was made Commander-in-Chief there after the Boers surrendered. God, we were sick of the sight of each other by then. So I pestered Lord Roberts over his promise to give me Ceylon.'

'Your own little island.'

'Exactly.' Macdonald sighed wistfully. 'A nice quiet little command all on its own. No one breathing down my neck.'

Crowley chuckled.

'You know that Don Quixote promised Sancho Panza an island if the rough little squire would follow him on his fantastical adventures,' he remarked.

'Did he?' the General asked. 'Aye, that's me all right. The rough little squire following the mad dream.'

A young woman arrived with the champagne.

'Of course, I was in Ceylon,' said the Beast, taking hold of a sparkling flute.

'So you said,' the General replied. 'When were you there?'

'I arrived in the summer of 1901 and left for India at the beginning of 1902.'

'Well, I just missed you,' said Macdonald with a grim smile. 'I first disembarked at Colombo on 25th March 1902. Good God, that's exactly a year ago.'

'It just proves that our paths were meant to cross, Sir Hector. Whether here, or in that enchanted isle. You know, of course, that the Persians called Ceylon Serendib. There's an old tale of three princes of Serendib, who were forever encountering good fortune by happenstance. Hence the term: serendipity.'

'Well, that's as may be. I believe the enchantment of Ceylon had quite the opposite effect on me.'

'How do you mean, sir?'

'It was no accident I took command there. It was a very well-laid plan. Yet it ended in disaster.'

'The scandal.'

'Aye.'

'What happened, exactly?'

'That's what everyone is so keen to know. Myself included.'

'You mean that there is some doubt about the matter?'

'Oh yes. Some terrible stories were made up. But then, I did behave disgracefully.'

'You followed your nature.'

243

'Many would say what I did was unnatural.'

'*Vamachara*,' said the Beast.

'I beg your pardon?'

'It's a term I learned in the study of yoga. That's what I was doing in Ceylon. Learning the power of the Tantra. Astrid knows of this, don't you?'

She frowned as they turned to her.

'Of course. The ancient Hindu knowledge of the Orient.' She struggled to sound convincing, awkwardly conscious that she had never travelled further east than Danzig.

'So you'll know of the way known as *vamachara*,' the Beast went on.

'Yes.' Astrid tried to concentrate and remember the instructions she had learned from Theodor Reuss. '*Vamachara* is transgressive energy. If explored in the correct ritual conditions it can release tremendous spiritual power.'

'Sometimes known as the left-hand path. I found it in Ceylon. Maybe you did too.'

'Och, I don't think so.'

'Sir Hector, you must let go of all your shame and self-disgust.'

The Beast reached out and touched the General gently on the arm.

'Sex is a sacrament of the will,' he went on. 'One must not have a horror of love. You must set yourself free.'

'You keep saying that. But how?'

'By accepting in yourself what is condemned by others. That's what it means to be damned.'

Crowley took a sip of champagne then let out a sigh.

'Let me explain what happened to me,' he went on. 'I had journeyed to Colombo in order to visit Allan Bennett, the friend and mentor I told you about. I needed to ask him for his version of the incident when Mathers pulled a pistol on him. I still had faith back then in Mathers' authority over the Golden Dawn. When I learned the truth from Bennett I knew that I had to take control of the Order myself. It may seem absurd to travel eight thousand miles to ask one question, but there you have it. Once there I found time to seek some enlightenment.

'Allan's health had much improved in the tropics. His asthma had gone and he was no longer dependent on the vast quantity of narcotics that I remembered from our experiments in Chancery Lane. He was well on the way to achieving his much sought after asceticism.

'Bennett had initially come to Ceylon to follow the Buddhist path but was disappointed to find the practice of it on the island had fallen into a kind of decadent paganism. He had however, taken the time to learn the fundamentals of yoga from a high-caste Hindu. We left Colombo and headed for the hills to the cooler and less humid climes of Kandy. Bennett had mastered enough yogic knowledge by then to continue to instruct me. And he needed the isolation and freedom from distraction to continue his own discipline. We took a bungalow on the terraced slopes overlooking the lake where we found conditions for work very favourable. We set our minds towards control of breath and body; to attain a higher level, one that would set one free from the miserable illusion of existence. Our life was delightfully simple. Within weeks we had sustained trance states that produced a blissful stillness. We were diligent in our practice, rigorous in our exercise. I felt calm and at peace, indifferent even. I was ready to achieve *samadhi* – the very obliteration of the self. Yet something was holding me back.

'Then the Esala Perahera began and our quiet world was plunged into chaos once more. As you might know, this is a preposterous festival where homage is paid to the Buddha's tooth that is kept in the main temple at Kandy. The locals go into quite a frenzy at the annual display of this unlikely relic. I was unimpressed by the supposed sanctity of this ceremony but rather taken by the absurdity of it all. And as a spectacle it was quite gorgeous. They bring out their elephants, dancers, monks, costumed officials, drums, horns, torches. Anything that makes a blaze of light or a blare of noise.

'But it had a woeful effect on poor Allan. He is so serious and single-minded, his soul so set on achieving a higher plane. The wilful madness and sensuality of the procession left him saddened and disillusioned. But then, like the Theosophists, he looks for a purity in the east that simply does not exist. I, on the other hand, loved the garish displays and "devil-dances", the very savagery of these practices was pleasing to me.

'The scene was wild and somewhat sinister. The darkened mountains, the silent lake below, the wide canopy of space above bejewelled with gaudy stars. It was a procession of ancient passions and primitive instincts. One caught shadows moving at the edge of torchlight, the night vibrating violently with a jubilant rage. There was a marvellous sense of insanity in the air. With the roar of the mob in my ears I was released from understanding and could let my mind go. I felt a tremendous impulse to do something wicked. It was the knowledge of God, not in a beautiful sense, no, but in all his brutal ugliness. God the terrible. It was the call of *vamachara*, the left-hand path.

'The very next day I made some excuses to Allan and caught the first train back to Colombo. As you know, travelling by rail from the hill country presents a vertiginous journey of descent. And so it was. I tumbled headlong into my own degradation in that wicked town, plunging into the lower depths of its shameful and secret worlds. Stews and brothels, opium dens and gambling houses. I performed my own devil-dance. Greedy for untrammelled pleasure I would stray into the native quarter where, amid foul poverty, humanity could be purchased cheaply and defiled without reproach. I had girls and boys of every hue, some scarcely more than children, others withered hags and toothless old men. I reached a state of ecstatic delirium, experiencing delicious horrors, terrifying pleasures.

'This was all, of course, for the sake of my spiritual progress. I had realised that morality can muddle mystical understanding and virtue is only necessary in so far as it favours success. All wisdom must be encompassed in order to achieve enlightenment. Once my soul was sated by its sublime debasement I returned, travelling up-country again, back to Kandy. I told nothing of what had passed to Allan, knowing his utter terror of the flesh. But I resumed my practice with renewed zeal and a broader sense of balance. Now I was ready for the higher plane, to surrender myself fully to oblivion.

'Then one day, after eight hours of *pranayama*, in deep contemplation and reciting endless mantras, arose a true Golden Dawn in my consciousness. I suddenly became aware of a shoreless space of darkness, shot through with a crimson glow. Out of the depths of mindfulness, the inner sun arose in melancholy splendour. The hollow sphere ascended, fiery with light, into the ether of space and began to revolve and coruscate, throwing out streams of jetted fire. In rapturous sorrow, I seemed to observe this vision from a blackened hillside, dark as any dying world, covered in dank and peaty wood, a few blasted pines standing stricken, unutterably alone.'

XXXI

Astrid watched Crowley's eyes as he talked, held in a half-trance by their unfocused stare. Pale blue moonstones, vibrant and restless in the gaslight. His voice had become low and hypnotic, leading her into the vision he was describing.

'*Vamachara*,' he intoned once more.

The word resonated melodiously through her mind. She felt herself swooning gently, her body sinking into the soft velvet of the couch. She tried to concentrate, to hold on to her sense of self. The Beast smiled and turned to the General.

'We need the way of abasement just as much as that of purity. I feel sure that something similar happened to you in Ceylon,' he suggested.

'What do you mean?' asked Macdonald.

'Well, the scandal, the terrible crimes that you are supposed to be guilty of. You were merely seeking enlightenment on the left-hand path.'

The General gave a bitter laugh.

'Well, you could say that,' he said.

'Astrid here would call it sex magic.'

As the Beast glanced across at her she felt a dread insistence in his gaze.

'Wouldn't you?' he demanded.

She glared back at him, summoning all her resolve to hold his stare, to maintain the struggle of will.

'Perhaps,' she conceded.

'Och, I went to Ceylon for peace and quiet,' Macdonald interjected. 'I felt I'd earned it after all those years of war.'

'But you found something else,' said the Beast.

'Aye. I should have been more careful but I'd acquired this stubborn arrogance by the time I was posted there. I didn't even realise it myself until it was too late. I'd become the great hero and thought that made me invulnerable. But it had quite the opposite effect. You want me to tell you about Ceylon?'

'Yes, yes,' the Beast hissed.

'I was proud and overbearing when I arrived and took the place as my own wee kingdom. I was Fighting Mac now and the whole world would know it. I was a damn fool. Though for all my clumsy vanity, deep down I had a sense of foreboding about the place.'

'A premonition maybe?' Crowley suggested.

'Aye, perhaps. There was this incessant cawing of crows. You get them in all parts of the island but particularly in Colombo. I remember thinking: what are all these ugly black birds doing here in paradise? It was like a warning of something. It was supposed to be an easy posting, but that just gave me the jitters. I had grown so used to conflict, to open hostilities. I was away from the action now, and I should have been able to relax at last, but I couldn't. I thought to myself: what is there for me to do here? *Nothing*, came a wee voice in my head. *Nothing except to get yourself into trouble.* Aye, Ceylon was a perplexing island for all its beauty.'

'Indeed, the Mohammedans contend that it is the very place Adam and Eve were cast into when they were driven out of Eden,' the Beast remarked. 'That it is a fallen paradise, a garden of earthly delights.'

'Aye,' the General agreed, 'and it seems the world has long dreamt of such a place and how they might take advantage of its charms. The Portuguese were there four hundred years ago, and before them Moorish traders who sailed down from the Gulf with their African slaves. Then the Dutch, then us. A long procession of masters. I found it a quiet place all right, but it had a sense of resignation about it. A weary resentment you'd notice in the eyes that watched you. Like they'd seen it all before and were just biding their time. Waiting for you to fall apart and the next lot to turn up.'

'Yes,' the Beast rejoined. 'I have to say I found the natives quite sullen and diffident.'

'And can you blame them? Not that there was ever much unrest; no, the whole island seems to be run by a handful of white officials with not much more than walking sticks. Civil authority is given a lazy hospitality but God knows what we in the military were supposed to do. I had the command of the Royal West Kent Regiment, along with a motley collection of auxiliaries, reserves and militias, though quite what their function was beyond the ceremonial was anybody's guess.

'In all my years of military service I'd scarce had any dealings with civil colonial society, one that was officially at peace. I imagined somehow that it would be polite, easy-going. Not a bit of it. Oh aye, it was all very restrained. But it was vicious underneath. When I arrived I was met at the harbour by an official in a gig. We drove to the Grand Oriental Hotel, where I was to be staying until proper quarters had been arranged, only a stone's throw from the quayside and we could just as easily have walked, for the road was cluttered with natives. The official shouted down at the throng whenever we were held up, scarcely breaking the genteel conversation he was having with me to mutter curses, saying: "Get out, out of the way you ugly stinking son of a black-buggered bitch, off, off, you greasy Tamil whore," and so on. As the crowd parted before us, the faces that gazed up looked indifferent and docile.

'This lethargic atmosphere was infectious and a kind of torpor descended on me. For the first time in my life I felt weak. Aye, feeble. And I soon took the easy advantages that almost seemed expected. On my first night at the Grand Oriental, the young Sinhalese man assigned as my temporary valet offered himself to me for ten rupees. I used him swiftly and with none of my usual caution or regret. Exploitation suddenly seemed so simple, necessary even. And I felt a sickly urge for possession. My own little island. I had no sense then that I was being watched all the time, nor that wicked talk spreads so quickly in what seemed such a tranquil place.

'I was either in a state of exhaustion or wound up in a terrible nervous anxiety. I was playing some ridiculous role, utterly uncertain of what to do next. To those around me I might well have appeared to swagger, but I was really sleepwalking. Of course I was Fighting Mac to them, a constant reminder of all the terror and bloodshed that had been necessary for their peaceful lives of commerce and speculation. What men like me had risked allowed them their casual cruelty. I had kept their world safe for them, aye and they surely resented me for it.'

'Well, they say colonial society is suburbia at its most ghastly,' Crowley concluded.

'Aye,' said Macdonald, 'and the planters are the worst of it. At least the civil service has some notion of improving the lot of the natives. In the tea plantations all they really care about is to squeeze as much labour as they can out of their coolies. And to keep up appearances. It seems a point of honour to act as if the coloured people around them are invisible. Even on remote estates the white masters and their wives insist on dressing for dinner, while the wretched Tamils who pick their tea go about ragged in coarse cotton cumblies. The plantation owners would always be complaining about whatever new initiative colonial government had come up with. Estate managers would regularly denounce surveys, inspections, reports on sanitation, anything that might even vaguely resemble liberal reform. The coolies in the country districts look half-starved and miserable. Most are Tamil, come in gangs from mainland India, to find that they are already in debt for the expenses of transit. Their wages can rarely catch up with the liability as the tea company acts as the agent selling them rice and other necessities, at vastly inflated prices. A planter once cheerfully assured me that they like to be in debt because they think that they are not doing their best unless they owe as much as the company will allow.

And when any arguments about conditions are finally exhausted, it always comes down to the fact that they are far better off here than back in India where there is outright starvation and so the conversation ends.

'Society moves up-country during the summer, as you know, to Kandy and to the hill stations. For the cooler climate, the golf courses and mock-Tudor country clubs. Aye, and at first I felt I would breathe easier up in the highlands. I remember seeing the mist rolling down the peaks of Nuwara Eliya just like on the mountains of Wester Ross. But instead I found it suffocating. Rules I never quite got the hang of, orders far stricter than military regulations. Those of the bridge table and the tennis court. Of knowing how to manoeuvre on the floor of a ballroom. I was absolutely hopeless. What's more, I developed a keen awareness of my lack of etiquette that made me appear all the more clumsy and boorish. In a wee while I managed to make most of the colony despise me. Och, I was so brash. When I was invited to inspect the volunteers of the Ceylon Militia, which is made up of either civil officials or planters, and instead of composing myself with a quiet decorum, I bawled them out with my colour-sergeant's howl. It was a big mistake, it made me many enemies, but I couldn't resist it. They were a useless bunch not fit to wear a uniform.

'I felt happier back in Colombo. Sultry and humid it was, the air always a bit on the close side, but the social atmosphere a lot less oppressive. And aye, here I found the temptations too. Along the left-hand path, as you call it. Like those around me I secretly bargained that I would take what I could from this world. I had a bungalow in Cinnamon Gardens, not far from garrison headquarters in Slave Island. There were plenty of places in the city where one could wander and find what one wanted. Along the Galle Face promenade, down by Colpetty railway station, in the gardens of Victoria Park. Aye, and that's where I first saw him.'

The General paused and let out a long sigh.

'Go on,' the Beast urged him.

'Well, the first thing I noticed was a peculiar assortment of western dress. A tweed jacket with cricket flannels, a pair of freshly blancoed tennis shoes but no socks. A green silk shirt and a flower-patterned cravat. His head was a pleasing shape, with a crown of light brown hair scraped tight against his scalp, coiled in a knot at the back. As he turned I saw his caramel skin, smooth and gleaming and much darker than his hair. His lips were full and crimson; his eyes were dark-rimmed but seemed to sparkle with a pale fire. As I came closer I saw that each of them was a different colour: one like mottled amber, the other sapphire.

'He was Burgher, that strange mix of Dutch, Portuguese, native and whatever. To call him half-caste would woefully understimate his inheritance. He had a bewildering genealogy, a mix of countless nations: Sinhalese, Tamil, Moor, Portuguese, Malay, Dutch, who knows what else.

'He told me proudly that his full name was Joseph Vijaya Baltasar van Wolfendaal de Saram, though I soon learned that to all the other street boys he was known as Jojoboy.'

XXXII

'Jojoboy,' the General said once more and stared wearily ahead.

'He sounds utterly charming.'

'Aye. He was indeed.' Macdonald muttered bitterly. 'But he was my downfall. And I his.'

The General paused again, trying to muster his thoughts. He knew now that Crowley was right. That he had to find an order to the words in his head, give them a grammar so that he could understand what had happened. He closed his eyes.

Jojoboy had a place that they could go back to in Pettah, the bazaar district east of the harbour. It was a squalid little room with a coloured print of St Anthony tacked on the wall above the bed. When the young man shook his locks free and they flowered into a hydra of ringlets, a myriad of lights sparkled from the shock, as if each innumerable filament was distinct and diverse. A bamboo blind striped sunlight on their bodies. Macdonald felt a shuttering of the senses, beguiled by the boy lying naked beside him.

'Where are you from?' he asked him.

'Here,' replied Jojoboy.

'No, I mean, what is your nationality?'

A soft laugh rippled through the room.

'God alone knows,' came the reply. 'I am becoming an unofficial European, I hope, sir.'

For all the time that he knew him, Macdonald felt confusion and uncertainty about Jojoboy's identity. At times he seemed to change colour with a capriciousness that challenged his surroundings rather than blended in with them. At night he could seem quite pale, by day dark and shadowy. From one occasion to the next he was able to appear so strikingly different that on the second time that he went with him there was a moment when Macdonald even wondered if it was the same person. Then he saw the variegation in his motley eyes, glowing like a permanent sunset.

'I am becoming to like you, Sir Hector,' the boy told him.

Yet despite their intimacy, there always seemed a yearning distance between them in time and space. Jojoboy looked so curious, unintelligible, unknowable. So many aspects, such variety bound up in him. He would fit in almost anywhere, but belong nowhere. So full of secrets and mystery, he aroused in Macdonald a boundless longing, an unquenchable desire and a lonely sense of doom. He knew then that he would never really get home, that there was no resting place.

Jojoboy liked to imply that he belonged to the leisured classes. He mentioned countless rich Burgher relatives: a certain Fernando Gomez who owned a warehouse in Fort, the eminent Oliver de Saram who had made a fortune on the stock market. As it was, most of his extensive family seemed to be working on the railways or in the dockyards. He was not even close to any of these supposed kin, only to his mother, who lived in a shack by the Main Street in Pettah.

He was bright and inquisitive and possessed a facility for ornate language. There was a constant use of the word 'becoming' in his speech, as if he were about to exist in some way. Jojoboy explained that besides any racial interpretation, 'burgher' simply meant town dweller. And it was certain that he was of a kind that could only really come into being within a city. He was, he insisted, cosmopolitan. It was clearly his favourite word, meaning as it did to him a universe of promise and possibility. And he loved all things urban: the theatres, bars, gambling houses, billiard halls, and indeed the Ceylon National Museum Library, for which he had somehow managed to obtain a reading pass. He had a fervent appetite for knowledge of all sorts. He candidly admitted that the library was also a convenient place to pick up men, but then he so often saw these encounters as part of his education. Having no formal schooling this contact with older gentlemen formed his strange and obscure learning, a wayward tutelage which tended towards the fantastical.

Jojoboy had recently developed an obsession with Taprobane, the ancient Greek name for Ceylon. A professor of classics who had come across him on a visit to Colombo had informed the lad that Onesicritus, a companion of Alexander the Great on his campaigns in north-western India, gave the first recorded account of the island. The Roman cartographer Pomponius Mela declared that Taprobane might not be merely an island but the commencement of another world. Beyond the boundaries of what was known, outside the cycles of history, it was imagined as a place where new beginnings could be made, without fear of repeating the errors of the past. Later Jojoboy learned, from a Jesuit priest he had importuned outside the Galle Face Hotel, of the heretic Tomasso Campanella who had used Taprobane as the location of his utopian 'City of the Sun'. All these mythological rumours appealed to him far more than actual history. He loved the gossip of antiquity. It gave him a brighter hope than any present reality.

He was a fabulous creature but one who preferred a western notion of exoticism. He would have much preferred the world around him to have remained undiscovered, or to have been some lost envoy of ancient imperialism. With Macdonald he liked to imagine that he was the catamite of some great proconsul, and that being so close to this power would set him above the rest. The General misheard him once, thinking that he was talking of other Burghers, then realising that Jojoboy referred to all other coloured inhabitants of the island as 'black buggers', with no sense of irony.

His declared status as 'unofficial European' reflected how those who could pass as white often thought of themselves.

Jojoboy's colour would never allow for this, but even down to the lowest castes, everybody in Ceylon suffered from some form of snobbishness. He belonged, however tenuously, to a peculiar set that could for the time being ride on the coat tails of the British. Living between worlds, in a dream that would one day disappear.

Macdonald was fooled by Jojoboy's forced arrogance and sense of sophistication. He didn't imagine that the boy might really want to be loved by him until it was too late. The loss of Bakhit had left him bitter, cynical even. Intoxicated by his desire for Jojoboy, he began to eye him with a lazy greed, as one of the earned pleasures of his former glory. Any tender feelings he might have had turned to a lustful possessiveness.

Consumed by his own weariness, he did not see how sad Jojoboy was. Macdonald fancied that all the dreams and aspirations the boy spoke of were merely part of a playful imagination. He soon realised the depths of the young man's fear of disappointment. One night all the terror about the future was confessed.

'I am becoming scared, Sir Hector,' Jojoboy told him.

'I found to my horror that in his mind I had become his hope. Me! He didn't see how utterly hopeless I was,' the General explained. 'I tried to reason with him that I was not rich, that I had no independent means. That all I had was my precarious status as Commander-in-Chief with all the eyes of the colony upon me. And I was terrified that he might make some sort of scene.'

'Circumstances were against you,' offered the Beast in a consoling tone.

'Yes, but what were mine compared with his? I didn't understand how trapped he felt. I took his desperation for something else. I should have helped him. Found some way for his hope of becoming.'

'Becoming?' asked Crowley.

Macdonald shook his head and continued.

'He had just turned twenty-two, a precarious age when all the hope of youth can easily curdle into bitterness. His genius did not allow him any reasonable prospects. You couldn't imagine him settling into a trade, or being content, as his cousins would be, with the routine of a dock clerk or a ticket collector, but he was getting too old for the street. He had acquired a taste for whisky and coconut arrack, and spent much of his money on the horses at Havelock racecourse. His conduct became more and more prodigal. His recklessness gave him an illusion of freedom but things were becoming increasingly dangerous for me.

'It became harder to find places to go or situations we could meet where I would not be recognised. He suggested that I should set him and his mother up in a nice bungalow in Mount Lavinia. I told him that this would be impossible, much as I would love to do so. I wanted him more than I could bear, but I could not keep him. I knew that.'

'He would get drunk and curse me, ask for large amounts of money, far beyond what I regularly paid him. He said it was to settle gambling debts, which was probably true, but soon his insistent demands had all the markings of blackmail. He constantly spoke of his desperation. Already there was a buzz of rumour about me and I knew that secrets got around among the Burghers faster than anywhere else in Ceylon, existing as they do between the whites and the natives. They are, of course, the perfect species for the spreading of gossip.

'So I avoided Jojoboy. I threw myself into work. Organising field exercises and a tour of inspection of the island's complex and quite unnecessary defences. I was about to depart for the Jaffna peninsula when a note appeared on my desk. He had somehow managed to get a letter to me. I remember the delicate copperplate handwriting, and every word he put down. *Dear Sir Hector*, he wrote, *may it please your honour to know that the undersigned is in the direst of conditions & humbly begs of*

*your honour one appointment before the desperate measures
might be taken to remedy his awful circumstance. I am becoming
on Galle Face Green tonight at seven thirty. I remain truly yours,*
and he signed with all the preposterousness of his full name. So
this was it, I concluded. The ransom note. I tore the ghastly
thing up and went to get my train.

'I bided my time up in the north, finding all kinds of excuses
to delay my return. On my way back I visited Anuradhapura,
the ruins of an ancient city in the jungle, which had once been
vast and populous, but is now desolate and choked with vines.
Overgrown shrines, scores of columns, statues, domed dagobas,
fragments of palaces, labyrinths hidden in a thick tangle. It
made me imagine London as a wilderness with St Paul's Cathedral
and the Albert Memorial merely confused heaps of grassy stone.
I felt as if I had been asleep for centuries and had returned to
witness our long dead empire.

'I eventually arrived in Colombo two weeks later fully expecting
some terrible consequence of the letter. But I heard nothing. In
the end I was driven quite out of my wits waiting for it. I went
to have tea at the Galle Face Hotel and, as discreetly as I could,
called over one of the waiters who I knew to be acquainted with
Jojoboy. There was a terror in his eyes that I could not fathom
and when I whispered the name he gasped and his tray clattered
to the floor. So I left as quickly as I could, feeling the genteel
eyes of the dining room following me, greedy with curiosity.

'Outside the hotel another waiter caught up with me, one
with enough composure to tell me the story. Jojoboy was dead.
He had been pulled out of the harbour the very morning after
I had left Colombo for the north. There had been an inquest
that heard that he had got very drunk that night and had
wandered down to the quayside. It seemed clear that in that
state he had fallen in by simple misadventure and had been
unable to save himself. But I knew better. I knew now that the
letter had not been blackmail. No, it was a suicide note.

'I went quite mad with grief and remorse. Measures that I

could have taken to save him were so simple, yet everything made them impossible. I was a coward. I knew it was not I alone that had killed him, that so much history and geography had pushed him over the edge that night. But I felt it all bear down upon me, the weight of it. It constituted my decline and fall. I was careless and inattentive of the full schedule of duties I had so recently prepared for myself. My negligence as to matters of dress and uniform was observed, I became slovenly in my habits, things quite out of character for me. And I started to drink. That cheap and disgusting coconut arrack that both reminded me of him and brought oblivion from his painful memory. Years of self-discipline fell away. God, how I dearly wished for some perilous action to engage in. But there was no dread battle to take me away from this, no real conflict. I had no one to fight but myself. There were mornings when I would wake, not sure of what had transpired the evening before. I was reckless for his sake. In death his wild spirit had taken me over.

'After many vague and unofficial complaints I was summoned by Ridgeway the Governor of the Colony, to the Queen's House in Colombo. I was fully expecting a dressing-down regarding my general conduct, but what transpired, well, it was horrifying. Several charges of sodomy were laid before me. All the idle talk of the island about me now piled itself up into a long list of ignominy.

'Some of it was true, of course, or at least bore a relation to the truth. The valet at the Grand Oriental had talked or had been made to talk. There was an accusation that I had misbehaved with a young sentry, one of the Volunteers it was said. Well, I couldn't remember that one, but if it had been night duty it might well have happened. The story that I had taken advantage of a young Boer prisoner – that was plainly ridiculous. The charges concerning misconduct with various Burgher youths, yes, but they could all have been Jojoboy at different times. But then the allegations became quite ugly, disgusting in fact. That I had interfered with a bugler in the Boys' Brigade, and with several boys at St Edward's School, sons of English gentlemen. I had no idea where all that might have come from except that all the sick imaginings of the colony had swirled around and settled upon me. They knew me for what I was and decided to condemn me in the foulest way they could think of.

'I refused to dignify these accusations with a response at first but Ridgeway had a simple solution to the dilemma. He suggested that I took leave and went back to London to arrange for another appointment. Foolishly I agreed. Now I realise what danger I was putting myself in by deserting my post in this way. But I had had quite enough of Ceylon. The place could only mean sadness for me now. I was so exhausted by it all, it almost came as a relief that I would be going back to England. There happened to be a liner docked in Colombo harbour on its way back to London. So I embarked quietly, with no fuss, with a vain confidence that this whole affair could be dealt with through careful consideration.

'But on my passage back a flurry of communication sealed my fate. Letters from the Governor to the War Office, questions in the Legislative Assembly, Reuters telegrams reporting my absence. I know now that by the time I arrived in London I was doomed. And that if I return to Ceylon I will be denounced there, but I cannot remain in the army unless I go back and clear my name. A court martial is being prepared for me, with Kitchener presiding. What on earth am I supposed to do?'

XXXIII

'THE SOLUTION IS OBVIOUS. You must not go back to Ceylon to face this court martial.'

'But if I do not I cannot remain in the army.'

'Is that such a bad thing?' asked the Beast.

Macdonald's eyes widened, his jaw dropped slightly. He stared open-mouthed for a moment.

Crowley laughed.

'You really cannot imagine a life outside the service, can you?' he asked.

'I, I,' the General stammered. 'I simply would not exist, man.'

'You would simply become somebody else. Yourself perhaps.'

'You think that I could just discharge myself? Dishonourably?'

'Why not? I know how seriously you take the word of honour, but you have been treated abominably.'

'I have behaved abominably.'

'No. You have been falsely accused.'

'Of some things, yes.'

'Then the whole case against you is flawed.'

'No,' said the General. 'It is all the same to them. The vile crimes against children they accuse me of, they consider them the same as the other matters. For them nothing is permitted, so everything is true.'

'Hmm.' The Beast nodded thoughtfully. 'If only it could be the other way around.'

'And what if I don't proceed to Ceylon? I can hardly go back to England.'

'Do you want to?'

'I beg your pardon?'

'I mean, is there anything back there for you?'

Macdonald thought about Christina and his son. He could tell Crowley everything but not this. He had always wanted to keep them from any awfulness that might befall him. And now it struck him that it was only this matter in his life that gave him any real sense of shame. His own perverse nature, well, that was an embarrassment perhaps. Why shouldn't it be? It was a delicate business after all. But no, he suddenly realised that he no longer felt that terrible fear any more. That's what this peculiar night with this extraordinary man had taught him. But Christina, that was shameful. How he had treated her that afternoon, how she had had to live all these years. The son he had never known. The guilt he had felt about it, that was at the heart of his life. But no, he wouldn't tell Crowley about that. He shook his head.

'Then you can go where you like,' the Beast reasoned.

'But—'

'And you can reject the double standards of polite society. Stop trying to be good. The so-called forces of good are those that have constantly oppressed me. I have seen them daily destroying the happiness of my fellow men. It is for that reason that I have made it my business to get into personal communication with the Devil. Accept your new-found status as one of the damned; it can set you free.'

'Where could I go?'

'Anywhere. You have spent most of your life abroad, for the most part it seems under canvas. It strikes me that you could survive almost anywhere. This whole matter will soon blow over. The establishment doesn't want a scandal. You know that they would much rather you were simply out of the way.'

'You're forgetting something.'

'What?'

The General gave an awkward cough.

'I have no means, sir,' he said. 'I've scarcely sixpence to my name beyond my army pay.'

'I'm a wealthy man. I'm in a position to offer you assistance.'

'I couldn't allow that.'

'Please.' The Beast smiled. 'Indulge me. I wouldn't be much of a magician if I couldn't make a man disappear now, would I?'

'No, really. I would not be able to accept.'

'It would merely be a loan, Sir Hector. I know that in good time you would be able to repay me anything I advanced you.'

'I don't know.'

'At least say you'll think about it. We'll meet for lunch again tomorrow. At the Regina. We can discuss it all then.'

The madame reappeared, leading a young man into the salon. Astrid sat up in her chair. She had drifted off to the drone of the two men telling their endless stories. Now she was suddenly alert to the lithe figure that had entered the room. He wore a striped *djellaba* with the hood down. He looked North African, Berber perhaps. Bright eyes danced beneath beetle brows and a mop of thick black hair. All at once the General wheeled all his attention to this new situation on his flank.

'*Je vous présente Abdul,*' the madame announced.

'How charming,' declared the Beast.

'*Salaam Alaikum,*' Macdonald murmured hoarsely at the youth.

'*Alaikum As'Salaam,*' the youth replied with a coy smile that revealed a set of well-shaped if slightly discoloured teeth.

The General rose and held out his hands and Abdul took hold of them with a short giggle, steadying the older man as he stood up. Macdonald stared into the deep brown eyes that beheld him with such indulgent amusement. In that moment they appeared so wide, immense and benign that they could comprehend his whole life, know and understand, and, yes, feel everything about him. They couldn't of course, but it didn't matter. The illusion of it was like a blessing. The General found himself muttering some more words in Arabic, thinking of the freedom that Crowley had spoken of. Only a few hours earlier it would have seemed ridiculous. Now escape from his awful fate seemed so easy. Absurd, but quite within the realms of possibility.

'I can see that you are already preparing for your many happy years in exile,' Crowley interjected.

'What?' Macdonald replied absently, already making his exit with the young man.

'Tomorrow, Sir Hector. Lunch at the Regina. I'll see you there.'

'Yes, yes.'

They walked out holding hands. The General let out a colossal yawn, his jaw stretching wide in an easeful howl. With the hope of repose at hand, the Great March into the night was nearly done.

The madame watched them depart, then turned to Astrid and Crowley with a wistful pout.

'Et pour vous, messieurs, dames?' she asked them both.

'A room,' the Beast requested hastily.

'What?' said Astrid.

She turned to him with an indignant frown. Crowley nonchalantly reached into his pocket and took out the box of *dragées*. He offered her one. She refused.

'*Une chambre?*' The madame gave a nod, a shrug. '*Seulement?*'

'*Une chambre spéciale,*' he said, picking out for himself one of the sugar almonds he had doctored earlier. He popped it in his mouth. It was time for a little astral flight of his own, he reasoned.

'*Ah! Oui.*'

'Now wait one moment,' Astrid interrupted.

'*Le temple secret,*' Crowley continued, pocketing the box of sweets.

'*Bien sûr, monsieur.*' The madame flashed a smile.

Astrid made a move to stand up. Crowley took hold of her arm.

'Wait,' he said, leaning across to look straight into her eyes. 'They have a special chamber here, fitted out for ceremonial magic. I've used it before for occult rituals. It has the exact proportions of the temple of Solomon.' He sucked at the sweet. 'Or something like that. Whatever, it is well appointed enough for our purposes.'

'Let go of me,' Astrid insisted.

The Beast held her arm firmly and she found that she could not break free of his wilful purblind stare. His countenance suddenly seemed bullish and reddened in the lamplight. His nostrils flared, the contused lower lip purpled and swollen. His eyes flashed wide as he spoke.

'That is,' he went on, rolling the *dragée* around his molars, 'if you really are what you claim to be.'

The madame cackled softly in the background. Astrid felt her stomach sink with unease and uncertainty. For a second she forgot who she was.

'What do you mean?' she asked cautiously.

'If you really are Dominatibur Astris, or at least her incarnation. Well' – he reached out with his free hand and patted the bound volume at his side – 'we have the sacred Cypher Manuscript. We can make contact with the Secret Chiefs.'

'What?'

'They will make themselves known to us through you. We can initiate a new Order of the Golden Dawn, with me as its Hierophant and you its High Priestess.'

All at once her fear exploded into loud laughter that broke the charm that had transfixed her. Her head reeled and she felt the sense of power surge through her once more. Yes, yes, she knew who she was. It came to her in a reverberation of ancient memory. Endless rebirth had brought her to this moment. Now she really could be Dominatibur Astris, the High Priestess. But only acting it out would make it come into being. The madame began to chuckle once more. Crowley crunched on the almond, threw his monstrous head back and let out a peal of laughter.

All three of them made for a dimly lit corridor, the procuress leading.

'Come,' the Beast called out in a sonorous voice. 'Let us inaugurate the new age!'

XXXIV

'I AM THE GOLDEN CHILD!' CROWLEY announced, pulling off his clothes. 'You are the Scarlet Woman!'

Candles blazed from all sides of the heptagonal vault in a labyrinth of flame. The All-Seeing Eye looked down on them from a niche between two pillars. Naked, the Beast moved into the centre of the chamber, where the stone floor was inlaid with a broad circle inscribed with Hebraic characters.

'What are you doing?' Astrid demanded.

'Come.' He beckoned to her. 'You are Isis, I am Osiris.'

There was a jolt within him: the first onslaught of the drug. Ah! The Chemical Wedding, he mused. The exuberance of life, the experience of death, all the sudden mysteries of creation would be revealed. He felt a sense of coming triumph. In his success with Macdonald, a whole empire of repression had been toppled. The world was his. Morality – it was just another set of codes to be deciphered. Now he would annihilate himself and God. He would shatter the limits of consciousness and reach the boundless continuity of the infinite.

'As above, so below.' The Beast uttered the hermetic oath of the Gnostics, stretching out both arms in the gesture of Baphomet.

As Astrid looked on, a thrill of terror ran through her. Despite his considerable girth, Crowley moved with fluid ease. In its rude state his frame acquired a brutal gravity. He carried his fat well, the weight of it adding to the unveiled potency. He turned his head towards her, his countenance morose and saturnine. Fearful as she was, Astrid affected a haughty and malevolent posture as she stood before him. Hers was the power of the Goddess, she told herself. Belief in it gave her a curious yearning.

'Come,' he whispered.

Astrid went closer. He lowered his face to her, his muzzle widening in a lupine grimace, as if catching her scent. The air buzzed with animal energy. In an instant he grabbed at her, a clawed hand snatching at her arm, trying to pull her into the circle.

She slapped him hard across the jaw and he let go, dropping down on one knee from the force of the blow. He let out a delighted whimper and gawped up at her.

'Yes,' he hissed. He brushed at his lips absently then looked at his fingers with a smile. 'Blood,' he declared, holding up his hand to show the evidence.

She was about to strike him again when she saw the curious shape on his chest. At first she fancied that it was a scar or a blemish, a tattoo even. But as she stooped lower it revealed itself as a whorl of black hairs that formed an intersecting mark. Four radials spiralled in on an axis. As she touched the tufted sigil she felt the beat of the heart below.

'A *haukenkreuz*,' she observed.

'Yes,' he replied. 'A *fylfot* or in the French a *croix gammée*. My birthmark is one of the most ancient symbols of power and good fortune. And an urgent signal from our remote ancestors. To the Greeks it is the gammadion or tetraskelion, found in abundance at the recent excavations of Troy. Its angles form a magic square, marking out sections of sacred geometry and it is, of course, a Nordic rune, thought to be a sun-wheel or the fire-whisk that whirls the cosmos into being.'

'Hmm,' Astrid purred, tracing the figure with her fingertips. The thing seemed alive, to move of its own accord, pulsing like an aperture.

'Sacred to the Buddhists, too,' the Beast went on. 'I saw it everywhere in Ceylon. In a ruined temple in the jungle with stone steps that cut into the forest, where black bulbous insects droned loud like the chant of long-dead monks; there at the top of the shrine, amid the lizards and monkeys, I saw this sign still victorious.'

'Yes,' she breathed, pushing him down on to the stone floor.

'To the Navajo tribe, who weave it into their blankets, it is the whirlwind; to the Indians of Panama, the tentacles of a great octopus that dragged the world into existence. For some it is the rotation of the heavens around the pole star; for others the tail of a comet bent by the gravitational pull of its orbit.'

Astrid pulled up her dress. Muscular legs bestrode him, taut and gleaming in the candlelight.

'It is most holy to the Hindus. And to the Jain *sadhus*.' He reached out and held the hand that touched his birthmark. The stigmata seemed to charge up with energy.

'In Sanskrit . . .' he whispered.

'Yes?' she gasped, a crackle of electricity at her fingertips.

'In Sanskrit, this sign is known as the *swastika*.'

She felt a surge of power, a sudden impulse of desire as she straddled him. Crowley put up his hand and at once the current was broken.

'What's the matter?' she groaned.

'I, I,' the Beast stuttered. 'I have to summon my Kundalini force.'

Astrid sighed impatiently. Crowley looked down. Although his mind was alive with passion, his body was not responding with the same enthusiasm. It was an occasional side effect of this drug, he remembered.

'I have an incantation that might help,' he suggested. 'I composed it myself.'

He took a deep breath and began to intone in a low and solemn voice:

> Rise, O my snake! It is now the hour
> Of the hooded and holy ineffable flower.
> Rise, O my snake, into brilliance of bloom
> On the corpse of Osiris afloat in the tomb!

But the snake did not rise. He started to make another pronouncement. Astrid quickly clamped her hand over his bloodied mouth to muffle it into an unintelligible moan. Deftly she flipped him on to his belly and he writhed beneath her, provoking her pitiless instincts. She reached out to the edge of the chamber and roughly pulled a thick candle from its sconce. As hot liquid wax splashed against the back of his legs the Beast let out a squeal of rapture and anticipation.

XXXV

MACDONALD AWOKE THINKING THAT HE was back in Cairo. Canopied by a brocade tapestry fringed with gold, he lay in a delicately carved wooden bed draped with a ruffled damask coverlet. Wrought-iron grilles on arched windows caged the dim light of dawn. He could just make out an ornate brass lantern hanging from the ceiling, tilework on polished plaster, a heavy Persian rug on the parquet floor. He turned to find the sleeping head of an Arab boy lolling on a velvet cushion. Then he remembered. Abdul. Of course. They had been put in the Moorish Room.

He reached out to touch the lad, gently stroking the delicate fuzz of hair at the nape of his neck. Abdul whimpered. Macdonald leaned over to take another look at him. At first glance the boy looked serene and at peace, but then the fringed eyelids bulged and fluttered; the mouth quivered and the jaw milled, giving out an occasional ratchet rasp of grinding teeth. God alone knew what disturbing dream possessed the slumbering youth. Macdonald slipped out of the bed, careful not to wake him.

He thought of the lads he had loved and lost: of Bakhit wandering away into the desert; Jojoboy with his desperate dreams of becoming; all of the brave boys he'd commanded, the wounded and the fallen. And he remembered Kenny Goss, the handsome, black-haired corporal from Lochaber, his other half all those years ago. Through decades of cruel and relentless guilt, love's loss had been empire's gain. But he could be true to that love now. He could fight for himself.

He dressed and negotiated his way through a maze of bizarre interiors. There was no sign of the indomitable madame, just a thickset doorman who beckoned him through to the cave-like entrance. Macdonald slipped him a five-franc note and the man winked as he held the door open to the street.

The sky was a wash of Prussian blue. The morning star burned heavily on the horizon, catching the oncoming light off the edge of the world. Lucifer, the bright one, he mused with a grin. Master of rebels and fugitives, patron saint of the damned. He caught a breath of air, cool and sharp, and let out a long redemptive sigh. At last he had found a moment of solace. There was hope yet. With calm lucidity he mustered his thoughts once more to measure his predicament.

Dawn is always the best time for any plan of attack, he reasoned. When the mind is at its clearest, the senses keenly whetted in a primal awareness. He would steal the march on the day, he decided, and began to walk with a new urgency. The whole empire would be buzzing with telegrams and communiqués. A fearsome net converging, closing him down. But there was still time. Now he had a new strategy, one he had rarely ever countenanced on the field. That of retreat, of flight.

As the first blush of sunrise caught the skyline he found that he was in Montmartre, up on the hill the city stretched out below him. He had the high ground over Paris. Helter-skelter down he went, on winding cobbled lanes and tiered stone staircases. He passed by a little park, branches dropping with blossom that reached over him through the high railings, their scent sweet and consoling.

Clear-headed and ready for action, there was exhilaration in his movement. A fleetness of thought in step with his vigorous, infantry pace. So much to organise in the coming days. If things were left inconclusive he would be able to escape it all. He would take Crowley's absurd offer, whatever that might mean. Stuart-Wortley could help him cover his tracks, if need be. Everything would be all right just as long as the scandal did not break. Ridgeway had promised a press silence if he did not return to Ceylon. And as for Roberts and Kitchener, he could damn their court martial. He could damn them all, now that he was one of the damned.

For a minute he dawdled as he thought of Christina and wee Hector. He would have to try to make some sort of provision for them. He tried not to dwell on this too much, it would slow him down when he needed to be swift. He humoured himself with the fact that his son had nearly come of age and would soon be able to look after his mother, but the worry of it dogged him as he picked up his stride once more.

He reached a small square with a wagon parked by a café on the corner. A short man in an apron was rolling a barrel towards the open hatch of the cellar. As Macdonald passed the man looked up briefly and caught his eye. His face was creased and weatherbeaten, the small stub of a cigarette clamped between pale and cracked lips.

'*Bonjour*,' Macdonald greeted him.

The man looked up at the gilded firmament, his wrinkled face stretching into a reckoning smile.

'*Ça va faire du soleil, n'est-ce pas?*' he remarked.

Yes, thought Macdonald as he strolled on. *Yes!* It was going to be a beautiful spring day. What a blessing. From now on he would be determined to have faith in his own good fortune. The sun was coming up over Paris. He looked out across the city. Crowley was right, he could live almost anywhere. He was at home in the world, after all. It would be a new adventure. He just needed a little luck. He patted the top pocket of his jacket, where he liked to keep Bakhit's charm.

By the time he reached rue de Rivoli he could feel the warmth of first light on his face. The concierge nodded to him as he entered the Hotel Regina. There would be time to bathe before breakfast. Then he would set to work. A note to Eddie at the Embassy. A telegram to Ridgeway, assuring him that he would not be returning to Ceylon. Crowley would be coming for lunch and together they would formulate some bold and mysterious stratagem. Then he would disappear. Become a new person. He was almost looking forward to it.

On the Louis Quatorze side table in the vestibule the foreign newspapers had just been laid out. He picked up a European edition of the *New York Herald* and made his way towards the staircase. He folded out the front page and looked down at a crude pen and ink sketch of a face. He froze.

It was himself.

A cruel and ugly drawing, a near caricature, obviously roughed out in some haste. Cross-hatching disfigured the left cheek, making him look scarred and battered. He had been given a walrus moustache, as huge and ridiculous as Kitchener's. But this gruesome defacement was undeniably meant as his likeness.

Oh, God.

He read the headline:

GRAVE CHARGE LIES ON SIR H. MACDONALD

Oh no, not this now.

Not Amenable to Law in Ceylon. He
Sails for England to Meet the Charge.

Please . . .

COLOMBO. Tuesday. – Charges of a grave character, involving the moral conduct of the gallant and popular general, Sir Hector Macdonald, commander of the Troops in Ceylon, have been made public here.

The offences alleged were not amenable to the law in Ceylon, but were such that the Governor had no choice but to summon Sir Hector Macdonald from Kandy to Colombo to answer the charge.

As a result of the conference with the Governor, Sir Hector decided to go to England to consult his friends and his Superiors at the War Office as to the course he should pursue.

In the Legislative Council to-day the Governor announced that Sir Hector MacDonald had decided to return to Ceylon to face a court martial.

War Office Unaware
He Had Left

(BY THE HERALD'S SPECIAL WIRE)

LONDON. Wednesday. The authorities at the War Office, says the 'Daily Express' were in utter ignorance of the reasons for Sir Hector Macdonald's departure from Ceylon until some days after he had sailed on the Ophir. They cabled to Colombo for details, and these were supplied without delay.

The purport of the charges cannot be entered into here, but it may be stated that while they do not constitute an offence under the laws of Ceylon, they are criminally punishable at home.

He staggered up the stairs to his room, closed the door and dropped the newspaper on to the bed. He knew what he had to do and that he would have to be quick about it. He gazed at himself in the mirror but could not remove the image of the badly drawn picture from his mind. There was no other way out now. Wherever he went he would be marked by the utter disgrace of it. He would be hunted down. They would never let him rest or be at peace.

He reached to his top pocket but Bakhit's charm was gone. He must have lost it in the night somewhere. All his luck had run out. His arms dropped and he quickly shoved his hands into his side pockets, pulling out the pornographic postcards he had stuffed there the previous day. And yes, there underneath them was the little pistol. Mathers' revolver. He took it out and held it before his eyes. A delicate little toy. Mother-of-pearl handle, small calibre, just the job. Much better than his service revolver. That heavy and cumbersome weapon would probably take the top of his head off. No, this was just the thing. It fitted snugly into the palm of his hand.

No time for a note. No need, thank God. Everybody would understand. It would be a great relief all round. *I would have had a better life had I been your widow*, Christina had told him. Well, now he would do the decent thing.

But as he lifted the gun his hand began to shake. He felt an awful terror that he might mess this up. The pistol was flailing around so much that he was worried that it might go off prematurely. *Steady*, he told himself. Just one last command. He had given the order to others so many times in his life. To hold one's fire until in correct range.

He cocked the revolver, lifted it up and rested it against his right temple. No, he thought, it might slip. Behind the ear. Yes. Easy does it.

Now. Just a little pressure on the trigger . . .

Part Five
RECESSIONAL

26th March 1903

To the Editor, *New York Herald*
Sir,
It was with feelings of intense disgust that I read the headings
in your issue of today which announced the tragic end of that
most gallant soldier, Sir Hector Macdonald. The publication
which you gave in your issue of yesterday, and the manner of
wording it, was sufficient to cause dismay to any man, whether
guilty or not of the crimes of which he was accused; but,
unfortunately, all public men and their lives are public property
nowadays as regards certain sections of the press. It might,
however, have been hoped that the comrades and friends of him
who is dead would have been spared the additional pain that
you inflict upon them by headings of such a sensational nature,
which are in the worst possible taste. The loss to the British
Army of one of the most distinguished officers, under
circumstances that were most distressing, is sufficiently great;
but you have considerably added to the pain of it by your manner
of announcing it.

Believe me, your obedient servant,

E.J. Stuart-Wortley, Lieut.-Colonel. Military Attaché.

Eddie called for a footman to post the letter and left the study
of his house in rue de la Faisanderie and went downstairs to
the drawing room. It was early evening and the past two days
had been harrowing. He had been called to the Hotel Regina
the previous afternoon to identify Mac's body. The newspaper
carrying news of the scandal lay open on the bed. Apparently

the poor man had stood before the looking-glass and shot himself through the head.

An officer from the Sûreté had questioned the hotel staff, made a cursory examination of the scene, and listed his meagre belongings, apart from a well-worn steamer trunk, as 'no jewellery and very little money'. A British surgeon, summoned by the Consul-General, had certified the death as suicide. The War Office in London had been informed; Macdonald's only known close relative, a brother in Scotland, had been notified.

It had been agreed that the Major-General might be buried in Paris without too much fuss and the next day Stuart-Wortley had set about making the grim arrangements. He contacted Messrs Sewell & Maugham, the English solicitors in rue de Faubourg St-Honoré, to arrange carriages, wreaths and a copy of the death certificate for the cemetery director at Père Lachaise. The funeral would be tomorrow, Friday.

Eddie went to the sideboard and poured himself a large brandy. Violet, his wife, looked up at him from the sofa.

'Are you done with all this ghastly business for tonight?' she asked him.

'Yes,' he replied, taking a long sip from the glass.

'What on earth happened?'

Eddie let out a sigh.

'It's altogether too sad for words,' he said.

'But they say that there was some dreadful scandal.'

'Please darling.'

'That he was, you know . . .'

'I'd really rather not talk about it.'

'It's everywhere now. I mean, they say that even K—'

'Violet!' He cut her short. 'You mustn't say such things. You shouldn't even think them.'

But he knew that it was foolish to be shocked at what she might know. As he caught her eye and saw the mischievous intelligence in it he remembered. Of course she knew. She was far too sophisticated not to. He had married into modernity. Her stepfather a liberal, her sister Agnes a wretched suffragette. The world was turning fast, spilling out its awful secrets. No one was safe from them.

'I saw Kitchener the night we met,' she went on. 'Do you remember? General Stephenson's ball in Cairo. He was pointed out to me. Frightful gorgon of a man. He didn't stay long in the ballroom, though. You, on the other hand, you looked so dashing in your Rifleman's uniform.'

She smiled at him and he couldn't help grinning back. He was bloody lucky to have her, he thought, musing again on the awful loneliness Mac must have felt at the end.

He hadn't told anybody about the night at Le Chat Blanc. He did not want to add to all the gossip and speculation. There were already wild rumours circulating about the circumstances of Macdonald's death. There was a knock on the door. The footman entered with a missive on a silver tray. It was a telegram forwarded from the War Office in London. He scanned it quickly:

HIGHLANDS MOST ANXIOUS SIR HECTOR MACDONALD SHOULD BE BURIED IN SCOTLAND. POSTPONE FUNERAL ARRANGEMENTS TILL MY ARRIVAL IN PARIS. MACDONALD HIS BROTHER.

The thought dawned that there was a kind of mania growing around this tragedy. He had hoped that they could have buried Macdonald quietly. But they would not leave him in peace. Not even in death.

'Darling, I'm afraid you'll have to dine on your own tonight. I've got to go back to the Embassy.'

'Oh how tiresome. When will you be back?'

'I don't know,' he replied. 'But I've got a feeling it's going to be a long night.'

He was right. It was gone midnight when the duty officer came through to his office with another message from London.

'New instructions from the WO, sir,' the man told him.

'Macdonald's heir is to claim the body and effects and take them for burial in Scotland.'

'Oh, Christ,' Eddie muttered. 'But wait a minute; heir you say? His brother might be his next of kin but he's hardly his heir.'

'Oh, it's not his brother, sir. It's his son.'

In his office two days later, Stuart-Wortley could not help staring at the young Hector as the family's solicitor, Peter Morison SSC, went through the new arrangements. His son. He had never known or imagined that Mac had a son. Not even the War Office was aware of his wife and child. Until now. Master Macdonald did not look much like the father. A slight and awkward young man nervously hunched over himself. Something about the eyes that was familiar, though. They had the same hunted look. He had inherited that from Mac, the poor lad.

'I've already been in communication with the brother,' Eddie explained. 'I understood from him—'

'I'm advised to inform you to ignore any such communications henceforth,' Morison insisted. 'I'm acting on behalf of the widow. Lady Macdonald.'

'Acting separately?' Eddie asked.

'If needs be, sir, yes.'

Stuart-Wortley nodded gloomily. He dreaded having to deal with a family row over the corpse along with everything else. Another War Office telegram came to his desk as they were talking. He glanced down at it:

GENERAL MACDONALD'S SON AND MR MORISON MUST BE MADE TO THOUROUGHLY UNDERSTAND THAT IN TAKING POSSESSION OF THE BODY THEY ARE ENTIRELY RESPONSIBLE FOR ALL FURTHER ARRANGEMENTS AND EXPENSES CONNECTED WITH ITS REMOVAL AND INTERMENT.

Stuart-Wortley tore the telegram to shreds, disturbing the sombre ambience of the room with his barely concealed anger.

'I'm sorry,' he said, tossing the fragments of the telegram into a waste-paper basket. 'I'm truly sorry. I knew him, you know. In the Sudan. I knew him in Afghanistan when he was a colour-sergeant in the 92nd.'

Eddie felt his eyes prick with tears, but a quiet fury held them back. Mac had been so ill-treated. The army had turned its back on him after all his years of service.

'Gentlemen,' he declared mutinously. 'I am at liberty to make any arrangements as to a military funeral. A gun carriage, for example.'

'No!' yelped young Hector.

'Please,' Morison added. 'It is the family's wishes that the interment be a quiet and private affair.'

Eddie sighed and nodded.

'Then so be it,' he said.

They went through all the necessary details together then Stuart-Wortley fired off a final message to his superiors:

BODY LEAVES PARIS TONIGHT VIA DIEPPE NEWHAVEN DUE LONDON BRIDGE 7.20 SUNDAY MORNING. ARRANGEMENTS HAVE BEEN COMPLETED FOR TRANSPORT TO KING'S CROSS. FROM KING'S CROSS MORISON WILL MAKE ALL ARRANGEMENTS FOR TRANSPORT TO EDINBURGH. MILITARY ATTACHE.

Now it was all done. He could find time for his own grief. He showed the solicitor and Mac's son out to the lobby of the Embassy. He shook their hands.

'Your father was a very brave man,' he told young Hector.

'Yes, sir,' the youth replied with a bitter glare on his face. 'I know.'

As the Berlin train rattled out of the Gare de l'Est, Astrid tottered along the corridor in search of a quiet carriage. She needed a secluded place to examine her treasure. She found an unoccupied compartment and settled herself in a corner by the window. With a cautious scan along the length of the coach, she opened her case and pulled out her loot.

She had left Crowley sprawled out in the temple room of the *maison de fantasie*, his body a prone device escutcheoned by the inscribed circle on the stone floor. By the time she had finished with him he was groaning insensibly in a state of deranged bliss. She had taken her own pleasure but the experience left her feeling somewhat perplexed and disappointed. The moment of sublime and sacramental ascendancy that she had sought in the act had eluded her. The ritual had descended into mere hedonism and debauchery. Crowley's desire to be subjugated was so greedy and demanding. Right to the depths of degradation he seemed determined to be the centre of attention. It seemed to her that men were helpless with power. It stupefied them, making them vain and contrary. Crowley and Theodor Reuss were much the same. Proud and imperious, they swaggered through life with arrogance and entitlement, yet begged to be dominated behind closed doors. The pale and nihilistic radicals she had known in the Jupiter café might preach freedom and emancipation, but gazed at the world with a hungry eye betraying wrathful yearnings for superiority. While the great tragedians like the General could conquer half the globe for Pax Britannica, yet hold no dominion over their emotions.

What was needed for the future, she decided, was an open honesty about power. Only then might men relinquish some of their insistent supremacy. For now all she hoped for was some means of personal enlightenment. And at this moment, she had what she wanted. She had taken it while Crowley lay dazed in the ceremonial chamber and crept out before he could regain his senses. She had not even dared look at it until she was sure that it was safe. It was only as she was leaving Paris, secure in the knowledge that she was on her way home, that she could finally take a proper look at the Cypher Manuscript.

Her hands trembled a little as they gripped the pale leather binding. She ran her fingers over the embossed seal on the cover, remembering the astonishment she felt on witnessing its contents. It was a true grimoire, its mystical imagery animated and transforming, capable of boundless divination.

But when she opened the book all she found was a scrawl of figures in dull brown ink on loosely bound quarto sheets. The paper had been yellowed to make it look older than it really was, its watermarks faint and unremarkable. It possessed none of the vibrant energy she had drawn from it before. The calligraphy was clumsy, the accompanying drawings lacking any finesse. It was merely a prosaic series of cryptograms, illustrated by a set of childish scribblings taken from the Kaballah, the Tarot and other esoterica. The train picked up speed, she leaned back and felt a hollow velocity in her stomach.

She flicked through the manuscript, still hoping that some real magic might be encrypted somewhere within the folios. But as the train reached open country she felt a growing sense of disenchantment. She had been tricked somehow. The strange epiphany beneath the lamplight had been a dream, a hallucination. A cold anger caught hold of her. She so much wanted to believe in magic, to have some proof of it. But just when she thought she was holding it in her hands it had been snatched away. This precious document was just an artless palimpsest of gibberish. Her heart hardened and she felt the bitter sense that power dwelt in the darkness, that a real black mass lurked somewhere distant, below the horizon. As she riffled through the last few pages of the Cypher Manuscript a marking caught her eyes, stark and familiar. The *haukenkreuz*, identical in shape to the one on Crowley's chest, blazoned its presence amid the chaos of text. It was some kind of sign to her, she decided, as she gazed out of the window at the passing landscape. She wondered what it could mean and tried to remember the Sanskrit name for the symbol.

Christina waited for the night train. She had taken a suite at the Great Northern Hotel by King's Cross Station. The body was in a parcel van on Platform Five, waiting to be entrained for Edinburgh that evening. Once she had heard the news of Hector's death she had moved fast. Sent her son with a solicitor to Whitehall with the marriage certificate, the birth certificate. She had made her claim and now there would be no more pretence. She had made herself known to the world.

But already there was a clamour for a public ceremony, a military burial. A crowd had started to gather outside, full of demands for glory and honour. They had no idea what such things had cost her. All the years of bitterness and regret. Now she was determined to lay them to rest quietly and in her own time.

So she took tea and waited. She would see no reporters or newsmen. Various representatives of Highland societies were turned away and she curtly informed her brother-in-law, who was now lobbying for a funeral with full ceremonial honours, that the matter was closed. It would be her rights that would be asserted now.

A knock came on the door. A valet entered.

'Lady Jeune to see you, ma'am,' he announced.

A woman in a fur-trimmed jacket came in. She had already removed her hat. Silver hair pulled back in a chignon presented a delicately boned face. The eyes were sharp and bright. Christina stood up.

'I'm afraid I am not receiving visitors,' she protested.

'Lady Macdonald, please let me apologise,' the woman implored breathlessly.

Christina had scarcely got used to being addressed in this way but she was beginning to like the protective formality of it. As Lady Jeune stepped forward and held out a gloved hand, she found herself taking it without thinking.

'You must forgive my intrusion at this time of sorrow,' the woman went on.

'Lady Jeune, is it?'

'The very same.'

She had seen the name in the court pages and diary columns.

Lady Jeune the prominent socialite, known for her parties in Mayfair, a great *mondaine* of London's elite. Christina willed herself not to be intimidated by her.

'Will you take some tea, Lady Jeune?' she offered.

'Well . . .'

'Or anything else. I can easily call down for something.'

'Tea would be most welcome. Thank you, Lady Macdonald.'

Christina smiled as her title was used once more. All at once she found that she could forget about what she felt inside, merely concern herself with the space she occupied, the part she was now playing. They sat together, the tea things laid out between them. Lady Macdonald served her guest.

'And now,' she declared. 'What may I do for you, Lady Jeune?'

'I was hoping to prevail upon you to think again about the funeral of your husband, Lady Macdonald.'

'But I have made my wishes quite clear, Lady Jeune. Why, only an hour ago I expressed them in a note to a Mr Mackenzie of the London Scottish Society.'

'I thought that if I could make a personal appeal, Lady Macdonald.'

'But why should you?'

'I beg your pardon?'

'I mean, might I ask what your interest is in this matter?'

Lady Jeune coughed.

'My family are from Cromarty,' she said.

'Indeed?'

'And your husband was a dear friend of mine.'

'Was he now?'

'A guest at my house.'

'At one of your famous parties?'

'Yes.'

'How charming. I'm afraid I myself have not been much for society. It's one of the few things I had in common with my husband. I imagine that you found him a dreadfully dull guest.'

'Not at all, Lady Macdonald. I always strive to bring together people from varying walks of life, all with different opinions and interests, and all remarkable in their own way.'

'How charming,' Christina intoned lightly, fixing her guest with an unassailable smile.

'Lady Macdonald, I deeply sympathise with your wishes for your husband's burial, but I ask you to remember the claim that the Scottish people have on him as a national hero. He does not solely belong to you.'

'He belongs to no one now but the Almighty.' Christina's eyes flashed suddenly. 'If He'll have him, that is.'

Lady Jeune coughed once more, but refused to be shocked. Lady Macdonald felt emboldened.

'To speak frankly, Lady Jeune, my husband never much belonged to me.'

'I understand that there was an estrangement.'

Christina broke into a sharp and unexpected laugh.

'Estrangement?' She found a mocking tone, quite alien to her usual mode of speech. 'Yes, well, what a peculiarly apt word that seems in respect to our relationship.'

She was light-headed, utterly detached, her mind floating freely above the tea table.

'Oh, I knew my husband well enough, Lady Jeune. Well enough to know that there is no need for all this hysterical behaviour. After all, I can't imagine that the Scottish people would have been so enthusiastic for him had he lived to face those terrible charges.'

'But nothing has been proven, Lady Macdonald.'

'Exactly,' Christina hissed through the clenched teeth of a grin. 'Then shouldn't we be grateful that we can now simply keep quiet about the whole affair?'

'It seems as if it might be too late for that. Already people are turning out in the manner of a public demonstration.'

Christina sighed.

'I will not change my mind, Lady Jeune. I'm sorry to deprive you of such a grand occasion, so near as it is to the beginning of the season, but I will not be made part of this morbid spectacle.'

For the briefest of moments Lady Jeune looked uncomfortable. Then she smiled and stood up.

'Thank you for your time, Lady Macdonald. I have only one further request. There are a great many people below wishing to pay their last respects, and a great many wreaths and bouquets. I wonder if provision might be made for that before the train departs.'

'I'm sure something could be arranged, Lady Jeune.'

Christina stood up and saw her to the door.

'And might I simply offer my deepest condolences.'

Lady Macdonald took the hand of her guest once more and smiled with all the grace she could muster.

By sundown, King's Cross was besieged, the station forecourt a tapestry of dark suits and bright plaid as the London clans gathered to mourn the passing of their great warrior hero. The vaulted arches echoed with a dismal drone and squeal as a lone piper struck up 'Flowers of the Forest'. At eight o'clock the night train for Edinburgh pulled in and the crowd surged forward on to the platform.

The London correspondent of the *New York Times* pushed his way through the dazed commotion, mentally composing his copy as he made for the baggage car. *Scotchmen gather at King's Cross Station, London – they want the funeral postponed*, he would suggest as the stand-first and then: *The dispatch of Major-General Sir Hector Macdonald, who committed suicide in Paris, to Scotland to-night by train was the occasion for a remarkable demonstration . . .*

The coffin was crated in a plain packing case simply marked *H.A.M. Edinburgh*, standing on the platform with the other northbound freight. As the train drew to a halt they began to load it on to the baggage car. The station-master ordered the lid of the crate prised open, the doors of the compartment opened wide.

Hundreds of Scotchmen, representing the Highland societies and several Scotch members of parliament gathered on the platform: the correspondent made sporadic markings in his notebook, but he was already wiring the copy in his mind. He watched as representatives of the Ross and Cromarty Society, the Argyllshire Association, and the London Clans Society laid wreaths of white heather on the coffin. Then came a slow procession of mourners bearing roses, purple heather, primroses and spring daffodils.

The correspondent lingered, trying to engage with the grim countenances that passed, in order maybe to get a quote to give his piece some local colour, but they all seemed too possessed with public grief. *Dour*, he noted. Then a portly figure in garish tartan and a lavender topcoat with what looked like a green carnation in its lapel came striding up officiously. The man stopped by the open car, plucked out his peculiar buttonhole and with a parting kiss sailed it on to the lid of the coffin. He turned and gave a knowing grin as he caught sight of the correspondent taking notes.

'A gentleman of the press?' the man enquired archly.

'Er, yes,' replied the correspondent. '*New York Times*.'

'Not the *Herald* then? Good. What your colleagues on that rag did was appalling. Quite appalling.'

'We're just here to report the news. A sad occasion, wouldn't you say?'

The man sniffed and looked around.

'It's the Celtic Twilight in all its pathetic glory,' he said. 'They much prefer their heroes to be dead.'

'I'm not sure that I follow.'

'Well, to paraphrase Voltaire: in this country it is good, from time to time, for a general to kill himself. *Pour encourager les autres*.'

'I don't quite understand.'

'That is because you are an American.'

'And you're a Scotchman? You don't sound like one.'

'If you please, sir,' the man countered with a supercilious gesture. 'I am the Laird of Boleskine and Abertaff.'

And with that the Beast turned on his heels and continued along the platform, followed by a porter wheeling a heavy crocodile-skin portmanteau.

Once settled in his sleeping compartment, Crowley made his way down to the dining car, the dirge of the bagpipes still droning in his ears. Poor Macdonald, he pondered. It was the open accusation of the scandal that had finally struck down his standard. Crowley had gone to the Regina for their luncheon appointment only to discover the terrible news. He had been too late. The brave fighter cornered, like a bull in a labyrinth. And now the empire had taken its blood sacrifice. The Great Power at its zenith, staring down at the abyss of decline. *Babylon the great is fallen, fallen . . .*

And he too was travelling north. Gerald Kelly was giving up the studio at the end of the month so it was time to move on. He would go back to his estate in Boleskine; it would be Easter in two weeks, the correct moment in the calendar to proceed with a magical retirement from the outside world. A time for silent contemplation and prayers for enlightenment. It would give him time to work out his next move.

He was finished with the Golden Dawn, that was for sure. He had lost the Cypher Manuscript, but Astrid was welcome to it. She had given him something far more precious in return. The Scarlet Woman had ridden the Beast just as prophesied, empowering him with the invocation of sex magic. He felt a quiver of pleasure as he remembered that night. If only he could have her as his sacred whore who knows what power could be manifested. He was left with the resonant knowledge of it. There would be other Scarlet Women, other such rituals to enact.

And he had gained something else of great portent. The *wafq*, the magic square of Macdonald's. He took it out and put it on the table in front of him to have a proper look at it. He noted down the reconfigured numbers in a grid on the back of an evening paper.

21	26	19
20	22	24
25	18	23

He realised his earlier mistake as he added up the columns correctly. Of course! The square's key was not ninety-nine, indicating the ninety-nine names of Allah. No, God was turned on his head. *Demon Est Deus Inversus*. It was an even better solution: sixty-six. His own number. *By all sorts of monkey tricks, adds up my name to Six Six Six*. His mother had always been right. He was the Beast. The Great Beast. He had always known it. Now the world would too.

All this had come from the fortuitous meeting with the General. What a fearsome combination they could have made, he lamented. As if chosen for the new age. The Beast and the lion-hearted man. Imperial and supernatural power unleashed on the modern world. An occult empire. A terrifying glimpse of something flashed before his eyes and he clasped a hand against his chest, over his sacred birthmark, as he pondered for a second on such a fearsome energy.

And what a wild century lay ahead. A devil-dance of sex and drugs, an orgy of exuberance and extermination. The new aeon would be tempted by the left-hand path. It would be a time of great conspiracy, of sects and cults. People would look back on the modern age and find it hard to distinguish it from the medieval as a time for hopeless certainties. Blasphemy, murder, rape, revolution, anything good or bad but strong. And above all the chatter would come the Devil's Paintbrush, to settle the argument. All the dark forces that had hidden in the shadow in the high noon of Western rationalism. Now was the time for unreason.

Of course a sense of humour would be needed to temper the dangerous fanaticism of the times. He had learned the importance of that from Pollitt, that this really was the only way to deal with the frightful indifference of the universe. *Credo quia absurdum*, that was the answer. It's what could save us all from the hideous fate of being sensible. If it was all a bit of a joke, then there was hope. But there could be terrible consequences, he thought in a moment of horror, if people took these things too seriously.

It was a bleak and brooding dawn. A bitter wind sent grey clouds scudding over Dean Cemetery. It was six o'clock in the morning when they took him to his grave. The Reverend Dr Alexander Whyte read the lesson from Revelation:

"'And the heaven departed as a scroll when it is rolled together, and every mountain and island were moved out of their places. And the kings of the earth, and the great men, and the generals, and the mighty men and every bondman, and every free man, hid themselves in the dens and in the rocks of the mountains.'"

A short benediction followed and the box was lowered into the hole. Christina scattered a handful of dirt on the lid of the coffin, then she led the small party of mourners as they walked slowly from the graveyard.

A motley crowd of onlookers huddled around the cemetery gates, muttering with curiosity as she passed. All the calumnies of speculation had begun. That the Major-General was the victim of an English plot to discredit the great Scottish hero. That he wasn't dead at all, the coffin was full of stones and Macdonald had been spirited away by some foreign power. Her husband was passing from history into the secret world of conjecture and conspiracy. Papers would go missing, War Office files would be lost, gaps would appear in diaries and memoirs. All manner of obscure theories would emerge from this strange tragedy. But she knew the truth.

And she could forgive him now. For that terrible afternoon when he had so desperately and pathetically tried to prove himself a man. She could forgive him for all the years since. He had spent his whole glorious career hiding. None of the gawping spectators understood that. They called him Fighting Mac. He had been fighting himself all his life.

She pulled the veil from her face as she walked out towards the waiting carriages. She looked across at the crags and spires of Edinburgh, that doleful city she had not seen in over fifteen years. The graveyard was up on a hill, overlooking a creek. She gazed down at the gentle river winding its way through Dean Village. It was the Water of Leith, she realised, feeling the abrupt closeness of memory. Here below she had met Hector Macdonald by St Bernard's Well, half a lifetime ago. Downstream a precocious girl was quoting Homer to a young subaltern. Andromache's mourning for Hector. The wind stung her eyes. Now the tears would come.

ACKNOWLEDGEMENTS

The Devil's Paintbrush is a true story. A brief account of the meeting between Aleister Crowley and Sir Hector Macdonald can be found in *The Confessions of Aleister Crowley* (© Ordo Templis Orientis). I merely offer a more elaborate version of what might have happened that night. I am indebted to the National Archives and the National Army Museum for primary sources, and also to the writings of: Thomas FG Coates, David L Coombe, John Montgomery, Kenneth IE Macleod, William Clive, Trevor Royle, Winston Churchill, Lord Edward Cecil, GW Steevens, Violet Stuart-Wortley, EF Benson, Leonard Woolf, Rudyard Kipling, JK Huysmans, Robert Baden-Powell, Somerset Maugham, Edward Carpenter, Michael Asher, 'Ismat Hasan Zulfo, Eve M Troutt Powell, Henry Keown-Boyd, Godfrey Lienhardt, EE Evans-Pritchard, Dominic Green, Douglas H Johnson, Richard Hill and Peter Hogg, Jamal Mahjoub, Jan Morris, David Bowie, Ronald Hyam, Philip Magnus, Wayland Young, Denis Judd, Piers Brendon, Lawrence Sutin, Hugh B Urban, Frank M Richardson, Tim Jeal, Elleke Boehmer, Aninyo Roy, Riccardo Orizio, Christopher Ondaatje, Michael Ondaatje, Richard Boyle, Shyam Selvadurai and Carl Muller.

I would like to thank Amira Kheir, Barnaby Rogerson and Hywel Willams for their advice and insight on an early manuscript; Jasper Stocker for the magic numbers; Michael Arnott for the Scottish background; Carole Welch for her glamour with grammar; Jonny Geller for keeping the faith; and Stephanie Theobald for many reasons, not least for her first-hand account of a black mass in Paris. Also thanks to: Ruth Tross, Crispin Hughes, Phil Griffiths, Francis Gooding, Oliver Bennett, Barry

Cole, Jeremy Brill, Fred Bolza, Mark Simpson, Simon Blow, Emma Bolland, John Lee, Olly Figg, Alan Hayder, Mohsin Hamid, Hugo Wilcken, Anne Harries, Giles Foden, Nicholas Blincoe, Tomaz Salamun, Ben Kane, Rehan Kultarnate, Michelle Franks, Stephen Lowenstein, Richard Clement, Louis Charalambous, Rose Collis, Stella Duffy and Shelley Silas, James Gardiner and Neil Bartlett, Jim MacSweeney and Gay's the Word Bookshop, Geraldine Beskin and the Atlantis Bookshop, Kenny Goss and the Terence Higgins Trust, Diego Mencaroni, Ben McManus, and Dr Charles S Landau. I am grateful for the inspiration of Ganesh, god of writers, with his fortuitous appearance as a rogue elephant with a broken tusk in Viharamahadevi Park, Colombo; and to the generous hospitality of the Civitella Ranieri Foundation, where this novel was started in autumn 2006.